A

IS FOR

ALIBI

OTHER SUE GRAFTON MYSTERIES

A
IS FOR
ALIBI

SUE GRAFTON

THE BEST MYSTERIES OF ALL TIME

THE BEST MYSTERIES OF ALL TIME

"A" IS FOR ALIBI

The author wishes to acknowledge the invaluable assistance of the
following people: Steven Humphrey, Roger Long, Alan Tivoli,
Barbara Stephans, Marlin D. Ketter of Investigations Unlimited and
Joe Driscoll of Driscoll and Associates Investigations, both of Columbus,
Ohio, and William Christensen, Police Captain, City of Santa Barbara.

ImPress is an imprint of Reader's Digest Select Editions,
Bedford Road, Pleasantville, New York 10570.

Library of Congress Cataloging-in-Publication Data is available.
ISBN 0-7621-8860-X

PRINTED IN THE UNITED STATES OF AMERICA

For my father,
CHIP GRAFTON,
who set me on this path

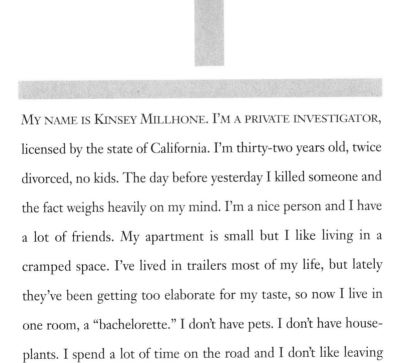

MY NAME IS KINSEY MILLHONE. I'M A PRIVATE INVESTIGATOR, licensed by the state of California. I'm thirty-two years old, twice divorced, no kids. The day before yesterday I killed someone and the fact weighs heavily on my mind. I'm a nice person and I have a lot of friends. My apartment is small but I like living in a cramped space. I've lived in trailers most of my life, but lately they've been getting too elaborate for my taste, so now I live in one room, a "bachelorette." I don't have pets. I don't have houseplants. I spend a lot of time on the road and I don't like leaving things behind. Aside from the hazards of my profession, my life

has always been ordinary, uneventful, and good. Killing someone feels odd to me and I haven't quite sorted it through. I've
already given a statement to the police, which I initialed page
by page and then signed. I filled out a similar report for the office files. The language in both documents is neutral, the ter-
minology oblique, and neither says quite enough.

NIKKI Fife first came to my office three weeks ago. I occupy
one small corner of a large suite of offices that house the California Fidelity Insurance Company, for whom I once worked.
Our connection now is rather loose. I do a certain number of
investigations for them in exchange for two rooms with a separate entrance and a small balcony overlooking the main street
of Santa Teresa. I have an answering service to pick up calls
when I'm out and I keep my own books. I don't earn a lot of
money but I make ends meet.

I'd been out for most of the morning, only stopping by the
office to pick up my camera. Nikki Fife was standing in the
corridor outside my office door. I'd never really met her but
I'd been present at her trial eight years before when she was
convicted of murdering her husband, Laurence, a prominent
divorce attorney here in town. Nikki was in her late twenties
then, with striking white-blonde hair, dark eyes, and flawless
skin. Her lean face had filled out some, probably the result of
prison food with its high starch content, but she still had the
ethereal look that had made the accusation of murder seem so
incongruous at the time. Her hair had grown out now to its
natural shade, a brown so pale that it appeared nearly color-
less. She was maybe thirty-five, thirty-six, and the years at the
California Institute for Women had left no visible lines.

I didn't say anything at first; just opened the door and let
her in.

"You know who I am," she said.

"I worked for your husband a couple of times."

She studied me carefully. "Was that the extent of it?"

I knew what she meant. "I was also there in court when you were being tried," I said. "But if you're asking if I was involved with him personally, the answer is no. He wasn't my type. No offense. Would you like coffee?"

She nodded, relaxing almost imperceptibly. I pulled the coffeepot from the bottom of the file cabinet and filled it from the Sparkletts water bottle behind the door. I liked it that she didn't protest the trouble I was going to. I put in a filter paper and ground coffee and plugged in the pot. The gurgling sound was comforting, like the pump in an aquarium.

Nikki sat very still, almost as though her emotional gears had been disengaged. She had no nervous mannerisms, didn't smoke or twist her hair. I sat down in my swivel chair.

"When were you released?"

"A week ago."

"What's freedom feel like?"

She shrugged. "It feels good, I guess, but I can survive the other way too. Better than you'd think."

I took a small carton of half-and-half out of the little refrigerator to my right. I keep clean mugs on top and I turned one over for each of us, filling them when the coffee was done. Nikki took hers with a murmured thanks.

"Maybe you've heard this one before," she went on, "but I didn't kill Laurence and I want you to find out who did."

"Why wait this long? You could have initiated an investigation from prison and maybe saved yourself some time."

She smiled faintly. "I've been claiming I was innocent for years. Who'd believe me? The minute I was indicted, I lost my credibility. I want that back. And I want to know who did me in."

I had thought her eyes were dark but I could see now that they were a metallic gray. Her look was level, flattened-out, as though some interior light were growing dim. She seemed to be a lady without much hope. I had never believed she was guilty myself but I couldn't remember what had made me so sure. She seemed passionless and I couldn't imagine her caring enough about anything to kill.

"You want to fill me in?"

She took a sip of coffee and then set the mug on the edge of my desk.

"I was married to Laurence for four years, a little more than that. He was unfaithful after the first six months. I don't know why it came as such a shock. Actually, that's how I got involved with him . . . when he was with his first wife, being unfaithful to her with me. There's a sort of egotism attached to being a mistress, I suppose. Anyway, I never expected to be in her shoes and I didn't like it much."

"According to the prosecutor, that's why you killed him."

"Look, they needed a conviction. I was it," she said with the first sign of energy. "I've just spent the last eight years with killers of one kind or another and believe me, the motive isn't apathy. You kill people you hate or you kill in rage or you kill to get even, but you don't kill someone you're indifferent to. By the time Laurence died, I didn't give a damn about him. I fell out of love with him the first time I found out about the other women. It took me a while to get it all out of my system . . ."

"And that's what the diary was all about?" I asked.

"Sure I kept track at first. I detailed every infidelity. I listened in on phone calls. I followed him around town. Then he started being more cautious about the whole thing and I started losing interest. I just didn't give a shit."

A flush had crept up to her cheeks and I gave her a moment to compose herself. "I know it looked like I killed him out of jealousy or rage, but I didn't care about that stuff. By the time he died, I just wanted to get on with my own life. I was going back to school, minding my own business. He went his way and I went mine . . ." Her voice trailed off.

"Who do you think killed him?"

"I think a lot of people wanted to. Whether they did or not is another matter. I mean, I could make a couple of educated guesses but I don't have proof of anything. Which is why I'm here."

"Why come to me?"

She flushed again slightly. "I tried the two big agencies in town and they turned me down. I came across your name in Laurence's old Rolodex. I thought there was a certain kind of irony hiring someone he had once hired himself. I did check you out. With Con Dolan down at Homicide."

I frowned. "It was his case, wasn't it?"

Nikki nodded. "Yes it was. He said you had a good memory. I don't like having to explain everything from scratch."

"What about Dolan? Does he think you're innocent?"

"I doubt it, but then again, I did my time so what's it to him?"

I studied her for a moment. She was forthright and what she said made sense. Laurence Fife had been a difficult man. I hadn't been all that fond of him myself. If she was guilty, I couldn't see why she would stir it all up again. Her ordeal was over now and her so-called debt to society had been taken off the books except for whatever remaining parole she had to serve.

"Let me think about it some," I said. "I can get in touch with you later today and let you know."

"I'd appreciate that. I do have money. Whatever it takes."

"I don't want to be paid to rehash old business, Mrs. Fife. Even if we find out who did it, we have to make it stick and that could be tough after all this time. I'd like to check back through the files and see how it looks."

She took a manila folder out of her big leather bag. "I have some newspaper clippings. I can leave those with you if you like. That's the number where I can be reached."

We shook hands. Hers was cool and slight but her grip was strong. "Call me Nikki. Please."

"I'll be in touch," I said.

I HAD to go take some photographs of a crack in a sidewalk for an insurance claim and I left the office shortly after she did, taking my VW out the freeway. I like my cars cramped and this one was filled with files and law books, a briefcase where I keep my little automatic, cardboard boxes, and a case of motor oil given to me by a client. He'd been cheated by two con artists who had "allowed" him to invest two grand in their oil company. The motor oil was real enough but it wasn't theirs; just some Sears thirty-weight with new labels pasted on. It had taken me a day and a half to track them down. In addition to the junk, I keep a packed overnight case back there, too, for God knows what emergency. I wouldn't work for anyone who wanted me *that* fast. It just makes me feel secure to have a nightgown, toothbrush, and fresh under-wear at hand. I have my little quirks I guess. The VW's a '68, one of those vague beige models with assorted dents. It needs a tune-up but I never have time.

I thought about Nikki as I drove. I had tossed the manila folder full of clippings on the passenger seat but I really didn't need to look at them. Laurence Fife had done a lot of divorce work and he had a reputation as a killer in court. He was cold, methodical, and unscrupulous, taking any advantage he could. In California, as in many states, the only grounds for divorce are irreconcilable differences or incurable insanity, which eliminates the trumped-up adultery charges that were the mainstay of divorce attorneys and private eyes in the old days. There is still the question of property settlements and custody—money and children—and Laurence Fife could get his clients anything. Most of them were women. Out of court, he had a reputation as a killer of another kind and the rumor was that he had mended many a broken heart in that difficult period between interlocutory and final decrees.

I had found him shrewd, nearly humorless, but exact; an easy man to work for because his instructions were clear and he paid in advance. A lot of people apparently hated him: men for the price he extracted, women for the betrayal of their trust. He was thirty-nine years old when he died. That Nikki was accused, tried, and convicted was just a piece of bad luck. Except for cases that clearly involve a homicidal maniac, the police like to believe murders are committed by those we know and love, and most of the time they're right—a chilling thought when you sit down to dinner with a family of five. All those potential killers passing their plates.

As nearly as I could remember, Laurence Fife had been having drinks with his law partner, Charlie Scorsoni, the night of his murder. Nikki was at a meeting of the Junior League. She got home before Laurence, who arrived about midnight. He was taking medication for numerous allergies and before he went to bed, he downed his usual capsule. Within two hours, he was awake—nauseated, vomiting, doubled over with violent stomach cramps. By morning, he was dead. An autopsy and lab tests showed that he'd died as a result of ingesting olean-

der, ground to a fine powder and substituted for the medication in the capsule he took: not a masterly plot, but one em-
ployed to good effect. Oleander is a common California
shrub. There was one in the Fifes' backyard as a matter of fact.
Nikki's fingerprints were found on the vial along with his. A
diary was discovered among her possessions, certain entries
detailing the fact that she'd found out about his adulteries and
was bitterly angry and hurt, contemplating divorce. The District Attorney established quite nicely that no one divorced
Laurence Fife without penalty. He'd been married and divorced once before and though another attorney had handled
his case, his impact was evident. He obtained custody of his
children and he managed to come out ahead financially. The
state of California is scrupulous in its division of assets, but
Laurence Fife had a way of maneuvering monies so that even
a fifty-fifty split gave him the lion's share. It looked as if Nikki
Fife knew better than to try disentangling herself from him
legally and had sought other means.

She had motive. She had access. The grand jury heard the
evidence and returned an indictment. Once she got into court,
it was simply a question of who could persuade twelve citizens
of what. Apparently the D.A. had done his homework. Nikki
hired Wilfred Brentnell from Los Angeles: a legal whiz with
a reputation as the patron saint of lost causes. In some sense,
it was almost like admitting her guilt. The whole trial had a
sensational air. Nikki was young. She was pretty. She was born
with money. The public was curious and the town was small.
It was all too good to miss.

SANTA TERESA IS A SOUTHERN CALIFORNIA TOWN OF EIGHTY thousand, artfully arranged between the Sierra Madres and the Pacific Ocean—a haven for the abject rich. The public buildings look like old Spanish missions, the private homes look like magazine illustrations, the palm trees are trimmed of unsightly brown fronds, and the marina is as perfect as a picture postcard with the blue-gray hills forming a backdrop and white boats bobbing in the sunlight. Most of the downtown area consists of two- and three-story structures of white stucco and red tile, with wide soft curves and trellises wound with gaudy maroon bougainvillea. Even the frame bungalows of the poor could hardly be called squalid.

The police department is located near the heart of town on a side street lined with cottages painted mint green with low stone walls and jacaranda trees dripping lavender blossoms. Winter in Southern California consists of an overcast and is heralded not by autumn but by fire. After the fire season come the mud slides. And then the status quo is restored and everything goes on as before. This was May.

After I dropped the roll of film off to be developed, I went into the Homicide Department to see Lieutenant Dolan. Con is in his late fifties with the aura of the unkempt: bags under his eyes, gray stubble or its illusion, a pouchy face, and hair that's been coated with some kind of men's product and combed across a shiny place on top. He looks like he would smell of Thunderbird and hang out under bridges throwing up on his own shoes. Which is not to say he isn't very sharp. Con Dolan is a lot smarter than the average thief. He and killers run about neck and neck. He catches them most of the time and only occasionally guesses wrong. Few people can outthink him and I'm not sure why this is true, except that his powers of concentration are profound and his memory clear and pitiless. He knew why I was there and he motioned me back to his office without a word.

What Con Dolan calls an office would do for a secretary anywhere else. He doesn't like being shut away and he doesn't much care for privacy. He likes to conduct his business tipped back in his chair with his attention half-turned to what's going on around him. He picks up a lot of information like that and it saves him needless talk with his men. He knows when his detectives come and go and he knows who's been brought in for questioning and he knows when reports aren't being done on time and why.

"What can I do for you?" he said, but his tone didn't indicate any particular desire to help.

"I'd like to look at the files on Laurence Fife."

He arched an eyebrow at me ever so slightly. "It's against department policy. We're not running a public library here."

"I didn't ask to take them out. I just want to look. You've let me do that before."

"Once."

"I've given you information more times than that and you know it," I said. "Why hesitate on this?"

"That case is closed."

"Then you shouldn't have any objections. It's hardly an invasion of anyone's privacy."

His smile then was slow and humorless and he tapped a pencil idly, loving, I imagined, the power to turn me down cold. "She killed him, Kinsey. That's all there is to it."

"You told her to get in touch with me. Why bother with it if you don't have a doubt yourself?"

"My doubts have nothing to do with Laurence Fife," he said.

"What then?"

"There's more to this one than meets the eye," he said evasively. "Maybe we'd like to protect what we've got."

"Are 'we' keeping secrets?"

"Oh I got more secrets than you ever dreamed about," he said.

"Me too," I said. "Now why are we playing games?"

He gave me a look that might have been annoyance and might have been something else. He's a hard man to read. "You know how I feel about people like you."

"Look, as far as I'm concerned, we're in the same business," I said. "I'm straight with you. I don't know what kind of gripes you have with the other private investigators in town, but I stay out of your way and I've got nothing but respect for the job you do. I don't understand why we can't cooperate with one another."

He stared at me for a moment, his mouth turning down with resignation. "You'd get more out of me if you'd learn to flirt," he said grudgingly.

"No I wouldn't. You think women are a pain in the ass. If I flirted, you'd pat me on the head and make me go away."

He wouldn't take the bait on that one but he did reach over and pick up the phone, dialing Identification and Records.

"This is Dolan. Have Emerald bring me the files on Laurence Fife." He hung up and leaned back again, looking at me with a mixture of speculation and distaste.

"I better not hear any complaints about the way you handle this. If I get one call from anyone—and I'm talking about a witness who feels harassed or anyone else, including my men or anybody else's men—you're up shit creek. You got that?"

I held up three fingers beside my temple dutifully. "Scout's honor."

"When were you ever a Scout?"

"Well, I was a Brownie once for almost a week," I said sweetly. "We had to paint a rose on a hanky for Mother's Day and I thought it was dumb so I quit."

He didn't smile. "You can use Lieutenant Becker's office," he said when the files arrived. "And stay out of trouble."

I went into Becker's office.

It took me two hours to sort through the mass of paperwork but I began to see why Con had been reluctant to let me look because just about the first thing that came to light was a series of Telexes from the West Los Angeles Police Department about a second homicide. At first, I thought it was a mistake— that communiqués from another case had been inadvertently sandwiched into the wrong file. But the details nearly leapt off the page and the implications made my heart go pitty-pat. An accountant named Libby Glass, Caucasian, female, age twenty-four, had died from ingesting ground oleander four days after Laurence Fife died. She had worked for Haycraft and Mc-Niece, a business-management firm representing the interests of Laurence Fife's law firm. Now what the hell was that about?

I flipped through copies of investigators' reports, trying to piece together the story from terse departmental memorandums and penciled summations of telephone calls flying back and forth between the Santa Teresa and West Los Angeles police departments. One memo noted that the key to her apartment had been found on the key ring in Laurence Fife's office desk drawer. A lengthy interview with her parents didn't add anything. There was an interview with a surly sounding ex-boyfriend named Lyle Abernathy, who seemed convinced that she was romantically involved with a "certain unnamed Santa Teresa attorney," but no one had pinned it down much beyond that. Still, the connection was ominous enough and it looked like Nikki Fife's alleged jealous rage might have included the object of her husband's philanderings as well as the man himself. Except that there wasn't any proof.

I made notes, jotting down last-known addresses and telephone numbers for whatever good that might do after all these years, and then I pushed my chair back and went to the door. Con was talking to Lieutenant Becker but he must have known what I wanted because he excused himself, apparently satisfied that I hadn't missed the point. I leaned on the doorframe, waiting. He took his sweet time ambling over.

"You want to tell me what that was about?"

His expression was bemused but there was an air of bitterness about it. "We couldn't make it stick," he said flatly.

"You think Nikki killed her too?"

"I'd be willing to bet on it," he snapped.

"I take it the D.A. didn't see it that way."

He shrugged, shoving his hands in his pockets. "I can read the California Evidence Code as well as the next man. They called off my dogs."

"The stuff in the file was all circumstantial," I said.

"That's right."

I shut my mouth, staring off at a row of windows that badly needed to be cleaned. I didn't like this little turn of events at all and he seemed to know that. He shifted his weight.

"I think I could have nailed her but the D.A. was in a big hurry and he didn't want to jeopardize his case. Bad politics. That's why you didn't like being a cop yourself, Kinsey. Working with a leash around your neck."

"I still don't like that," I said.

"Maybe that's why I'm helping you," he said and the look in his eyes was shrewd.

"What about follow-up?"

"Oh we did that. We worked on the Libby Glass angle for months, off and on. So did the West LAPD. We never turned up anything. No witnesses. No informants. No fingerprints that could have placed Nikki Fife at the scene. We couldn't even prove that Nikki *knew* Libby Glass."

"You think I'm going to help you make your case?"

"Well, I don't know about that," he said. "You might. Believe it or not, I don't think you're a bad investigator. Young yet, and sometimes off the wall, but basically honest at any rate. If you turn up evidence that points to Nikki, I don't think you'd hold that back now, would you?"

"*If* she did it."

"If she didn't, then you don't have anything to worry about."

"Con, if Nikki Fife has something to hide, why would she

open this whole thing up again? She couldn't be that kind of fool. What could she possibly gain?"

"You tell me."

"Listen," I said, "I don't believe she killed Laurence in the first place so you're going to have a hell of a time persuading me she killed someone else as well."

The phone rang two desks over and Lieutenant Becker held up a finger, looking over at Con. He gave me a fleeting smile as he moved away.

"Have a good time," he said.

I scanned the file again quickly to make sure I hadn't overlooked anything and then I closed it up and left it on the desk. He was deep in conversation with Becker again when I passed the two of them and neither looked up at me. I was troubled by the idea of Libby Glass but I was also intrigued. Maybe this was going to be more than a rehash of old business, maybe there was more to be turned up than a trail that was eight years cold.

By the time I got back to the office, it was 4:15 and I needed a drink. I got a bottle of Chablis out of my little refrigerator and applied the corkscrew. The two coffee mugs were still sitting on my desk. I rinsed out both and filled mine with wine tart enough to make me shudder ever so slightly. I went out onto the second-floor balcony and looked down at State Street, which runs right up the middle of downtown Santa Teresa, eventually making a big curve to the left and turning into a street with another name. Even where I stood, there were Spanish tile and stucco arches and bougainvillea growing everywhere. Santa Teresa is the only town I ever heard of that made the main street narrower, planted trees instead of pulling them up, and constructed cunning telephone booths that look like small confessionals. I propped myself up on the waist-high ledge and sipped my wine. I could smell the ocean and I let my mind go blank, watching the pedestrians down below. I already knew that I would go to work for Nikki but I needed just these few moments for myself before I turned my attention to the job to be done.

At 5:00 I went home, calling the service before I left.

OF ALL the places I've lived in Santa Teresa, my current cubbyhole is the best. It's located on an unpretentious street that parallels the wide boulevard running along the beach. Most of the homes in the neighborhood are owned by retired folk whose memories of the town go back to the days when it was all citrus groves and resort hotels. My landlord, Henry Pitts, is a former commercial baker who makes a living now, at the age of eighty-one, by devising obnoxiously difficult crossword puzzles, which he likes to try out on me. He is usually also in the process of making mammoth batches of bread, which he leaves to rise in an old Shaker cradle on the sunporch near my room. Henry trades bread and other baked goods to a nearby restaurant for his meals and he has also, of late, become quite crafty about clipping coupons, declaring that on a good day he can buy $50.00 worth of groceries for $6.98. Somehow these shopping expeditions seem to net him pairs of panty hose, which he gives to me. I am halfway in love with Henry Pitts.

The room itself is fifteen feet square, outfitted as living room, bedroom, kitchen, bathroom, closet, and laundry facility. Originally this was Henry's garage and I'm happy to say that it sports no stucco, red Spanish tile, or vines of any kind. It is made of aluminum siding and other wholly artificial products that are weather-resistant and never need paint. The architecture is completely nondescript. It is to this cozy den that I escape most days after work and it was from here that I called Nikki and asked her to meet me for a drink.

I DO MOST OF MY HANGING OUT IN A NEIGHBORHOOD BAR called Rosie's. It's the sort of place where you look to see if the chair needs brushing off before you sit down. The plastic seats have little rips in them that leave curls of nylon on the underside of your stockings and the tables have black Formica tops hand-etched with words like *hi*. To the left above the bar, there's a dusty marlin, and when people get drunk, Rosie lets them shoot rubber-tipped arrows at it with a toy gun, thus averting aggressions that might otherwise erupt into vicious barroom snits.

The place appeals to me for a couple of reasons. Not only is it close to my home but it is never attractive to tourists, which means that most of the time it's half-empty and perfect for private conversations. Then, too, Rosie's cooking is inventive, a sort of devil-may-care cuisine with a Hungarian twist. It is with Rosie that Henry Pitts barters baked goods, so I get to eat his breads and pies as a dividend. Rosie is in her sixties with a nose that almost meets her upper lip, a low forehead, and hair dyed a remarkable shade of rust, rather like the color of cheap redwood furniture. She also does tricky things with an eyebrow pencil that makes her eyes look small and suspect.

When Nikki walked in that night, she hesitated, scanning the place. Then she spotted me and moved through the empty tables to the booth where I usually sit. She slid in across from me and eased out of her jacket. Rosie ambled over, eyeing Nikki with uneasiness. Rosie is convinced that I do business with Mafia types and drug crazies and she was probably trying to determine the category into which Nikki Fife might fit.

"So are you eating something or what?" Rosie said, getting straight to the point.

I glanced at Nikki. "Have you had dinner?"

She shook her head. Rosie's eyes moved from Nikki to me as though I might be translating for a deaf-mute.

"What have you got tonight?"

"It's veal porkolt. Veal cubes, lotta onion, paprika, and tomato paste. You'll love it. You'll go nuts. It's the best kinda stew I make. Henry's rolls and everything, and on a plate I'm gonna put some good soft cheese and a coupla gherkins."

She was already writing the order down as she spoke, so it didn't require much from us in the way of consent. "You gonna have wine too. I'll pick the kind."

When Rosie had left, I related the information I'd picked up in the files about the murder of Libby Glass, including the telephone calls that had been traced to Laurence's home phone.

"Did you know about her?"

Nikki shook her head. "I heard the name but it was through my attorney, sometime during the trial, I think. I can't even remember now what was said."

"You never heard Laurence mention her? Never saw her name written down anyplace?"

"No little love notes if that's what you mean. He was meticulous about that sort of thing. He was once named as co-respondent in a divorce action because of some letters he wrote and after that, he seldom put anything personal in writing. I usually knew when he was involved with someone but never because he left cryptic notes or telephone numbers on matchbook covers or anything like that."

I thought about that one for a minute. "What about phone bills though? Why leave those around?"

"He didn't," Nikki said. "All the bills were sent to the business-management firm in Los Angeles."

"And Libby Glass handled the account?"

"Apparently she did."

"So maybe he called her on business matters."

Nikki shrugged. She was a little less remote than she had been but I still had the feeling that she was one step removed from what was happening. "He was having an affair with *someone*."

"How do you know?"

"The hours he kept. The look on his face." She paused, apparently thinking back. "Sometimes he would smell of someone else's soap. I finally accused him of that and afterwards he had a shower installed at the office and used the same kind of soap there that we used at home."

"Did he see women down at the office?"

"Ask his partner," she said with the faintest tinge of bitterness. "Maybe he even screwed 'em on the office couch, I don't know. Anyway it was little things. It sounds stupid now, but once he came home and the edge of his sock was turned down. It was summer and he said he'd been out playing tennis. He had on tennis shorts and he'd worked up a sweat all right, but not out on a public court. I really zapped him that time."

"But what would he say when you confronted him?"

"He'd admit it sometimes. Why not? I didn't have any proof and adultery isn't grounds for divorce in this state anyway."

Rosie arrived with the wine and two paper napkins wrapped around some silverware. Nikki and I were both silent until she'd departed again.

"Why did you stay married to him if he was such a jerk?"

"Cowardice I guess," she said. "I would have divorced him eventually, but I had a lot at stake."

"Your son?"

"Yes." Her chin came up slightly, whether from pride or defensiveness I wasn't sure. "His name is Colin," she said. "He's twelve. I have him in a boarding school up near Monterey."

"You also had Laurence's kids living with you at the time, didn't you?"

"Yes, that's right. A boy and a girl, both in school."

"Where are they now?"

"I have no idea. His ex-wife is here in town. You might check with her if you're curious. I don't hear from them."

"Did they blame you for his death?"

She leaned forward, her manner intense. "Everyone blamed me. Everyone believed I was guilty. And now I take it Con Dolan thinks I killed Libby Glass too. Isn't that what you were getting at?"

"Who cares what Dolan thinks? I don't think you did it and I'm the one going to work on this thing. Which reminds me. We ought to get the financial end of it clarified. I charge thirty bucks an hour plus mileage. I'd like to have at least a grand up front. I'll send you an itemized accounting from week to week indicating what time I've put in doing what. Also, you have to understand that my services are not exclusive. I sometimes handle more than one case at a time."

Nikki was already reaching into her purse. She took out a checkbook and a pen. Even looking at it upside down, I could see that the check was for five thousand dollars. I admired the carelessness with which she dashed it off. She didn't even have to check her bank balance first. She pushed it across the table to me and I tucked it into my purse as though I disposed of such matters as casually as she.

Rosie appeared again, this time with our dinner. She put a plate down in front of each of us and then stood there until we began to eat. "Mmm, Rosie, it's wonderful," I said.

She wiggled slightly in place, not yielding her ground.

"Maybe it don't suit your friend," she said, looking at me instead of Nikki.

"Marvelous," Nikki murmured. "Really it is."

"She loves it," I said. Rosie's gaze slid across to Nikki's face and she finally seemed satisfied that Nikki's appreciation of the dish was equaled only by my own.

I let the conversation wander while we ate. Between the good food and the wine, Nikki seemed to be letting down her guard. Under that cool, unruffled surface, signs of life were beginning to show, as though she were just wakening from a curse that had rendered her immobile for years.

"Where do you think I should start?" I asked.

"Well I don't know. I've always been curious about his secretary back then. Her name was Sharon Napier. She was already working for him when he and I met, but there was something not right about her, something in her attitude."

"Was she involved with him?"

"I don't think so. I really don't know what it was. I could just about guarantee they didn't have any sexual ties, but something had gone on. She was sometimes sarcastic with him, which Laurence never tolerated from anyone. The first time I heard her do it, I thought he'd cut her down, but he never batted an eye. She never took any guff from him at all, wouldn't stay late, wouldn't come in on weekends when he had a big case coming up. He never complained about her either, just went out and hired temporary help when he needed it. It wasn't like him, but when I asked him about it, he acted as if I were crazy, reading significance into the situation when there wasn't any. She was gorgeous, too, hardly the run-of-the-mill office type."

"Do you have any idea where she is now?"

Nikki shook her head. "She used to live up on Rivera but she's not there now. At least, she's not listed in the telephone book."

I made a note of her last-known address. "I take it you never knew her well."

Nikki shrugged. "We had the customary exchanges when I called the office but it was just routine stuff."

"What about friends of hers or places she might hang out?"

"I don't know. My guess is she lived way beyond her means. She traveled every chance she could and she dressed a lot better than I did back then."

"She testified at the trial, didn't she?"

"Yes, unfortunately. She'd been a witness to a couple of nasty quarrels I had with him and that didn't help."

"Well, it's worth looking into," I said. "I'll see if I can get a line on her. Is there anything else about him? Was he in the middle of any hassles when he died? Any kind of personal dispute or a big legal case?"

"Not that I knew. He was always in the middle of something big."

"Well, I think the first move is to talk to Charlie Scorsoni and see what he has to say. Then we'll figure it out from there."

I left money on the table for the dinner check and we walked out together. Nikki's car was parked close by, a dark green Oldsmobile ten years out of date. I waited until she'd pulled away and then I walked the half block to my place.

When I got in, I poured myself a glass of wine and sat down to organize the information I'd collected so far. I have a system of consigning data to three-by-five index cards. Most of my notes have to do with witnesses: who they are, how they're related to the investigation, dates of interviews, follow-up. Some cards are background information I need to check out and some are notes about legal technicalities. The cards are an efficient way of storing facts for my written reports. I tack them up on a large bulletin board above my desk and stare at them, telling myself the story as I perceive it. Amazing contradictions will come to light, sudden gaps, questions I've overlooked.

I didn't have many cards for Nikki Fife and I made no attempt to assess the information I had. I didn't want to form a hypothesis too early for fear it would color the entire course of the investigation. It did seem clear that this was a murder where an alibi meant little or nothing. If you go to the trouble to substitute poison for the medication in someone's antihistamine capsules, all you have to do afterward is sit back and wait. Unless you want to risk killing off others in the household, you have to be sure that only your intended victim takes that particular prescription, but there are plenty of pills that would satisfy that requirement: blood-pressure medication, antibiotics, maybe even sleeping pills. It doesn't matter much as long as you have access to the supply. It might take your victim two days or two weeks but eventually he'd dose himself properly and you could probably even manufacture a reasonable facsimile of surprise and grief. The plan has a further advantage in that you don't actually have to be there to shoot, bludgeon, hack up, or manually strangle your intended. Even where the motivation to kill is overpowering, it'd be pretty distasteful (one would think) to watch someone's eyes bug out and listen to his or her last burbling cries. Also, when done in person there's always that unsettling chance that the tables might be turned and you'd wind up on a slab in the morgue yourself.

As methods go, this little oleander number was not half bad. In Santa Teresa, the shrub grows everywhere, sometimes ten feet tall with pink or white blossoms and handsome narrow leaves. You wouldn't need to bother with anything so blatant as buying rat poison in a town where there are clearly no rats, and you wouldn't have to sport a false mustache when you went into your local hardware store to ask for a garden pest control with no bitter aftertaste. In short, the method for killing Laurence Fife, and apparently Libby Glass as well, was inexpensive, accessible, and easy to use. I did have a couple of questions and I made notes of those before I turned out the light. It was well after midnight when I fell asleep.

I WENT INTO THE OFFICE EARLY TO TYPE UP MY INITIAL notes for Nikki's file, indicating briefly what I'd been hired to do and the fact that a check for five thousand dollars had been paid on account. Then I called Charlie Scorsoni's office. His secretary said he had some time free midafternoon, so I set up an appointment for 3:15 and then used the rest of the morning to do a background check. When interviewing someone for the first time, it's always nice to have a little information up your sleeve. A visit to the county clerk's office, the credit bureau, and the newspaper morgue gave me sufficient facts to dash off a

quick sketch of Laurence Fife's former law partner. Charlie
Scorsoni was apparently single, owned his own home, paid his
bills on time, did occasional public-speaking stints for worthy
causes, had never been arrested or sued—in short, was a rather
conservative, middle-aged man who didn't gamble, speculate
on the stock market, or jeopardize himself in any way. I had
caught glimpses of him at the trial and I remembered him as
slightly overweight. His current office was within walking distance of mine.

The building itself looked like a Moorish castle: two stories
of white adobe with windowsills two feet deep, inset with
wrought-iron bars, and a corner tower that probably housed the
rest rooms and floor mops. Scorsoni and Powers, Attorneys-at-
Law, were on the second floor. I pushed through a massive
carved wooden door and found myself in a small reception area
with carpeting as soft underfoot as moss and about the same
shade. The walls were white, hung with watercolors in various
pastels, all abstract, and there were plants here and there; two
plump sofas of asparagus green wide-wale corduroy sat at right
angles under a row of narrow windows.

The firm's secretary looked to be in her early seventies, and
I thought at first she might be out on loan from some geriatric
agency. She was thin and energetic, with bobbed hair straight
out of the twenties and "mod" glasses replete with a rhinestone
butterfly on the lower portion of one lens. She was wearing a
wool skirt and a pale mauve sweater, which she must have knit
herself, as it was a masterpiece of cable stitches, wheat ears,
twisted ribs, popcorn stitches, and picot appliqué. She and
I became instant friends when I recognized the afore-
mentioned—my aunt having raised me on a regimen of such
accomplishments—and we were soon on a first-name basis.
Hers was Ruth; nice biblical stuff.

She was a chatty little thing, full of pep, and I wondered if she wasn't about perfect for Henry Pitts. Since Charlie Scorsoni was keeping me waiting, I took my revenge by eliciting as much information from Ruth as I could manage without appearing too rude. She told me she had worked for Scorsoni and Powers since the formation of their partnership seven years ago. Her husband had left her for a younger woman (fifty-five) and Ruth, on her own for the first time in years, had despaired of ever finding a job, as she was then sixty-two years old, "though in perfect health," she said. She was quick, capable, and of course was being aced out at every turn by women one-third her age who were cute instead of competent.

"The only cleavage I got left, I sit on," she said and then hooted at herself. I gave Scorsoni and Powers several points for their perceptiveness. Ruth had nothing but raves for them both. Still her rhapsodizing hardly prepared me for the man who shook my hand across the desk when I was finally ushered into his office forty-five minutes late.

Charlie Scorsoni was big, but any excess weight I remembered was gone. He had thick, sandy hair, receding at the temples, a solid jaw, cleft chin, his blue eyes magnified by big rimless glasses. His collar was open, his tie askew, sleeves rolled up as far as his muscular forearms would permit. He was tilted back in his swivel chair with his feet propped up against the edge of the desk, and his smile was slow to form and smoldered with suppressed sexuality. His air was watchful, bemused, and he took in the sight of me with almost embarrassing attention to detail. He laced his hands across the top of his head. "Ruth tells me you have a few questions about Laurence Fife. What gives?"

"I don't know yet. I'm looking into his death and this seemed like the logical place to start. Mind if I sit down?"

He gestured with one hand almost carelessly, but his expression had changed. I sat down and Scorsoni eased himself into an upright position.

"I heard Nikki was out on parole," he said. "If she claims she didn't kill him, she's nuts."

"I didn't say I was working for her."

"Well it's for damn sure nobody else would bother."

"Maybe not. You don't sound too happy about the idea."

"Hey listen. Laurence was my best friend. I would have walked on nails for him." His gaze was direct and there was something bristly under the surface—grief, misdirected rage. It was hard to tell what.

"Did you know Nikki well?" I asked.

"Well enough I guess." The sense of sexuality that had seemed so apparent at first was seeping away and I wondered if he could turn it off and on like a heater. Certainly his manner was wary now.

"How did you meet Laurence?"

"We went to the University of Denver together. Same fraternity. Laurence was a playboy. Everything came easily to him. Law school, he went to Harvard, I went to Arizona State. His family had money. Mine had none. I lost track of him for a few years and then I heard he'd opened his own law firm here in town. So I came out and talked to him about going to work for him and he said fine. He made me a partner two years later."

"Was he married to his first wife then?"

"Yeah, Gwen. She's still around town someplace but I'd be a little careful with her. She ended up bitter as hell and I've heard she's got surly things to say about him. She has a dog-grooming place up on State Street somewhere if that's any help. I try to avoid running into her myself."

He was watching me steadily and I got the impression that

he knew exactly how much he would tell me and exactly how much he would not.

"What about Sharon Napier? Did she work for him long?"

"She was here when I hired on, though she did precious little. I finally ended up hiring a girl of my own."

"She and Laurence got along okay?"

"As far as I know. She hung around until the trial was over and then she took off. She stiffed me for some money I'd advanced against her salary. If you run into her, I'd love to hear about it. Send her a bill or something just to let her know I haven't forgotten old times."

"Does the name Libby Glass mean anything to you?"

"Who?"

"She was the accountant who handled your business down in L.A. She worked for Haycraft and McNiece."

Scorsoni continued to look blank for a moment and then shook his head. "What's she got to do with it?"

"She was also killed with oleander right about the time Laurence died," I said. He didn't seem to react with any particular shock or dismay. He made a skeptical pull at his lower lip and then shrugged.

"It's a new one on me but I'll take your word for it," he said.

"You never met her yourself?"

"I must have. Laurence and I shared the paperwork but he had most of the actual contact with the business managers. I pitched in occasionally though, so I probably ran into her at some point."

"I've heard he was having an affair with her," I said.

"I don't like to gossip about the dead," Scorsoni said.

"Me neither, but he did play around," I said carefully. "I don't mean to push the point, but there were plenty of women who testified to that at the trial."

Scorsoni smiled at the box he was drawing on his legal pad. The look he gave me then was shrewd.

"Well, I'll say this. One, the guy never forced himself on anyone. And two, I don't believe he would get himself involved with a business associate. That was not his style."

"What about his clients? Didn't he get involved with them?"

"No comment."

"Would *you* get in bed with a female client?" I asked.

"Mine are all eighty years old so the answer is no. I do estate planning. He did divorce." He glanced at his watch and then pushed his chair back. "I hate to cut this short but it's four-fifteen now and I have a brief to prepare."

"Sorry. I didn't mean to take up your time. It was nice of you to see me on such short notice."

Scorsoni walked me out toward the front, his big body exuding heat. He held the door open for me, his left arm extending up along the doorframe. Again, that barely suppressed male animal seemed to peer out through his eyes. "Good luck," he said. "I suspect you won't turn up much."

I PICKED up the eight-by-ten glossies of the sidewalk crack I'd photographed for California Fidelity. The six shots of the broken concrete were clear enough. The claimant, Marcia Threadgill, had filed for disability, asserting that she'd stumbled on the jutting slab of sidewalk that had been forced upward by a combination of tree roots and shifting soil. She was suing the owner of the craft shop whose property encompassed the errant walkway. The claim, a "slip and fall" case, wasn't a large one—maybe forty-eight hundred dollars, which included her medical bills and damages, along with compensation for the time she'd been off work. It looked like the insurance company would pay, but I had been instructed to give a cursory look on the off chance that the claim was trumped-up.

Ms. Threadgill's apartment was in a terraced building set into a hill overlooking the beach, not that far from my place. I parked my car about six doors down and got my binoculars out of the glove compartment. By slouching down on my spine, I could just bring her patio into focus, the view clear enough to disclose that she wasn't watering her ferns the way she ought. I don't know a lot about houseplants, but when all the green things turn brown, I'd take it as a hint. One of the ferns was that nasty kind that grow little gray hairy paws that begin, little by little, to creep right out of the pot. Anyone who'd own a thing like that probably had an inclination to defraud and I could just picture her hefting a twenty-five-pound sack of fern mulch with her alleged sprained back. I watched her place for an hour and a half but she didn't show. One of my old cohorts used to claim that men are the only suitable candidates for surveillance work because they can sit in a parked car and pee discreetly into a tennis-ball can, thus avoiding unnecessary absences. I was losing interest in Marcia Threadgill and in truth, I had to pee like crazy, so I put the binoculars away and found the nearest service station on my way back into town.

I STOPPED in at the credit bureau again and talked to my buddy who lets me peek into files not ordinarily made public. I asked him to see what he could find out about Sharon Napier and he said he'd get back to me. I did a couple of personal errands and then went home. It had not been a very satisfying day but then most of my days are the same: checking and cross-checking, filling in blanks, detail work that was absolutely essential to the job but scarcely dramatic stuff. The basic characteristics of any good investigator are a plodding nature and infinite patience. Society has inadvertently been grooming women to this end for years. I sat down at my desk and consigned Charlie Scorsoni to several index cards. It had been an unsettling interview and I had a feeling that I wasn't done with him.

LIVING WITH THE CLIMATE IN SANTA TERESA IS RATHER LIKE functioning in a room with an overhead light fixture. The illumination is uniform—clear and bright enough—but the shadows are gone and there is a disturbing lack of dimension. The days are blanketed with sunlight. Often it is sixty-seven degrees and fair. The nights are consistently cool. Seasonally it does rain but the rest of the time, one day looks very much like the next and the constant, cloudless blue sky has a peculiar, disorienting effect, making it impossible to remember where one is in the year. Being in a building with no exterior windows gives the same impression: a subliminal suffocation, as though some, but not all, of the oxygen has been removed from the air.

I left my apartment at 9:00, heading north on Chapel. I stopped for gasoline, using the self-service pump and thinking, as I always do, what a simple but absurd pleasure it is to be able to do that sort of thing myself. By the time I found K-9 Korners, it was 9:15. The discreet sign in the window indicated that the place opened for business at eight. The grooming establishment was attached to a veterinarian's office on State Street just where it made the big bend. The building was painted flamingo pink, one wing of it housing a wilderness supply store with a mummy bag hanging in the window and a dummy, in a camping outfit, staring blankly at a tent pole.

I pushed my way into K-9 Korners to the accompaniment of many barking dogs. Dogs and I do not get along. They inevitably stick their snouts right in my crotch, sometimes clamping themselves around my leg as though to do some kind of two-legged dance. On certain occasions, I have limped gamely along, dog affixed, their masters swatting at them ineffectually, saying "Hamlet, get down! What's the matter with you!?" It is hard to look such a dog in the face, and I prefer to keep my distance from the lot of them.

There was a glass showcase full of dog-care products, and many photographs of dogs and cats affixed to the wall. To my right was a half door, the upper portion opening into a small office with several grooming rooms adjoining. By peering around the doorjamb, I could spot several dogs in various stages of being done up. Most were shivering, their eyes rolling piteously. One was having a little red bow put in its topknot, right between its ears. On a worktable were some little brown lumps I thought I could recognize. The groomer, a woman, looked up at me.

"Can I help you?"

"The dog just stepped on that brown lump," I said.

She looked down at the table. "Oh Dashiell, not again. Excuse me a minute," she said. Dashiell remained on the table, trembling, while she grabbed for some paper towels, deftly scooping up Dashiell's little accident. She seemed pretty good-natured about it. She was in her mid-forties with large brown eyes and shoulder-length gray hair, which was pulled back and secured with a scarf. She wore a dark wine-colored smock and I could see that she was tall and slim.

"Are you Gwen?"

She glanced up with a quick smile. "Yes, that's right."

"I'm Kinsey Millhone. I'm a private investigator."

Gwen laughed. "Oh Lord, what's this all about?" She disposed of the paper towel and moved over to the half door and opened it. "Come on in. I'll be right back."

She lifted Dashiell from the table and carried him into a back room just off to the left. More dogs began to bark and I could hear a blower being turned off. The air in the place was dense with heat, scented with the smell of damp hair, and the odd combination of flea syrup and dog perfume. The brown linoleum tile floor was covered with assorted clippings, like a barber shop. In the adjoining room, I could see a dog being bathed by a young girl who worked over an elevated bathtub. To my left several dogs, beribboned, were waiting in cages to be picked up. Another young woman was clipping a poodle on a second grooming table. She glanced at me with interest. Gwen returned with a little gray dog under her arm.

"This is Wuffles," she said, half clamping the dog's mouth shut. Wuffles gave her a few licks in the mouth. She pulled her head back, laughing, and made a face.

"I hope you don't mind if I finish this up. Have a seat," she said affably, indicating a metal stool nearby. I perched, wishing I didn't have to mention Laurence Fife's name. From what Charlie Scorsoni had told me, it would rather spoil her good humor.

Gwen began to clip Wuffles's toenails, tucking the dog against her body to prevent sudden moves. "You're local, I assume," she said.

"Yes, I have an office downtown here," I said, pulling out my I.D. automatically. I held it toward her so she could read it. She gave it a glance, apparently accepting it without much suspicion or concern. It always amazes me when people take me on faith.

"I understand you used to be married to Laurence Fife," I ventured.

"Yes, that's right. Is this about him? He's been dead for years."

"I know. His case is being opened up again."

"Oh, *that's* interesting. By whom?"

"Nikki. Who else?" I said. "The Homicide Department knows I'm looking into it and I have their cooperation, if that helps you any. Could you answer some questions for me?"

"All right," she said. Her tone was cautious but there was also a note of interest, as though she considered it a curious inquiry but not necessarily bad.

"You don't sound that surprised," I said.

"Actually I am. I thought that was finished business."

"Well, I'm just starting to look into it and I may come up with a blank. We don't have to talk here if it's inconvenient. I don't like to interrupt your work."

"This is fine with me, as long as you don't mind watching me clip a few dogs. I really can't afford a time-out right now. We're loaded today. Hold on," she said. "Kathy, could you hand me that flea spray? I think we missed a few here."

The dark-haired groomer left the poodle long enough to reach up for the flea spray, which was passed over to Gwen. "That's Kathy, as you might have gathered," Gwen said. "The one up to her elbows in soapsuds is Jan."

Gwen began to spray Wuffles, turning her face away to avoid the fumes. "Sorry. Go ahead."

"How long were you married to Fife?"

"Thirteen years. We met in college, his third year, my first. I'd known him about six months I guess."

"Good years? Bad years?"

"Well I'm mellowing some on that," she said. "I used to think it was all a big waste but now I don't know. Did you know Laurence yourself?"

"I met him a couple of times," I said, "just superficially."

Gwen's look was wry. "He could be very charming if he wanted to, but at heart he was a real son of a bitch."

Kathy glanced over at Gwen and smiled. Gwen laughed. "These two have heard my version about a hundred times," she said by way of explanation. "Neither has ever been married so I tend to play devil's advocate. Anyway, in those days I was the dutiful wife, and I mean I played the part with a dedication few could match. I cooked elegant meals. I made lists. I cleaned the house. I raised the kids. I'm not saying I'm anything unique for that, except that I took it awfully to heart. I wore my hair up in this French roll, not a pin out of place, and I had these outfits to put on and take off, kind of like a Barbie doll." She stopped and laughed at the image of herself, pretending to pull a string from her neck. "Hello, I'm Gwen. I'm a good wife," she burbled in a kind of nasal parrot tone. Her manner was rather affectionate as though she, instead of Laurence, had died but was remembered fondly by dear friends. Part of the time she was looking at me, and part of the time she combed and clipped the dog on the table in front of her, but in any event her manner was friendly—hardly the bitter, withdrawn account I'd expected.

"When it was over, I was pretty angry—not so much at him as at myself for buying into the whole gig. I mean, don't get me wrong. I liked it at the time and it suited me fine, but there was also a form of sensory deprivation going on so that when the marriage blew up, I was totally unequipped to deal with the real world. He managed the money. He pulled the strings. He made the major decisions, especially where the kids were concerned. I bathed and dressed and fed them and he shaped their lives. I didn't realize it at the time because I was just running around anxious to please him, which was no easy task, but now that I look back on it, it was really fucked."

She glanced up at me to see if I'd react to the language, but I just smiled back.

"So now I sound like all the other women who came out of marriages in that era. You know, we're all faintly grumpy about it because we think we've been had."

"You said you'd mellowed some," I said. "How did that come about?"

"Six thousand dollars' worth of therapy," she said flatly.

I smiled. "What made the marriage blow?"

Her cheeks tinted slightly at that but her gaze remained just as frank. "I'd rather save that for later if you're really interested."

"Sure, fine," I said. "I didn't mean to interrupt anyway."

"Well. It wasn't all his fault," she said. "But it wasn't all mine either and he hosed me with that divorce. I'm telling you, I got beat up."

"How?"

"How many ways are there? I was scared and I was also naïve. I wanted Laurence out of my life and I didn't care much what it cost. Except the kids. I fought him tooth and nail over them, but what can I tell you? I lost. I've never quite recovered from that."

I wanted to ask her about the grounds for the custody battle but I had the feeling it was touchy stuff. Better to let that slide for the moment and come back to it later if I could. "The kids must have come back to you after he died, though. Especially with his second wife going to prison."

Gwen pushed at a strand of gray hair with a capable-looking hand. "They were almost college age by then. In fact, Gregory had left that fall and Diane left the year after. But they were very messed-up kids. Laurence was a strict disciplinarian. Not that I have any quarrel with that—I think kids need structure—but he was a very controlling person, really out of touch with anything emotional, rather aggressive in his manner of dealing with anyone, the kids in particular. So the two of them, after five years of that regime, were both withdrawn and shut-down. Defensive, uncommunicative. From what I could tell, his relation to them was based on attack, being held accountable, much like what he had done with me. Of course, I'd been seeing them alternate weekends and that sort of thing, and I had the usual summer visitation. I just didn't have any idea how far it had gone. And his death was a kick in the head to them on top of that. I'm sure they both had a lot of feelings that were never resolved. Diane went straight into therapy. And Gregory's seen someone since, though not regularly." She paused a moment. "I feel like I'm giving you case histories here."

"Oh no, I appreciate your candor," I said. "Are the kids here in town too?"

"Greg's living south of Palm Springs. Salton Sea. He has a boat down there."

"What sort of work does he do?"

"Well, he doesn't have to do anything. Laurence did provide for them financially. I don't know if you've checked on the insurance yet, but his estate was divided equally between the three kids—Greg, Diane, and Nikki's son, Colin."

"What about Diane? Where is she?"

"She's in Claremont, going to school. Working on another degree. She's interested in teaching deaf children and she seems to do very well. It worried me some at first because I suspect, in her mind, it was all tied up—my divorce, Nikki, Colin, and her responsibility—even though it had nothing to do with her."

"Wait a minute. I don't understand what you mean," I said.

Gwen glanced up at me with surprise. "I thought you'd already talked to Nikki."

"Well, I talked to her once," I said.

"Didn't she tell you Colin was deaf? He was deaf from birth. I don't really remember what caused it, but there was nothing they could do about it apparently. Diane was very upset. She was thirteen, I think, when the baby was born and maybe she resented the intrusion. I don't mean to be so analytical at every turn but some of this came out with her psychiatrist and it seems pertinent. I think now she can articulate most of it herself—in fact she does—so I don't think I'm violating any confidence."

She selected a couple of strands of ribbon from about twenty spools hung on pegboard on the wall above the grooming table. She laid a blue and an orange on Wuffles's head. "What do you think, Wuf? Blue or orange?"

Wuffles raised her (I assumed) eyes and panted happily, and Gwen chose the orange, which I must admit made a certain jaunty sense against Wuffles's silver-gray mop of hair. The dog was docile, full of trust, loving every move even though half of Gwen's attention was turned to me.

"Gregory was into drugs for a while," Gwen said conversationally. "That's what his generation seemed to do while mine was playing house. But he's a good kid and I think he's okay now. Or as okay as he'll ever be. He's happy, which is a lot more than most of us can say—I mean, *I'm* happy but I know a lot of people who aren't."

"Won't he get tired of boating?"

"I hope so," Gwen said lightly. "He can afford to do anything he wants, so if the leisure begins to pall, he'll find something useful to do. He's very smart and he's a very capable kid, in spite of the fact that he's idle right now. Sometimes I envy him that."

"Do you think it would distress the kids if I talked to them?"

Gwen was startled at that, the first time she'd seemed disconcerted by anything. "About their father?"

"I may have to at some point," I said. "I wouldn't like to do it without your knowledge, but it might really help."

"I suppose it would be all right," she said, but her tone was full of misgivings.

"We can talk about it later. It may not be necessary at all."

"Oh. Well. I don't see how it could hurt. I must say, I don't really understand why you're into this business again."

"To see if justice was done, I guess," I said. "It sounds melodramatic, but that's what it amounts to."

"Justice to whom. Laurence or Nikki?"

"Maybe you should tell me what you think. I'm assuming there was no love lost between you and them, but do you think he got his 'just desserts'?"

"Sure, why not? I don't know about her. I figure she had a

fair trial and if that's the way it came out, well she must have done it. But there were times I'd have done it myself if I had thought of some way."

"So if she killed him, you wouldn't blame her?"

"Me and half a dozen others. Laurence alienated a lot of people," she said carelessly. "We could have formed a club and sent out a monthly newsletter. I still run into people who sidle up to me and say 'Thank god he's dead.' Literally. Out of the corner of their mouths." Gwen laughed again. "I'm sorry if that sounds irreverent but he was not a nice man."

"But who in particular?"

She put her hand on her hip and gave me a jaded look. "If you got an hour, I'll give you a list," she said.

I laughed then. Her humor seemed irrepressible or maybe she was only feeling ill at ease. Talking to a private eye is often unnerving to people.

Gwen put Wuffles in an empty cage and then went into the other room and led out a big English sheepdog. She lifted its front feet first, placing them on the table, and then she heaved its hind legs up while the dog whined uneasily.

"Oh come on, Duke," she snapped. "This one is such a sissy."

"Do you think we could talk again soon?" I asked.

"Sure, I'd like that. I close up here at six. If you're free then, we can have a drink. By the end of the day, I'm ready for one."

"Me too. I'll see you then," I said.

I hopped down off my stool and let myself out. When the door closed, she was already chatting with the dog. I wondered what else she knew and how much of it she was willing to share. I also hoped to hell I could look that good in another ten years.

I STOPPED OFF AT A PAY PHONE AND GAVE NIKKI A CALL. SHE
picked up on the third ring.

"Nikki? This is Kinsey. I have a request. Is there any way I can
get into the house where you and Laurence lived?"

"Sure. I still own it. I'm just leaving to drive up to Monterey
to bring Colin back but it's en route. I can meet you there if
you like."

She gave me the address and said she'd be there in fifteen minutes or so. I hung up and headed for my car. I wasn't sure what I
was after but I wanted to walk through the place, to get a feel for

what it was like, living as they lived. The house was in Montebello, a section of town where there are rumored to be more millionaires per square mile than in any other part of the country. Most of the houses are not even visible from the road. Occasionally you can catch a glimpse of a tiled roof hidden away in tangles of olive trees and live oak. Many parcels of land are bordered by winding walls of hand-hewn stone overgrown with wild roses and nasturtiums. Towering eucalyptus trees line the roads, with intermittent palms looking like Spanish exclamation points.

The Fifes' house was on the corner of two lanes, shielded from view by ten-foot hedges that parted at one point to admit a narrow brick driveway. The house was substantial: two stories of putty-colored stucco with white trim. The facade was plain and there was a portico to one side. The surrounding land was equally plain except for patches of California poppies in shades of peach and rich yellow, gold, and pink. Beyond the house, I could see a double garage with what I guessed was a caretaker's quarters above. The lawns were well tended and the house, while it had an unoccupied look, didn't seem neglected. I parked my car on the portion of the drive that circled back on itself to permit easy exit. In spite of the red-tiled roof, the house looked more French than Spanish: windows without cornices, the front door flush with the drive.

I got out of my car and walked around to the right, my footsteps making no sound on the pale rosy bricks. In the rear, I could see the outline of a swimming pool and for the first time, I felt something chill and out of place. The pool had been filled to the brim with dirt and trash. An aluminum lawn chair was half-sunk in the sod, weeds growing through the rungs. The diving board extended now over an irregular surface of grass clippings and dead leaves, as though the water had thickened and congealed. A set of steps with handholds disappeared into the depths and the surrounding concrete apron was riddled with dark splotches.

I found myself approaching with uneasiness and I was startled out of my concentration by the sound of malicious hissing. Waddling toward me with remarkable speed were two huge white geese, their heads thrust forward, mouths open like snakes with their tongues protruding, emitting a terrifying sound. I gave a low involuntary cry and began to backtrack toward my car, afraid to take my eyes off them. They covered the ground between us at a pace that forced me into a run. I barely reached my car before they caught up with me. I wrenched the door open and slammed it again with a panic I hadn't felt in years. I locked both doors, half expecting the viperous birds to batter at my windows until they gave way. For a moment they balanced, half lifted, wings flapping, black eyes bright with ill-will, their hissing faces even with mine. And then they lost interest and waddled off, honking and hissing, pecking savagely at the grass. Until that moment, it had never even occurred to me to include crazed geese among my fears, but they had suddenly shot straight to the top of the list along with worms and water bugs.

Nikki's car pulled in behind mine. She got out with perfect composure and approached as I rolled my window down. The two geese appeared again around the corner of the house, making their flat-footed beeline for the flesh of her calves. She gave them an idle glance and then laughed. Both raised up again, short wings flopping ineffectually, their manner suddenly benign. Nikki had a bread bag in her hand and she tossed them some crumbs.

"What the hell *are* those things?" I eased out of the car cautiously but neither paid the slightest attention to me.

"That's Hansel and Gretel," she said amicably. "They're Embden geese."

"The geese part I could tell. What happened? Did somebody train them to kill?"

"It keeps little kids off the property," she said. "Come on in." She inserted a key in the lock and the front door swung open. Nikki stooped to pick up some junk mail that had been pushed through the slot. "The mailman gives them saltines," she said as an afterthought. "They'll eat anything."

"Who else had keys to this place?" I asked. I noticed an alarm-system panel, which was apparently turned off.

She shrugged. "Laurence and me. Greg and Diane. I can't think of anyone else."

"Gardener? Maid?"

"Both have keys now but I don't think they did at the time. We did have a housekeeper. Mrs. Voss. She probably had one."

"Did you have a security system then?"

"We do now but that's only been in the last four years. I should have sold the place years ago but I didn't want to make decisions like that when I was in prison."

"It must be worth a lot."

"Oh sure. Real-estate values have tripled and we paid seven hundred and fifty thousand at the time. He picked it out. Put it in my name for business reasons, but it never did appeal to me much."

"Who did the decorating?" I asked.

Nikki smiled sheepishly. "I did. I don't think Laurence knew any better, but I took a subtle revenge. He insisted that we buy the place so I left all the color out."

The rooms were large, ceilings high, and plenty of light came in. The floors were dark-stained tongue and groove. The layout was very conventional: living room to the right, dining room to the left, with the kitchen behind. There was a sitting room beyond the living room and a long glassed-in porch along that side, running the length of the house. There was a curious air to the house, which I assumed was because no one had lived there for years, like a department-store display of especially elegant appointments. The furniture was still in place and there was no sign of dust. There were no plants and no magazines, no evidence of ongoing activity. Even the silence had a hollow tone, barren and lifeless.

The whole interior was done in neutral tones: grays and oyster whites, hazel and cinnamon. The couches and chairs were soft upholstered pieces with rounded arms and thick cushions, a sort of art deco look without any attempt at flash. There was a nice blend of modern and antique and it was clear that Nikki knew what she was doing even when she didn't care.

Upstairs, there were five bedrooms, all with fireplaces, all with bathrooms of remarkable size, deep closets, dressing rooms, the whole of it carpeted in thick fawn-colored wall-to-wall wool shag.

"This is the master suite?"

Nikki nodded. I followed her into the bathroom. Fat chocolate towels were stacked near the sink. There was a sunken tub, the surrounding ceramic tile a pale tobacco shade. There was a separate glassed-in shower that had been outfitted as a steam room. Soap, toilet paper, Kleenex.

"Do you stay here?" I asked as we came down the stairs.

"I haven't as yet, but I may. I have someone come in every two weeks to clean and of course there's a gardener on the premises all the time. I've been staying at the beach."

"You have another house out there?"

"Yes. Laurence's mother left it to me."

"Why you and not him?"

She smiled slightly. "Laurence and his mother didn't get along. Would you like some tea?"

"I thought you had to hit the road."

"I have time."

I followed her out to the kitchen. There was a cooking island in the center of the room with a big copper hood above the burners, a wide expanse of chopping block counter, and all manner of pans, baskets, and kitchen implements hanging on a circular metal rack that extended from the ceiling. All of the other counters were white ceramic tile; a double stainless-steel sink was sunk into one. There was a regular oven, a convection oven, a microwave, a refrigerator, two freezers, and impressive storage space.

Nikki put some water on to boil and perched herself on a wooden stool. I took up a stool across from her, the two of us sitting in the center of the room, which looked as much like a chem lab as a cook's dream.

"Who have you talked to so far?" she asked.

I told her about my conversation with Charlie Scorsoni.

"They seem like an odd pair of friends to me," I said. "My recollection of Laurence is a little hazy, but he always struck me as very elegant and cerebral. Scorsoni's very physical. He reminds me of a guy in an ad for chain saws."

"Oh Charlie's a real scrapper. From what I hear, he came up the hard way, bulldozing his way past all obstacles. Kind of like the blurb on a paperback: 'stepping over the bodies of those he loved . . .' Maybe Laurence liked that. He always talked about Charlie with grudging respect. Laurence had everything handed to him. Of course Charlie thought Laurence could do no wrong."

"That seemed clear enough," I said. "I don't suppose he had any motive for murder. Did you ever think he might have had a hand in it?"

Nikki smiled, getting up to take out cups, saucers, and tea

bags. "At one time or another, I've considered everyone, but Charlie seems unlikely to me. He certainly didn't benefit financially or professionally . . ." She poured boiling water into both cups.

"As far as the eye can see," I said, dunking my tea bag.

"Well yes, that's true. I suppose there might have been some kind of hidden dividend, but surely that would have come to light at some point in the last eight years."

"One would think." I went on to tell her about my interview with Gwen. Nikki's cheeks went ever so faintly pink.

"I feel bad about her," she said. "By the time they divorced, Laurence really hated her and I tended to fan the flames a bit. He never could take any responsibility for the failure of that marriage and as a result, he had to blame her and punish her. I didn't help. At first I really believed what he was saying about her. I mean, I personally thought she seemed like a capable person and I knew Laurence had been very dependent on her but it was safer to wean him away by feeding his bad feelings. You know what I mean? In some ways, his hating her so strongly was no different from his loving her, but it made me feel more secure to widen the breach. I'm ashamed of that now. When I fell out of love with him myself and he began to turn on me, I suddenly recognized the process."

"But I thought you were the downfall of that relationship," I said, looking at her carefully through the steam rising from my teacup.

Nikki ran both hands into her hair, lifting it away from her head and letting it fall again, giving her head a slight toss. "Oh no," she said, "I was his revenge. Never mind the fact that he'd been screwing around on her for years. He found out she was having an affair so he had me. Nice, huh? I didn't realize all this until much later, but that's how it was."

"Wait a minute. Let me see if I got this straight," I said. "He found out *she* was involved with someone, so he gets involved with you and then divorces her. From what I understand she got reamed."

"Oh yes. That's exactly what he did. The affair with me was his way of proving he didn't care. Taking the kids and the money was her punishment. He was very vindictive. It was one reason he made such a good attorney. He identified passionately with anyone who'd been wronged. He'd whip himself into a frenzy over the least little thing and then he'd use that as a driving force until he'd ground the opposition down. He was merciless. Absolutely merciless."

"Who did Gwen have the affair with?"

"You'd have to ask her that. I'm not sure I ever knew. It was certainly something he never talked about."

I asked her about the night Laurence died and she filled me in on those details.

"What was he allergic to?"

"Animal hair. Mostly dogs but cat dander too. For a long time he wouldn't tolerate pets in the house but then when Colin was two, someone suggested that we get him a dog."

"I understand Colin's deaf."

"He was born deaf. They test newborns' hearing so we knew right away, but nothing could be done for him. Apparently I had a mild case of German measles before I even realized I was pregnant. Fortunately that was the only damage he seemed to suffer. We were lucky to that extent."

"And the dog was for him? Like a guard dog or something?"

"Something like that. You can't watch a kid night and day. That's why we had the pool filled in. Bruno was a big help too."

"A German shepherd."

"Yes," Nikki said and then hesitated slightly. "He's dead now. He got hit by a car right out there on the road, but he was a great dog. Very smart, very loving, very protective of Colin. Anyway, Laurence could see what it did for him, having a dog like Bruno, so he went back on the allergy medication. He really did love Colin. Whatever his faults, and he had lots of them, believe me, he did love that little boy."

Her smile faded and her face went through an odd alteration. She was suddenly gone, disengaged. Her eyes were blank and the look she gave me was empty of emotion.

"I'm sorry, Nikki. I wish we didn't have to go into all of this."

We finished our tea and then got up. She removed the cups and saucers, tucking them into the dishwasher. When she looked back at me, her eyes were that flat gun-metal gray again. "I hope you find out who killed him. I'll never be happy until I know."

The tone of her voice made my hands numb. There was a flash in her eyes like the one I'd seen in the eyes of the geese: malevolent, unreasoning. It was just a flicker and it quickly disappeared.

"You wouldn't try to get even, would you?" I asked.

She glanced away from me. "No. I used to think about that in prison a lot but now that I'm out, it doesn't seem that important to me. Right now, all I want is to have my son back. And I want to lie on the beach and drink Perrier and wear my own clothes. And eat in restaurants and when I'm not doing that, I want to cook. And sleep late and take bubble baths . . ." She stopped and laughed at herself and then took a deep breath. "So. No, I don't want to risk my freedom."

Her eyes met mine and I smiled in response. "You better hit the road," I said.

I STOPPED OFF AT THE MONTEBELLO PHARMACY WHILE I was in the neighborhood. The pharmacist, whose name tag said "Carroll Sims," was in his fifties, medium height, with mild brown eyes behind mild tortoiseshell frames. He was in the midst of explaining to quite an old woman exactly what her medication was and how it should be taken. She was both puzzled and exasperated by the explanation but Sims was tactful, answering her flustered inquiries with a benign goodwill. I could imagine people showing him their warts and cat bites, describing chest pains and urinary symptoms across the counter. When it was my turn,

I wished I had some little ill I could tell him about. Instead, I showed him my I.D.

"What can I do for you?"

"Did you happen to work here eight years ago when Laurence Fife was murdered?"

"Well I sure did. I own the place. Are you a friend of his?"

"No," I said, "I've been hired to look into the whole case again. I thought this was a logical place to start."

"I don't think I can be much help. I can tell you the medication he was taking, dosage, number of refills, the doctor who prescribed it, but I can't tell you how the switch was made. Well, I can tell you that. I just can't tell you who did it."

Most of the information Sims gave me I already knew. Laurence was taking an antihistamine called HistaDril, which he'd been on for years. He consulted an allergist about once a year and the rest of the time the refill on the medication was automatically okayed. The only thing Sims told me that I hadn't known was that HistaDril had recently been taken off the market because of possible carcinogenic side-effects.

"In other words, if Fife had just taken the medication for a few more years, he might have gotten cancer and died anyway."

"Maybe," the pharmacist said. We stared at one another for a moment.

"I don't suppose you have any idea who killed him," I said.

"Nope."

"Well, I guess that's that. Did you see any of the trial?"

"Just when I testified. I identified the pill bottle as one of ours. It had been pretty recently refilled but Fife himself had done that and we'd chitchatted at the time. He'd been taking HistaDril for so long we hardly needed to talk about that."

"Do you remember what you did talk about?"

"Oh, the usual thing. I think there was a fire burning across the backside of the city about that time and we talked about that. A lot of people with allergies were bothered by the increase in air pollution."

"Was it bothering him?"

"It bothered everyone a little bit but I don't remember him being any worse off than anyone else."

"Well," I said, "I thank you for your time. If you think of anything else, will you give me a buzz? I'm in the book."

"Sure, if I think of anything," he said.

It was midafternoon and I wasn't meeting Gwen again until 6:00. I felt restless and out of sorts. Bit by bit, I was putting together background information, but nothing was really happening yet, and as far as I knew nothing might ever come of it. As far as the state of California was concerned, justice had been served and only Nikki Fife stood in contradiction of this. Nikki and the nameless, faceless killer of Laurence Fife who had enjoyed eight years of immunity from prosecution, eight years of freedom that I was now being hired to violate. At some point, I was bound to tread on someone's toes and that someone was not going to be happy with me.

I decided to go spy on Marcia Threadgill. At the time she tripped on that crack in the sidewalk, she had just come from the craft shop, having purchased items necessary to make one of those wooden purses covered with assorted shells. I imagined her decoupaging orange crates, making clever hanging ornaments out of egg cartons festooned with plastic sprigs of lily of the valley. Marcia Threadgill was twenty-six years old and she suffered from bad taste. The owner of the craft shop had filled me in on the projects she had done and every bit of it reminded me of my aunt. Marcia Threadgill was cheap at heart. She turned common trash into Christmas gifts. This is the mentality, in my opinion, that leads to cheating insurance companies and other sly ruses. This is the kind of person who would write to the Pepsi-Cola bottling plant claiming to have found a mouse hair in her drink, trying to net herself a free case of soda.

I parked a few doors down from her apartment and got out my binoculars. I slouched, focusing on her patio, and then sat up. "Well I'll be damned," I breathed.

In place of the nasty brown withered fern was a hanging plant of mammoth proportions, which must have weighed twenty pounds. Now how had she lifted that up to attach to a hook high above her head? A neighbor? A boyfriend? Had she done it herself perchance? I could even see the price tag stuck to one side of the pot. She'd bought it at a Gateway supermarket for $29.95, which was quite a price considering that it was probably full of fruit flies.

"Shit," I said. Where was I when she hoisted that mama up? Twenty pounds of glossy plant and moist soil on a chain at shoulder height. Had she stood on a chair? I drove straight over to the nearby Gateway supermarket and headed back to the produce department. There were five or six such plants— Dumbo ears or elephant tongues, whatever the damn things are called. I lifted one. Oh my God. It was worse than I had thought. Awkward and heavy, impossible to manage without help. I picked up some film in the Ten Items or Less, No Checks line and loaded my camera. "Marcia, you little sweetheart," I cooed, "I'm gonna nail your ass."

I drove back to her apartment and got out my binoculars again. I'd no more than settled down on my spine, glasses trained on her patio, than Ms. Threadgill herself appeared, trailing one of those long plastic hoses, which must have been attached to her faucet inside. She misted and sprayed and watered and carried on, poking a finger down into the dirt, plucking a yellowing leaf from another potted plant on the patio rail. A real obsessive type by the look of it, inspecting the underside of leaves for God knows what pests. I studied her face. She looked like she'd spent about forty-five dollars having a free makeup demonstration in some department store. Mocha and caramel on her eyelids. Raspberry on her cheekbones. Lipstick the color of chocolate. Her fingernails were long and painted the approximate shade of cherry syrup in the sort of boxed candies you wish you hadn't bitten into so eagerly.

An old woman in a nylon jersey dress came out onto the patio above Marcia's and the two had a conversation. I guessed that it was some kind of complaint because neither looked happy and Marcia eventually flounced away. The old lady yelled something after her that looked dirty even in pantomime. I got out of the car and locked it, taking a clipboard and legal pad.

Marcia's apartment was listed on the register as 2-C. The apartment above hers was listed under the name Augusta White. I bypassed the elevator and took the stairs, pausing first outside Marcia's door. She was playing a Barry Manilow album full-blast, and even as I listened she cranked up the volume a notch or two. I went up another flight and tapped on Augusta's door. She was there in a flash, her face thrust forward through the crack like a Pekingese, complete with bulging eyes, pug nose, and chin whiskers. "Yes?" she snapped. She was eighty years old if a day.

"I'm in the building next door," I said. "We've had some complaints about the noise and the manager asked me to look into it. Could I talk to you?" I held up my official-looking clipboard.

"Hold on."

She moved away from the door and stomped back into her kitchen to get her broom. I heard her bang on the kitchen floor a few times. From below, there was a mighty thump, as though Marcia Threadgill had whacked on the ceiling with a combat boot.

Augusta White stomped back, squinting at me through the crack. "You look like a real-estate agent to me," she said suspiciously.

"Well, I'm not. Honest."

"You look like one anyway so just go on off with your papers. I know all the people next door and you aren't one." She slammed the door shut and shot the bolt into place.

So much for that. I shrugged and made my way back down the stairs. Outside again, I made an eyeball assessment of the terraces. The patios were staggered in a pyramid effect and I had a quick flash of myself climbing up the outside of the building like a second-story man to spy on Marcia Threadgill at close range. I had really hoped I could enlist someone's aid in getting a firsthand report of Ms. Threadgill, but I was going to have to let it slide for a moment. I took some pictures of the hanging plant from the vantage point of my car, hoping it would soon wither and perish from a bad case of root rot. I wanted to be there when she hung a new one into place.

I went back to my apartment and jotted down some notes. It was 4:45 and I changed into my jogging clothes: a pair of shorts and an old cotton turtleneck. I'm really not a physical fitness advocate. I've been in shape maybe once in my life, when I qualified for the police academy, but there's something about running that satisfies a masochistic streak. It hurts and I'm slow but I have good shoes and I like the smell of my own sweat. I run on the mile and a half of sidewalk that tracks the beach, and the air is usually slightly damp and very clean.

Palm trees line the wide grassy area between the sidewalk and the sand and there are always other joggers, most of them looking lots better than I.

I did two miles and then called it quits. My calves hurt. My chest was burning. I huffed and puffed, bending from the waist, imagining all kinds of toxic wastes pumping out through my pores and lungs, a regular purge. I walked for half a block and then I heard a car horn toot. I glanced over. Charlie Scorsoni had pulled in at the curb in a pale blue 450 SL that looked very good on him. I wiped the sweat trickling down my face on an upraised shirt sleeve and crossed to his car.

"Your cheeks are bright pink," he said.

"I always look like I'm having an attack. You should see the looks I get. What are you doing down here?"

"I felt guilty. Because I cut you short yesterday. Hop in."

"Oh no." I laughed, still trying to catch my breath. "I don't want to get sweat all over your seats."

"Can I follow you back to your place?"

"Are you serious?"

"Sure," he said. "I thought I'd be especially winsome so you wouldn't put me on your 'possibly guilty' list."

"Won't help. I'm suspicious of everyone."

When I came out of the shower and stuck my head around the bathroom door, Scorsoni was looking at the books stacked up on my desk. "Did you have time to search through the drawers?" I asked.

He smiled benignly. "They were locked."

I smiled and closed the bathroom door again, getting dressed. I noticed that I was pleased to see him and that didn't sit well with me. I'm a real hard-ass when it comes to men. I don't often think of a forty-eight-year-old man as "cute" but that's how he struck me. He was big and his hair had a nice curl to it, his rimless glasses making his blue eyes look almost luminous. The dimple in his chin didn't hurt either.

I left the bathroom, moving toward the kitchenette in my bare feet. "Want a beer?"

He was sitting on the couch by then, leafing through a book about auto theft. "Very literate taste," he said. "Why don't you let me buy you a drink?"

"I have to be somewhere at six," I said.

"Beer's fine then."

I uncapped it and handed it to him, sitting down at the other end of the couch with my feet tucked up under me. "You must have left the office early. I'm flattered."

"I'll go back tonight. I have to go out of town for a couple of days and I'll have to get my briefcase packed, tidy up some loose ends for Ruth."

"Why take time out for me?"

Scorsoni gave me a quizzical smile with the barest hint of irritation. "God, so defensive. Why not take time out for you? If Nikki didn't kill Laurence, I'm as interested as anyone in finding out who did it, that's all."

"You don't believe she's innocent for a minute," I said.

"I believe you believe it," he said.

I looked at him carefully. "I can't give you information. I hope you understand that. I could use any help you've got and if you have a brainstorm, I'd love to hear it, but it can't be a two-way street."

"You want to lecture an attorney about client privilege, is that it? Jesus Christ, Millhone. Give me a break."

"Okay, okay. I'm sorry," I said. I looked down at his big hands and then up at his face again. "I just didn't want my brain picked, that's all."

His expression relaxed and his smile was lazy. "You said you didn't know anything anyway," he pointed out, "so what's to pick? You're such a goddamn *grouch*."

I smiled then. "Listen, I don't know what my chances are on this thing. I don't have a feel for it yet and it's making me nervous."

"Yeah and you've been working on it—what—two days?"

"About that."

"Then give yourself a break while you're at it." He took a sip of beer and then with a small tap set the bottle on the coffee table. "I wasn't very honest with you yesterday," he said.

"About what?"

"Libby Glass. I did know who she was and I suspected that he was into some kind of relationship with her. I just didn't think it was any of your business."

"I don't see how it could make any difference at this point," I said.

"That's what I decided. And maybe it's important to your case—who knows? I think since he died, I've tended to invest him with a purity he never really had. He played around a lot. But his taste usually ran to the moneyed class. Older women. Those slim elegant ones who marry aristocracy."

"What was Libby like?"

"I don't really know. I ran into her a couple of times when she was setting up our tax account. She seemed nice enough. Young. She couldn't have been more than twenty-five or twenty-six."

"Did he tell you he was having an affair with her?"

"Oh no, not him. I never knew him to kiss and tell."

"A real gentleman," I said.

Scorsoni shot me a warning look.

"I'm not being facetious," I said hastily. "I've heard he kept his mouth shut about the women in his life. That's all I meant."

"Yeah, he did. He played everything close to his chest. That's what made him a good attorney too. He never tipped his hand, never telegraphed. The last six months before he died, he was odd though, protective. There were times when I almost thought he wasn't well, but it wasn't physical. It was some kind of psychic pain, if you'll excuse the phrase."

"You had drinks with him that night, didn't you?"

"We had dinner. Down at the Bistro. Nikki was off someplace and we played racquetball and then had a bite to eat. He was fine as far as I could tell."

"Did he have the allergy medication with him then?"

Scorsoni shook his head. "He wasn't much for pills anyway. Tylenol if he had a headache, but that was rare. Even Nikki admitted that he took the allergy cap after he got home. It had to be someone who had access to that."

"Had Libby Glass been up here?"

"Not for business as far as I know. She might have come up to see him but he never said anything to me. Why?"

"I don't know. I was just thinking that somebody might have dosed them both somehow at the same time. She didn't die until four days later but that's not hard to explain if the caps were self-administered."

"I never heard much about her death. I don't even think it hit the papers here. He was down in Los Angeles though, I do know that. About a week and a half before he died."

"That's interesting. I'm going down there anyway. Maybe I can check that out."

He glanced at his watch. "I better let you go," he said, getting up. I got up and ambled to the door with him, oddly reluctant to see him go.

"How'd you lose the weight?" I said.

"What, this?" he asked, slapping his midsection. He leaned toward me slightly as though he meant to confide some incredible regimen of denial and self-abuse.

"I gave up candy bars. I used to keep 'em in my desk drawer," he murmured conspiratorially. "Snickers and Three Musketeers, Hershey's Kisses, with the silver wrappers and the little paper wick at the top? A hundred a day . . ."

I could feel a laugh bubble up because his tone was caressing and he sounded like he was confessing to a secret addiction to wearing panty hose. Also because I knew if I turned my face, I'd be closer to him than I thought I could cope with at that point.

"Mars Bars? Baby Ruths?" I said.

"All the time," he said. I could almost feel the heat of his face and I slid a look up at him sideways. He laughed at himself then, breaking the spell, and his eyes held mine only a little longer than they should. "I'll see you," he said.

We shook hands as he left. I didn't know why—maybe just an excuse to touch. Even a contact that casual made the hairs stand up along my arm. My early-warning system was clanging away like crazy and I wasn't sure how to interpret it. It's the same sensation I have sometimes on the twenty-first floor when I open a window—a terrible attraction to the notion of tumbling out. I go a long time between men and maybe it was time again. Not good, I thought, not good.

WHEN I PULLED UP IN FRONT OF K-9 KORNERS AT 6:00, Gwen was just locking up. I rolled down my car window and leaned across the seat. "You want to go in my car?"

"I better follow you," she said. "Do you know where the Palm Garden is? Is that all right with you?"

"Sure, that's fine."

She moved off toward the parking lot and a minute later she pulled out of the driveway in a bright yellow Saab. The restaurant was only a few blocks away and we pulled into the parking lot side by side. She had stripped off her smock and was brushing haphazardly at the lap of her skirt.

"Pardon the dog hair," she said. "Usually I head straight for a bath."

The Palm Garden is located in the heart of Santa Teresa, tucked back into a shopping complex, with tables outside and the requisite palms in big wooden tubs. We found a small table off to one side and I ordered white wine while she ordered Perrier.

"You don't drink?"

"Not much. I gave that up when I got divorced. Before that I was knocking back a *lot* of Scotch. How's your case?"

"It's hard to tell at this point," I said. "How long have you been in the dog-grooming business?"

"Longer than I'd like," she said and laughed.

We talked for a while about nothing in particular. I wanted time to study her, hoping to figure out what she and Nikki Fife had in common that both of them had ended up married to him. It was she who brought the conversation back around to the subject at hand. "So fire away," she said.

I curtsied mentally. She was very deft, making my job much easier than I'd thought she would. "I didn't think you'd be so cooperative."

"You've been talking to Charlie Scorsoni," she said.

"It seemed like a logical place to start," I said with a shrug. "Is he on your list?"

"Of people who might have killed Laurence? No. I don't think so. Am I on his?"

I shook my head.

"That's odd," she said.

"How so?"

She tilted her head, her expression composed. "He thinks

I'm bitter. I've heard it from a lot of different sources. Small town. If you wait long enough, anyone's opinion about you will be reported back."

"It sounds like you'd be entitled to a little bitterness."

"I worked that through a long time ago. By the way, this is where you can reach Greg and Diane if you're interested." She pulled an index card out of her purse with the two names, addresses, and telephone numbers.

"Thanks. I appreciate that. Any advice about how they should be approached? I was serious when I said I didn't want to upset them."

"No, no. They're straight shooters, both of them. If anything, you might find them a little *too* up front."

"I understand they haven't kept in touch with Nikki."

"Probably not, but that's too bad. Old business. I'd much rather see them let that go. She was very good to them." She reached back then and pulled the scarf out of her hair, shaking her hair slightly so that it would fall loose. It was shoulder-length, an interesting shade of gray that I didn't imagine had been tampered with. The contrast was nice . . . gray hair, brown eyes. She had strong cheekbones, nice lines around her mouth, good teeth, a tan that suggested health without vanity.

"What did you think of Nikki?" I asked, now that the subject had been broached.

"I'm not really sure. I mean, I resented the hell out of her back then but I'd like to talk to her sometime. I feel like we might understand each other a lot better. You want to know why I married him?"

"I'd be interested in that."

"He had a big cock," she said impishly and then laughed. "Sorry. I couldn't resist that. Actually he was awful in the sack.

A regular screwing machine. Terrific if you like your sex de-personalized."

"I'm not crazy about that kind myself," I said dryly.

"Neither was I when I figured it out. I was a virgin when I married him."

"Jesus," I said. "That's a bore."

"It was an even bigger bore back then but it was all part of the message I was raised on. I always thought the failure was mine in terms of our sex life . . ." She trailed off and the faintest tint came to her cheeks.

"Until what," I ventured.

"Maybe I should have wine too," she said and signaled to the waitress. I ordered a second glass. Gwen turned to me.

"I had an affair when I turned thirty."

"Shows you had *some* sense."

"Well yes and no. It only lasted about six weeks but it was the best six weeks of my life. In a way, I was glad to see it end. It was powerful stuff and it would have turned my life around. I wasn't ready for that." She paused and I could see her reviewing the information in her head. "Laurence was always very critical of me and I believed I deserved it. Then I ran into a man who thought I could do no wrong. At first I resisted. I knew what I was feeling for this man but it went against the grain. Finally I just gave in. For a while I told myself it was good for my relationship with Laurence. I was suddenly getting something I'd needed for a long time and it made me feel very giving with him. And then the double life began to take its toll. I deceived Laurence for as long as I could but he began to suspect something was going on. I got so I couldn't tolerate his touch—too much tension, too much deceit. Too much good stuff somewhere else. He must have felt the change come over me because he began to probe and question, wanted to know where I was every minute of the day. Called at odd hours in the afternoon and of course I was out. Even when I was with Laurence, I was somewhere else. He threatened me with divorce and I got scared so I 'fessed up. That was the biggest mistake of my life because he divorced me anyway."

"As punishment."

"As only Laurence Fife knew how. In spades."

"Where is he now?"

"My lover? Why do you ask?"

Her tone was instantly guarded, her expression wary.

"Laurence must have known who he was. If he was punishing you, why not punish the other guy too?"

"I don't want to cast suspicion on him," she said. "That would be a lousy thing to do. He had nothing to do with Laurence's death. I'll give you a written guarantee."

"What makes you so sure? A lot of people were mistaken about a lot of things back then and Nikki paid a price for it."

"Hey," she said sharply, "Nikki was represented by the best lawyer in the state. Maybe she got a few bad breaks and maybe not, but there's no point in trying to lay the blame on someone who had nothing to do with it."

"I'm not trying to blame anyone. I'm just trying to come up with a direction on this thing. I can't force you to tell me who he is . . ."

"That's right and I think you'd have a hell of a time finding out from anyone else."

"Look, I'm not here to pick a fight. I'm sorry. Skip that for now."

Two patches of red appeared on her neck. She was fighting back anger, trying to get control of herself again. I thought, for a moment, she would bolt.

"I'm not going to press the point," I said. "That's a whole separate issue and I came here to talk to you. You don't want to talk about that then it's fine with me."

She still seemed poised for flight so I shut my mouth and let her work it out for herself. Finally I could see her relax a little and I realized then that I was as tense as she. This was too valuable a contact for me to blow.

"Let's go back to Laurence. Tell me about him," I said. "What were all the infidelities about?"

She laughed self-consciously then and took a sip of wine, shaking her head. "Sorry. I didn't mean to get upset but you took me by surprise."

"Yeah, well that happens now and then. Sometimes I surprise myself."

"I don't think he liked women. He was always expecting to be betrayed. Women were the people who did you in. He liked to get there first, or at least that's my guess. I suspect an affair for him was always a power relationship and he was top dog."

" 'Do unto others before they do unto you.' "

"Right."

"But who had an ax to grind with him? Who could have hated him that much?"

She shrugged and her composure seemed restored. "I've thought about that all afternoon and what's odd is that when it comes right down to it, I'm not sure. He had awful relationships with a lot of people. Divorce attorneys are never very popular, but most of them don't get murdered."

"Maybe it wasn't related to business," I suggested. "Maybe it wasn't an irate husband pissed off about alimony and child support. Maybe it was something else—'a woman scorned.' "

"Well there were a lot of those. But I think he was probably very slick about breaking things off. Or the women themselves were sufficiently recovered to recognize the limits of the relationship and move on. He did have an awful affair with the wife of a local judge, a woman named Charlotte Mercer. She'd have run him down in the street given half a chance. Or that's what I've heard since. She wasn't the type to let go gracefully."

"How'd you find out about it?"

"She called me up after he broke off with her."

"Before your divorce or afterwards?"

"Oh afterwards, because I remember thinking at the time that I wished she'd called sooner. I went into court with nothing."

"I don't understand," I said. "What good would it have done? You couldn't have gotten him on adultery even back then."

"He didn't get *me* on that either but it sure would have given me a psychological edge. I felt so guilty about what I'd done that I hardly put up a fight except when it came to the kids, and even then he beat me down. If she'd wanted to cause trouble, she could have been a big help. He still had his reputation to protect. Anyway, maybe Charlotte Mercer can fill you in."

"Wonderful. I'll tell her she's my number-one suspect."

Gwen laughed. "Feel free to mention my name if she wants to know who sent you. It's the least I can do."

AFTER Gwen left, I looked up Charlotte Mercer's address in the telephone book by the pay phone in the rear. She and the judge lived up in the foothills above Santa Teresa in what turned out to be a sprawling one-story house with stables off to the right, the land all dust and scrub brush. The sun was just beginning to go down and the view was spectacular. The ocean looked like a wide lavender ribbon stitched up against a pink-and-blue sky.

A housekeeper in a black uniform answered the bell and I

was left in a wide cool hallway while "the missus" was fetched. Light footsteps approached from the rear of the house and I thought at first the Mercers' teenage daughter (if there was one) had appeared in Charlotte's place.

"Yes, what is it?"

The voice was low and husky and rude and the initial impression of adolescence gave way rapidly.

"Charlotte Mercer?"

"Yes, that's right."

She was petite, probably five-four, maybe a hundred pounds if that. Sandals, tank top, white shorts, her legs tawny and shapely. Not a line on her face. Her hair was a dusty blond, cut short, her makeup subdued. She had to be fifty-five years old and there was no way she could have looked that good without a team of experts. There was an artificial firmness to her jaw and her cheeks had that sleek tucked-up look that only a face-lift can provide at that late date. Her neck was lined and the backs of her hands were knotted with veins but those were the only contradictions to the appearance of slim, cool youth. Her eyes were a pale blue, made vivid by the skillful application of mascara and an eye shadow in two shades of gray. Gold bracelets jangled on one arm.

"I'm Kinsey Millhone," I said. "I'm a private investigator."

"Goody for you. What brings you here?"

"I'm looking into Laurence Fife's death."

Her smile faltered, sinking from minimal good manners into something cruel. She gave me a cursory inspection, dismissing me in the same glance. "I hope it won't take long," she said, and looked back. "Come out to the patio. I've left my drink there."

I followed her toward the back of the house. The rooms we passed looked spacious and elegant and unused: windows sparkling, the thick powder-blue carpeting still furrowed with vacuum-cleaner tracks, fresh-cut flowers in professional arrangements on glossy tabletops. The wallpaper and drapes were endless repetitions of the same blue floral print and everything smelled of Lemon Pledge. I wondered if she used it to disguise the mild scent of bourbon on the rocks that wafted after her. As we passed the kitchen, I could smell roast lamb laced with garlic.

The patio was shaded by latticework. The furniture was white wicker with bright green canvas cushions. She took up her drink from a coffee table of glass and wrought iron, plunking herself down on a padded chaise. She reached automatically for her cigarettes and a slim gold Dunhill. She seemed amused, as though I'd arrived solely to entertain her during the cocktail hour.

"Who sent you up here? Nikki or little Gwen?" Her eyes slid away from mine and she seemed to require no response. She lit her cigarette, pulling the half-filled ashtray closer. She waved a hand at me. "Have a seat."

I chose a padded chair not far from hers. An egg-shaped swimming pool was visible beyond the shrubs surrounding the patio. Charlotte caught my look.

"You want to stop and have a swim or what?"

I decided not to take offense. I had the feeling that sarcasm came easily to her, an automatic reaction, like someone with a smoker's cough.

"So who sent you up here?" she said, repeating herself. It was the second hint I had that she wasn't as sober as she should have been, even at that hour of the day.

"Word gets around."

"Oh, I'll bet it does," she said with a snort of smoke. "Well, I'll tell you this, sweetie pie. I was more than a piece of ass to that man. I wasn't the first and I wasn't the last but I was the fucking *best*."

"Is that why he broke it off?"

"Don't be a bitch," she said with a quick sharp look, but she laughed at the same time, low in her throat, and I suspected I might have gone up in her estimation. She apparently played fast and loose and didn't object to a cut now and then in the interest of a fair game. "Sure he broke it off. Why should I have secrets these days? I had a little wingding with him before he divorced Gwen and then he came back around a few months before he died. He was like some old tomcat, always sniffin' around the same back porch."

"What happened this last time?"

She gave me a jaded look as if none of it seemed to matter much. "He got involved with somebody else. Very hush-hush. Very hot. Screw him. He discarded me like yesterday's under-pants."

"I'm surprised you weren't a suspect," I said.

Her brows shot up. "Me?" She hooted. "The wife of a prominent judge? I never even testified and they knew damn well that I was involved with him. The cops tiptoed around me like I was a fussy baby taking an unexpected nap. And who asked 'em to? I would have told 'em anything. Hell, I didn't give a shit. Besides, they already had their suspect."

"Nikki?"

"Sure, Nikki," she said expansively. Her gestures were re-laxed, the hand with the cigarette waving languidly as she spoke. "You ask me, she was way too prissy to kill anyone. Not that anyone cared much what I thought. I'm just your Mrs. Loud-Mouth Drunk. What does she know? Who's going to listen to her? I could tell you things about anybody in this town and who'd pay attention to me? And you know how I find out? I'll tell you this. You'll be interested in this because that's what you do, too, find out about people, right?"

"More or less," I murmured, trying not to interrupt the flow. Charlotte Mercer was the type who'd barge right on if she didn't get sidetracked. She took a long drag on her cigarette, blowing smoke through her nose in two fierce streams. She coughed, shaking her head.

"Pardon me while I choke to death," she said, pausing to cough again. "You tell secrets," she went on, taking up from where she left off. "You tell the dirtiest damn thing you know and nine times out of ten, you'll net yourself something worse. You can try it yourself. I say anything. I tell stories on myself just to see what I get back. You want gossip, honey, you came to the right place."

"What's the word out on Gwen?" I asked, testing the waters.

Charlotte laughed. "You don't trade," she said. "You got nothing to swap."

"Well no, that's true. I wouldn't be in business long if I didn't keep my mouth shut."

She laughed again. She seemed to like that. My guess about her was that it made her feel important to know what she knew. I was hoping she liked to show off a little bit too. She might well have heard about Gwen's affair but I couldn't ask without tipping my hand so I just waited her out, hoping to pick up what I could.

"Gwen was the biggest chump who ever lived," she said without much interest. "I don't like the type myself and I don't know how she held on to him as long as she did. Laurence Fife was one cold cookie, which was why I was so crazy about him if you haven't guessed. I can't stand a man who *fawns*, you know what I mean? I can't stand a man sucking up to me, but he was the kind who took you right on the floor and he didn't even look at you afterwards when he zipped up his pants."

"That sounds crude enough," I said.

"*Sex* is crude, which is why we all run around doing it, which is why I was such a good match for him. He was crude as he was mean and that's the truth about him. Nikki was too refined, too lah-de-dah. So was Gwen."

"So maybe he liked both extremes," I suggested.

"Well now, I don't doubt that. Probably so. Maybe he married the snooty ones and fooled around with flash."

"What about Libby Glass? Did you ever hear about her?"

"Nope. No dice. Who else?"

God, this woman made me wish I had a list. I thought fast, trying to milk her while she was in the mood. I had the feeling the moment would pass and she'd turn sullen again.

"Sharon Napier," I said, as though it were a parlor game.

"Oh yeah. I checked that one out myself. The first time I ever laid eyes on that little snake, I knew something was off."

"You think he was involved with her?"

"Oh no, it's better yet. Not her. Her *mother*. I hired a private dick to look that up. Ruined her life and Sharon knew about it, too, so up she pops years later and sticks it to him. Her parents broke up over him and Mommy had a nervous breakdown or turned to drink, some damn thing. I don't know all the details except he fucked everyone over but good and Sharon collected on that for *years*."

"Was she *blackmailing* him?"

"Not for bucks. For her livelihood. She couldn't *type*. She barely knew how to spell her own name. She just wanted revenge, so she shows up every day for work and she does what she feels like doing and thumbs her nose at him. He took anything she dished out."

"Could she have killed him?"

"Sure, why not? Maybe the gig wore thin or maybe just taking his pay from week to week wasn't good enough." She paused, pushing the ember out on her cigarette with a number of ineffectual stabs. She smiled over at me with cunning.

"I hope you don't think I'm rude," she said with a glance at the door. "But school's out. My esteemed husband, the good judge, is due home any second now and I don't want to sit and explain what you're doing in my house."

"Fair enough," I said. "I'll let myself out. You've been a big help."

"I'll bet." She got to her feet, setting her drink down on the glass-topped table with a resounding crack. There was no harm done and she recovered herself with a long slow look of relief.

She studied my face briefly. "You're gonna have to get your eyes done in a couple of years. Right now, you're okay," she pronounced.

I laughed. "I like lines," I said. "I earn mine. But thanks anyway."

I left her on the patio and went around the side of the house to where my car was parked. The conversation wasn't sitting that well with me and I was glad to be on my way. Charlotte Mercer was shrewd and perhaps not above using her drunkenness for its effect. Maybe she'd been telling the truth and maybe not. Somehow the revelation about Sharon Napier seemed too pat. As a solution, it seemed too obvious. On the other hand, the cops are sometimes right. Homicide usually isn't subtle and most of the time, you don't have that far to look.

IT TOOK ME A DAY AND A HALF TO COME UP WITH AN ADDRESS on Sharon Napier. By means I'd just as soon not spell out, I tapped into the Department of Motor Vehicles computer and discovered that her driver's license had expired some six years back. I checked with the Auto Title Department, making a quick trip downtown, and found that a dark green Karmann Ghia was registered in her name with an address that matched the last-known address I had for her locally, but a side note indicated that the title had been transferred to Nevada, which probably meant that she'd left the state.

I placed a call to Bob Dietz, a Nevada investigator whose name I looked up in the National Directory. I told him what information I needed, and he said he'd call me back, which he did that afternoon. Sharon Napier had applied for and had been issued a Nevada driver's license; it showed a Reno address. His Reno sources, however, reported that she'd skipped out on a big string of creditors the previous March, which meant that she'd been gone for approximately fourteen months. He'd guessed that she was probably still in the state so he'd done some further nosing around. A small Reno credit company showed requests for information on her from Carson City and again from Las Vegas, which he thought was my best bet. I thanked him profusely for his efficiency and told him to bill me for his time but he said he'd just as soon trade tit for tat at some point, so I made sure he had my address and home phone if he needed it. I tried Information in Las Vegas, but there was no listing for her so I called a friend of mine down there and he said he'd check around. I told him I'd be driving to Los Angeles early in the week and gave him the number so he could reach me there in case it took him a while to pick up a lead on her.

The next day was Sunday and I devoted that to myself: laundry, housecleaning, grocery shopping. I even shaved my legs just to show I still had some class. Monday morning I did clerical work. I typed up a report for Nikki and put in another call to the local credit bureau just to double-check. Sharon Napier had apparently left town with a lot of money owed and a lot of people mad. They had no forwarding address so I gave them the information I had. Then I had a long talk with California Fidelity on the subject of Marcia Threadgill. For forty-eight hundred dollars, the insurance company was almost ready to settle with her and move on, and I had to argue with as much cunning as I could muster. My services on that one weren't costing them anything out of pocket and it pissed me off that they were halfway inclined to look the other way. I even had to stoop so low as to mention principles, which never sits that well with the claims manager. "She's cheating your *ass*," I kept saying, but he just shook his head as though there were forces at work that I was too dim to grasp. I told him to check with his boss and I'd get back to him.

By 2:00, I was on the road to Los Angeles. The other piece of the puzzle was Libby Glass and I needed to know how she fit into all of this. When I reached L.A., I checked into the Hacienda Motor Lodge on Wilshire, near Bundy. The Hacienda is not even remotely hacienda-like—an L-shaped, two-story structure with a cramped parking lot and a swimming pool surrounded by a chain-link fence with a padlock. A very fat woman named Arlette doubles as manager and switchboard operator. I could see straight into her apartment from the desk. It's furnished, I'm told, from her profits as a Tupperware lady, a little hustling she does on the side. She leans toward Mediterranean-style furniture upholstered in red plush.

"Fat is beautiful, Kinsey," she said to me confidentially as I filled out the registration card. "Looka here."

I looked. She was holding out her arm so that I could admire the hefty downhang of excess flesh.

"I don't know, Arlette," I said dubiously. "I keep trying to avoid it myself."

"And look at all the time and energy it takes," she said. "The problem is that our society shuns tubbos. Fat people are heavily discriminated against. Worse than the handicapped. Why, they got it easy compared to us. Everywhere you go now, there are signs out for them. Handicapped parking. Handicapped johns. You've seen those little stick figures in wheelchairs. Show me the international sign for the grossly overweight. We got rights."

Her face was moon-shaped, surrounded by a girlish cap of wispy blonde hair. Her cheeks were permanently flushed as though vital supply lines were being dangerously squeezed.

"But it's so unhealthy, Arlette," I said. "I mean, don't you have to worry about high blood pressure, heart attacks . . ."

"Well there's hazards to everything. All the more reason we should be treated decently."

I gave her my credit card and after she made the imprint she handed me the key to room #2. "That's right up here close," she said. "I know how you hate being stuck out back."

"Thanks."

I've been in room #2 about twenty times and it is always dreary in a comforting sort of way. A double bed. Threadbare wall-to-wall carpeting in a squirrel gray. A chair upholstered in orange plastic with one gimpy leg. On the desk, there is a lamp shaped like a football helmet with "UCLA" printed on the side. The bathroom is small and the shower mat is paper. It is the sort of place where you are likely to find someone else's underpanties beneath the bed. It costs me $11.95 plus room tax in the off-season and includes a "Continental" breakfast—instant coffee and jelly doughnuts, most of which Arlette eats herself. Once, at midnight, a drunk sat on my front step and yelled for an hour and a half until the cops came and took him away. I stay there because I'm cheap.

I set my suitcase on the bed and took out my jogging clothes. I did a fast walk from Wilshire to San Vicente and then headed west at a trot as far as Twenty-sixth Street, where I tagged a stop sign and turned around, jogging back up to Westgate and across to Wilshire again. The first mile is the one that hurts. I was panting hard when I got back. Given the exhaust fumes I'd taken in from passing motorists on San Vicente, I figured I was about neck-and-neck with toxic wastes. Back in room #2 again, I showered and dressed and then checked back through my notes. Then I made some phone calls. The first was to Lyle Abernathy's last-known work address, the Wonder Bread Company, down on Santa Monica. Not surprisingly, he had left and the personnel office had no idea where he was. A quick check in the phone book showed no listing for him locally, but a Raymond Glass still lived in Sherman Oaks and I verified the street number I had noted from the police files up in Santa Teresa. I placed another call to my friend in Vegas. He had a lead on Sharon Napier but said it would take him probably half a day to pin it down. I alerted Arlette that he might be calling and cautioned her to make sure the information, if she took it, was exact. She acted a little injured that I didn't trust her to take phone messages for me, but she'd been negligent before and it had cost me plenty last time around.

I called Nikki in Santa Teresa and told her where I was and what I was up to. Then I checked my answering service. Charlie Scorsoni had called but left no number. I figured if it was important he'd call back. I gave my service the number where I could be reached. Having tagged all those bases, I went next door to a restaurant that seems to change nationalities every time I'm there. Last time I was in town, it was Mexican fare, which is to say very hot plates of pale brown goo. This time it was Greek: turdlike lumps wrapped in leaves. I'd seen things in roadside parks that looked about that good but I washed them down with a glass of wine that tasted like lighter fluid and who knew the difference? It was now 7:15 and I didn't have anything to do. The television set in my room was on the fritz so I wandered down to the office and watched TV with Arlette while she ate a box of caramel Ayds.

IN THE morning, I drove over the mountain into the San Fernando Valley. At the crest of the hill, where the San Diego Freeway tips over into Sherman Oaks, I could see a layer of smog spread out like a mirage, a shimmering mist of pale yellow smoke through which a few tall buildings yearned as though for fresh air. Libby's parents lived in a four-unit apartment building set into the crook of the San Diego and Ventura freeways, a cumbersome structure of stucco and frame with bay windows bulging out along the front. There was an open corridor dividing the building in half, with the front doors to the two downstairs apartments opening up just inside. On the right, a stairway led to the second-floor landing. The building itself affected no particular style and I guessed that it had gone up in the thirties before anybody figured out that California architecture should imitate southern mansions and Italian villas. There was a pale lawn of crab and Bermuda grasses intermixed. A short driveway along the left extended back to a row of frame garages, with four green plastic garbage cans chained to a wooden fence. The juniper bushes growing along the front of the building were tall enough to obscure the ground-floor windows and seemed to be suffering from some peculiar molting process that made some of the branches turn brown and the rest go bald. They looked like cut-rate Christmas trees with the bad side facing out. The season to be jolly, in this neighborhood, was long past.

Apartment #1 was on my left. When I rang the bell, it sounded like the br-r-r-r of an alarm clock running down. The door was opened by a woman with a row of pins in her mouth

that bobbed up and down when she spoke. I worried she
would swallow one.

"Yes?"

"Mrs. Glass?"

"That's right."

"My name is Kinsey Millhone. I'm a private investigator. I
work up in Santa Teresa. Could I talk to you?"

She took the pins out of her mouth one by one and stuck
them into a pin cushion that she wore on her wrist like a bris-
tling corsage. I handed her my identification and she studied
it with care, turning it over as though there might be tricky
messages written in fine print on the back. While she did that,
I studied her. She was in her early fifties. Her silky brown hair
was cut short, a careless style with strands anchored behind
her ears. Brown eyes, no makeup, bare-legged. She wore a
wraparound denim skirt, a washed-out Madras blouse in
bleeding shades of blue, and the kind of cotton slippers I've
seen in cellophane packs in grocery stores.

"It's about Elizabeth," she said, finally returning my I.D.

"Yes. It is."

She hesitated and then moved back into the living room,
making way for me. I picked my way across the living-room
floor and took the one chair that wasn't covered with lengths
of fabric or patterns. The ironing board was set up near the
bay window, the iron plugged in and ticking as it heated.
There were finished garments hanging on a rack near the
sewing machine on the far wall. The air smelled of fabric siz-
ing and hot metal.

In the archway to the dining room, a heavyset man in his
sixties sat in a wheelchair, his expression blank, his pants un-
done in front, heavy paunch protruding. She crossed the room
and turned his chair around so that it faced the television set.

She put headphones on him and then plugged the jack into the TV, which she flipped on. He watched a game show whether he liked it or not. A couple were dressed up like a boy and girl chicken but I couldn't tell if they were winning anything.

"I'm Grace," she said. "That's her father. He was in an automobile accident three years ago last spring. He doesn't talk but he can hear and any mention of Elizabeth upsets him. Help yourself to coffee if you like."

There was a ceramic percolator on the coffee table, plugged into an extension cord that ran back under the couch. It looked as if all the other appliances in the room were radiating from the same power source. Grace eased down onto her knees. She had about four yards of dark green silk spread out on the hardwood floor and she was pinning a handmade pattern into place. She held a magazine out to me, opened to a page that showed a designer dress with a deep slit up one side and narrow sleeves. I poured myself a cup of coffee and watched her work.

"I'm running this up for a woman married to a television star," she said mildly. "Somebody's sidekick. He got famous overnight and she says he's recognized even in the car wash now. People asking for his autograph. Has facials. Him, not her. He was poor, I hear, for the last fifteen years and now they go to all these parties in Bel Air. I do her clothes. He buys his on Rodeo Drive. She could, too, on the money he makes but it makes her feel insecure, she says. She's much nicer than he is. I already read in the *Hollywood Reporter*, 'New Two You,' him and somebody else 'pulling up steaks at Stellini's.' She'd be smart to put an expensive wardrobe together before he leaves her if you ask me."

Grace seemed to be talking to herself, her tone distracted,

a smile warming her face now and then. She picked up a pair of pinking shears and began to cut along the straight edge, the scissors making a crunching sound against the wood floor. For a while I didn't say anything. There was something hypnotic about the work and there seemed to be no compulsion to converse. The television flickered, and from an angle I could see the girl chicken jumping up and down, hands to her face. I knew the audience was urging her to do something— choose, pass, change boxes, take what was behind the curtain, give back the envelope, all of it taking place in silence while Libby's father looked on from his wheelchair incuriously. I thought she should consult her boy-chicken mate but he just stood there self-consciously like a kid who knew he was too old to be out in costume on Halloween. The tissue paper pattern rustled as Grace removed it, folding it carefully before she laid it aside.

"I sewed for Elizabeth when she was young," she said. "Once she left home, of course, she only wanted store-bought. Sixty dollars for a skirt that only had twelve dollars' worth of wool at most, but she did have a good eye for color and she could afford to do as she pleased. Would you like to see a picture of her?" Grace's eyes strayed up to mine and her smile was wistful.

"Yes. I'd appreciate that."

She took the silk first and placed it on the ironing board, testing the iron with a wet index finger as she passed. The iron spat back and she turned the lever down to "wool." There were two snapshots of Libby in a double frame on the windowsill and she studied them herself before she handed them to me. In one, Libby was facing the camera but her head was bent, her right hand upraised as though she were hiding her face. Her blonde hair was sun-streaked, cut short like her mother's but feathered back across her ears. Her blue eyes were amused, her grin wide, embarrassed to be caught, I couldn't think why. I'd never seen a twenty-four-year-old look quite so young or quite so fresh. In the second snapshot, the smile was only partially formed, lips parted over a flash of white teeth, a dimple showing near the corner of her mouth. Her complexion was clear, tinted with gold, lashes dark so that her eyes were delicately outlined.

"She's lovely," I said. "Really."

Grace was standing at the ironing board, touching up folds of silk with the tip of the iron, which sailed across the asbestos board like a boat on a flat sea of dark green. She turned the iron off and wiped her hands briefly down along her skirt, then took the pieces of silk and began to pin them together.

"I named her after Queen Elizabeth," she said and then she laughed shyly. "She was born on November 14, the same day Prince Charles was born. I'd have named her Charles if she'd been a boy. Raymond thought it was silly but I didn't care."

"You never called her Libby?"

"Oh no. She did that herself in grade school. She always had such a sense of who she was and how her life should be. Even as a child. She was very tidy—not prissy, but neat. She would line her dresser drawers with pretty floral wrapping papers and everything would be arranged just so. She liked accounting for the same reason. Mathematics was orderly and it made sense. The answers were always there if you worked carefully enough, or that's what she said." Grace moved over to the rocking chair and sat down, laying the silk across her lap. She began to baste darts.

"I understand she worked as an accountant for Haycraft and McNiece. How long was she there?"

"About a year and a half. She had done the accounts for her

father's company—he did small-appliance repair—but it really didn't interest her, working for him. She was ambitious. She passed her CPA exam when she was twenty-two. She took a couple of computer courses, too, in night school, after that. She made very good grades. She had two junior accountants working under her, you know."

"Was she happy there?"

"I'm sure she was," Grace said. "She spoke of going to law school at one point. She enjoyed business management and finance. She liked working with figures and I know she was impressed because that company represented very wealthy people. She said you could learn a lot about someone's character by the way they spent money, what they bought and where—whether they lived within their means, that kind of thing. She said it was a study of human nature." Grace's voice was tinged with pride. It was hard for me to reconcile the idea of this prim-sounding CPA with the girl in the photographs who looked pretty, animated, bashful, and rather sweet, hardly a woman with a hard-driving purpose in life.

"What about her old boyfriend? Do you have any idea where he is now?"

"Who, Lyle? Oh, he'll be around in a bit."

"Here?"

"Oh my, yes. He stops by every day at noon to help me with Raymond. He's a lovely boy but of course you probably knew she broke off her engagement with him a few months before . . . she passed on. She went with Lyle all through high school and they both attended Santa Monica City College together until he dropped out."

"Is that when he went to work for Wonder Bread?"

"Oh no, Lyle's had many jobs. At the time Lyle left school, Elizabeth was in her own apartment and she didn't confide much in me but I feel she was disappointed in him. He was going to be a lawyer and then he simply changed his mind. He said law was too dull and he didn't like details."

"Did they live together?"

Grace's cheeks tinted slightly. "No, they didn't. It may sound odd and Raymond thought it was very wrong of me, but I encouraged them to move in together. I sensed that they were drifting apart and I thought it would help. Raymond was like Elizabeth, disenchanted with Lyle for quitting school. He told her she could do much better for herself. But Lyle adored her. I thought that should count for something. He would have found himself. He had a restless nature, like many boys that age. He would have come to his senses and I told her so. He needed responsibility. She could have been a very good influence because she was so responsible herself. But Elizabeth said she didn't want to live with him and that was that. She was strong-willed when she wanted to be. And I don't mean that as criticism. She was as nearly perfect as a daughter could be. Naturally I wanted whatever she wanted but I couldn't bear to see Lyle hurt. He's very dear. You'll see when you meet him."

"And you have no idea what actually caused the breakup between them? I mean, could she possibly have been involved with someone else?"

"You're talking about that attorney up in Santa Teresa," she said.

"It's his death I'm looking into," I said. "Did she ever talk to you about him?"

"I never knew anything about him until the police came down from Santa Teresa to talk to us. Elizabeth didn't like to confide her personal affairs, but I don't believe Elizabeth would fall in love with a married man," Grace said. She began to fuss with the silk, her manner agitated. She closed her eyes and then pressed a hand to her forehead as though checking to see if she'd contracted a sudden fever. "I'm sorry. Sometimes I forget. Sometimes I pretend she got sick. The other makes me cringe, that someone might have done that to her, that someone could have hated her that much. The police here don't do anything. It isn't solved but no one cares anymore so I just . . . I simply tell myself she got sick and was taken. How could someone have done that to her?" Her eyes welled with tears. Her grief rolled across the space between us like a wash of salt water and I could feel tears form in my own eyes in response. I reached out and took her hand. For a moment, she clutched my fingers hard and then she seemed to catch herself, pulling back.

"It's been like a weight pressing on my heart. I will never recover from it. Never."

I phrased my next question with care. "Could it have been an accident?" I said. "The other man—Laurence Fife—died from oleander, which someone put in an allergy capsule. Suppose they'd been doing business together, going over accounts or something. Maybe she was sneezing or complaining about a stuffy nose and he just volunteered his own medication. People do that all the time."

She considered that for a moment uneasily. "I thought the police said the attorney died before she did. Days before."

"Maybe she didn't take the pill right away," I said, shrugging. "With something like that, you never know when someone will take a doctored capsule. Maybe she put it in her purse and swallowed it later without even realizing there was any jeopardy. Did she have allergies? Could she have been coming down with a cold?"

Grace began to weep, a small mewing sound. "I don't remember. I don't think so. She didn't have hay fever or anything like that. I don't even know who'd remember after all these years."

Grace looked at me then with those large, dark eyes. She had a good face, almost childlike, with a small nose, a sweet mouth. She took out a Kleenex and wiped her cheeks. "I don't think I can talk about it anymore. Stay for lunch. Meet Lyle. Maybe he can tell you something that would help."

I SAT ON A STOOL IN THE KITCHEN AND WATCHED GRACE
make tuna fish salad for lunch. She had seemed to shake herself,
as though wakening from a brief but vital nap and then she had
put on her apron and cleared the dining-room table of the rest
of her sewing paraphernalia. She was a woman who worked
with care, her movements restful as she assembled placemats
and napkins. I set the table for her, feeling like a well-behaved
kid again while she rinsed lettuce and patted it dry, placing a layer
on each plate like a doily. She neatly pared thin ribbons of skin
from several tomatoes and coiled them like roses. She fluted a

mushroom for each plate, added two thin spikes of asparagus so that the whole of it looked like a flower arrangement. She smiled at me timidly, taking pleasure in the picture she had created. "Do you cook?"

I shook my head.

"I don't have much occasion to myself except when Lyle's here. Raymond wouldn't notice and I probably wouldn't bother at all if it were just for me." She lifted her head. "There."

I hadn't heard the truck pull into the driveway but she must have been tuned to Lyle's arrival. Her hand strayed unconsciously to a strand of hair, which she tucked back. He came in through a utility room off to the left, pausing around the corner, apparently to take off his boots. I heard two thunks. "Hey, babe. What's for lunch?"

He came around into the dining room with a grin, giving her cheek a noisy buss before he caught sight of me. He halted, the animation flickering off and on, then draining out of his face. He looked at her hesitantly.

"This is Miss Millhone," she said to him.

"Kinsey," I filled in, holding out my hand. He reached out and shook my hand automatically, but the central question still hadn't been answered. I suspected that I was intruding on an occasion that ordinarily admitted no variation. "I'm a private investigator from Santa Teresa," I said.

Lyle moved over to Raymond without another glance at me. "Hey, Pops. How's it going today? You feeling okay?"

The old man's face registered nothing, but his eyes came into focus. Lyle took the headphones off, turning the set off too. The change in Lyle had been immediate and I felt as if I'd just seen snapshots of two different personalities in the same body, one joyful, the other keeping watch. He was not much taller than me and his body was trim, his shoulders wide. He had his shirt pulled out, unbuttoned down the front. His chest muscles were spare but well formed like those of a man who's been lifting weights. I guessed him to be about my own age. His hair was blond, worn long and faintly tinted with the green of a chlorinated swimming pool and hot sun. His eyes were a washed-out blue, too pale for his tan, his lashes bleached, his chin too narrow for the breadth of his cheeks. The overall effect was of a face oddly off—good looks gone slightly askew, as though under the surface there were a hairline crack. Some subterranean tremor had caused the bones to shift minutely and the two halves of his face seemed not quite to match. He wore faded jeans slung low on his hips and I could see the silky line of darkish hair pointing like an arrow toward his crotch.

He went about his business, ignoring me completely, talking to Grace while he worked. She handed him a towel, which he tucked under Raymond's chin, and then he proceeded to lather and shave him with a safety razor, which he rinsed in a stainless-steel bowl. Grace was taking out bottles of beer, removing the caps, pouring liquid into tulip glasses which she set at each place. There was no plate prepared for Raymond at all. When the shaving process had been completed, Lyle brushed Raymond's thinning white hair and then fed him a jar of baby food. Grace shot me a satisfied look. See what a dear he is? Lyle reminded me of an older brother caring for a toddler so that Mom would approve. She did. She looked on affectionately while Lyle scraped Raymond's chin with the bowl of the spoon, easing the drooling vegetable puree back into Raymond's slack mouth. Even as I watched, a stain began to spread across the front of Raymond's pants.

"Hey, don't worry about it, Pops," Lyle crooned, "we'll get you cleaned up after lunch. How's that?"

I could feel the muscles in my face setting with distaste.

During lunch, Lyle ate quickly, saying nothing to me and very little to Grace.

"What sort of work do you do, Lyle?" I said.

"Lay brick."

I looked at his hands. His fingers were long and dusted with mortar gray that had seeped down into the crevices of his skin. At this range, I could smell sweat, overlaid with the delicate scent of dope. I wondered if Grace noticed at all or if, perhaps, she thought it might be some exotic aftershave.

"I've got to make a run up to Vegas," I said to Grace, "but I'd like to stop back on my way up to Santa Teresa. Do you have any of Libby's belongings?" I was relatively certain she did.

Grace consulted Lyle with a quick look but his eyes were lowered to his plate. "I believe so. There are some boxes in the basement, aren't there, Lyle? Elizabeth's books and papers?"

The old man made a sound at the mention of her name and Lyle wiped his mouth, tossing the napkin down as he got up. He wheeled Raymond down the hallway.

"I'm sorry. I shouldn't have mentioned Libby," I said.

"Well that's all right," she said. "If you'll call or come by when you get back to Los Angeles, I'm sure it'd be all right if you looked at Elizabeth's belongings. There isn't much."

"Lyle doesn't seem to be in a very good mood," I remarked. "I hope he doesn't think I'm intruding."

"Oh no. He's quiet around people he doesn't know," she said. "I don't know what I'd do without him. Raymond is too heavy for me to lift. I have a neighbor who stops by twice a day to help me get him in and out of his chair. His spine was crushed in the accident."

Her conversational tone gave me the willies. "Do you mind if I use the bathroom?" I said.

"It's down the hall. The second door on the right."

As I passed the bedroom, I could see that Lyle had already lifted Raymond into bed. There were two straight-backed wooden chairs pushed up against the side of the double bed to keep him from falling out. Lyle was standing between the two chairs, cleaning Raymond's bare ass. I went into the bathroom and closed the door.

I helped Grace clear the table and then I left, waiting in my car across the street. I made no attempt to conceal myself and no pretense at driving away. I could see Lyle's pickup truck still parked in the driveway. I checked my watch. It was ten minutes to one and I figured he must be on a limited lunch hour. Sure enough, the side door opened and Lyle stepped out onto the narrow porch, pausing to lace his boots. He glanced over at the street, spotting my car, and seemed to smile to himself. Ass, I thought. He got into his truck and backed out of the driveway rapidly. I wondered for a moment if he intended to back straight across the street and into the side of my car, crushing me. He wheeled at the last minute, though, and flung the truck into gear, taking off with a chirp of rubber. I thought maybe we were going to have a little impromptu car chase but it turned out he didn't have that far to go. He drove eight blocks and then pulled into the driveway of a modest-sized Sherman Oaks house that was being refaced with red brick. I guessed it was a status symbol of some sort because brick is very expensive on the West Coast. There probably aren't six brick houses in the whole city of L.A.

He got out of his truck and ambled around to the back, tucking in his shirt, his manner insolent. I parked on the street and locked my car, following him. I wondered idly if he intended to smash my head in with a brick and then mortar me into a wall. He was not pleased with my arrival on the scene and he made no bones about that. As I rounded the corner, I could see that the owner of the house was disguising his little cottage with a whole new facade. Instead of looking like a modest California bungalow, it would look like certain pet hospitals in the Midwest, real high-rent stuff. Lyle was already mixing up mortar in a wheelbarrow in the back. I picked my way across some two-by-fours with crooked rusty nails protruding. A little kid would have to have a lot of tetanus shots after falling on those.

"Why don't we start all over again, Lyle," I said conversationally.

He snorted, taking out a cigarette, which he tucked into the corner of his mouth. He lit it, cupping crusty hands around the match, and then blew out the first mouthful of smoke. His eyes were small and one of them squinted now as the smoke curled up across his face. He reminded me of early photographs of James Dean—that defensive hunched stance, the crooked smile, the pointed chin. I wondered if he was a secret admirer of *East of Eden* reruns, staying up late at night to watch on obscure channels piped in from Bakersfield.

"Hey, come on. Why don't you talk to me," I said.

"I don't have nothin' to say to you. Why stir up all that shit again?"

"Aren't you interested in who killed Libby?"

He took his time about answering. He picked up a brick, holding it upright while he applied a thick layer of mortar to one end with a trowel, beveling the soft cement as if it were a gritty gray cheese. He laid the brick on the chest-high line of bricks where he'd been working and gave it a few taps with a hammer, bending down then to pick up the next brick.

I cupped my right hand to my ear. "Hello?" I said, as if I might have gone temporarily deaf.

He smirked, cigarette bobbing in his mouth. "You think you're real hot shit, don't you?"

I smiled. "Listen, Lyle. There's no point in this. You don't have to tell me anything and you know what I can do? Spend about an hour and a half this afternoon finding out anything I want to know about you. I can do it in six phone calls from a motel room in West Los Angeles and I've even got someone paying me for my time, so it's nothing to me. It's fun, if you really want to know the truth. I can get your service records, credit rating. I can find out if you've ever been arrested for anything, job history, library books overdue . . ."

"Go right ahead. I got nothin' to hide."

"Why put us through all that stuff?" I said. "I mean, I can go check you out but I'll just come back around here tomorrow and if you don't like me now, you ain't gonna like me any better then. I might be in a bad mood. Why don't you just loosen up?"

"Aw, I'm real loose," he said.

"What happened to your plans to go to law school?"

"I dropped out," he said sullenly.

"Maybe the dope smoking got to you," I suggested mildly.

"Maybe you can go get fucked," he snapped. "Do I look like a lawyer to you? I lost interest, okay? That's no fuckin' crime."

"I'm not accusing you of anything. I just want to figure out what happened to Libby."

He flipped the ash off the cigarette and dropped it, chunking it into the dirt with the toe of his boot. I sat down on a pile of bricks that had been covered with a tarp. Lyle glanced over at me through lowered lids.

"What makes you think I smoke dope anyway?" he asked abruptly.

I tapped my nose, letting him know I'd smelled it on him. "Also laying brick doesn't seem that interesting," I said. "I figure if you're smart, you gotta do something to keep from going nuts."

He looked at me, his body relaxing just a little bit. "What makes you think I'm smart?"

I shrugged. "You went with Libby Glass for ten years."

He thought about that for a while.

"I don't know anything," he said, almost gruffly.

"You know more than I do at this point."

He was beginning to relent, though his shoulders were still tense. He shook his head, going back to his work. He took the trowel and moved the damp mass of mortar around like cake icing that has gone all granular. "She dumped me after she met that guy from up north. That attorney . . ."

"Laurence Fife?"

"Yeah, I guess it was. She wouldn't tell me anything about him. At first, it was business—something about some accounts. His law firm had just hooked up with the place she worked and she had to get all this stuff on the computer, you know? Set up to run smoothly from month to month. It was all real complicated, calls goin' back and forth, things like that. He came down a few times and she'd have drinks when they finished up, sometimes dinner. She fell in love. That's all I know."

He took out a small metal brace at right angles and hammered it into the wooden siding on the house, placing a mortar-laden brick on top.

"What's that do?" I asked out of curiosity.

"What? Oh. That keeps the brick wall from falling away from the rest," he said.

I nodded, halfway tempted to try laying brick myself.

"And she broke up with you after that?" I asked, getting back to the point.

"Pretty much. I'd see her now and again, but it was over and I knew it."

He was beginning to drop the tension in his tone and he sounded more resigned than angry. Lyle buttered another brick with soft mortar and set it in place. The sun felt good on my back and I settled on my elbows, leaning back on the tarp.

"What's your theory?" I asked.

He looked at me slyly. "Maybe she killed herself."

"Suicide?" The thought hadn't even crossed my mind.

"You asked. I'm just tellin' you what I thought at the time. She sure was hung up on him."

"Yeah, but enough to kill herself when he died?"

"Who knows?" He lifted one shoulder and let it drop.

"How did she find out about his death?"

"Someone called her and told her about it."

"How do you know that?"

"Because she called me up. At first she didn't know what to make of it."

"She was grieving for him? Tears? Shock?"

He seemed to think back. "She was just real confused and upset. I went over there. She asked me to come and then she changed her mind and said she didn't want to talk about it. She was shaky, couldn't concentrate. It kind of made me mad that she was jerking me around, so I left. Next thing I knew, she was dead."

"Who found her?"

"The apartment manager where she lived. She didn't show up for work for two days and didn't call in, so her boss got worried and went over to her place. The manager tried peeping in the windows but the drapes were shut. They knocked some, front and back, and finally got in with a passkey. She was lying on the bathroom floor in her robe. She'd been dead for three days."

"What about her bed? Had it been slept in?"

"I don't know. The police didn't give that out."

I thought about that for a minute. It sounded like she might have taken a capsule at night, just as Laurence Fife had. It still seemed to me it might have been the same medication—some kind of antihistamine capsule in which someone had substituted oleander.

"Did she have allergies, Lyle? Was she complaining of a head cold or anything like that when you saw her last?"

He shrugged. "She might have, I guess. I don't remember anything like that. I saw her Thursday night. Wednesday or Thursday of that week when she heard that attorney was dead. She died on Saturday night late, they said. That much they put in the paper when it happened."

"What about this attorney she was involved with? Do you know if he kept anything at her place? Toothbrush? Razor? Things like that? Maybe she took medication that was meant for him."

"How do I know?" he said testily. "I don't stick my nose where it doesn't belong."

"Did she have a girl friend? Someone she might have confided in?"

"Maybe from work. I don't remember anyone in particular. She didn't have 'girl friends.' "

I took out my notebook and jotted down the telephone number at my motel. "This is where I can be reached. Will you give me a call if you think of anything else?"

He took the slip of paper and tucked it carelessly into the back pocket of his jeans. "What's in Las Vegas?" he asked. "How does that tie in?"

"I don't know yet. There may be a woman down there who can fill in some blanks. I'll be back through Los Angeles toward the end of the week. Maybe I'll look you up again."

Lyle had already tuned me out, tapping the next brick into place, troweling away the excess mortar that had drooled out between the cracks. I glanced at my watch. I still had time to check out the place where Libby Glass had worked. I didn't think Lyle was telling the whole truth, but I had no way to be sure. So I let it slide—for the time being anyway.

HAYCRAFT AND McNIECE WAS LOCATED IN THE AVCO EMBASSY building in Westwood, not far from my motel. I parked in an expensive lot adjacent to the Westwood Village Mortuary and went into the entranceway near the Wells Fargo Bank, taking the elevator up. The office itself was just to the right as I got off. I pushed through a solid teak door, lettered in brass. The interior was done with polished uneven red-tile flooring, mirrors floor to ceiling, and panels of raw gray wood, hung here and there with clusters of dried corn. A receptionist sat behind a corral to my left. A placard reading "Allison, Receptionist" sat on the corral post, the letters burned into the wood as though by some charred stick. I gave her my card.

"I wonder if I might talk to a senior accountant," I said. "I'm looking into the murder of a CPA who used to work here."

"Oh yeah. I heard about her," Allison said. "Hang on."

She was in her twenties with long dark hair. She wore jeans and a string tie, her western-cut shirt looking like it had been stuffed with many handfuls of hay. Her belt buckle was shaped like a bucking mustang.

"What is this? A theme park or something?" I asked.

"Huh?"

I shook my head, not willing to pursue the point, and she clopped away in her high-heeled boots through some swinging doors. After a moment, she returned.

"Mr. McNiece isn't in but the man you probably want to talk to is Garry Steinberg with two *r*'s."

"B-e-r-r-g?"

"No, G-a-r-r-y."

"Oh, I see. Excuse me."

"That's okay," she said. "Everybody makes that mistake."

"Would it be possible to see Mr. Steinberg? Just briefly."

"He's in New York this week," she said.

"What about Mr. Haycraft?"

"He's dead. I mean, you know, he's been dead for years," she said. "So actually now it's McNiece and McNiece but nobody wants to have all the stationery changed. The other McNiece is in a meeting."

"Is there anybody else who might remember her?"

"I don't think so. I'm sorry."

She handed me my card. I turned it over and jotted down my motel number and my answering service up in Santa Teresa.

"Could you give this to Garry Steinberg when he gets back? I'd really appreciate a call. He can make it collect if I'm not at the motel here."

"Sure," she said. She sat down and I could have sworn she eased the card straight into the trash. I watched her for a moment and she smiled at me sheepishly.

"Maybe you could just leave that on his desk with a note," I suggested.

She leaned over slightly and came up again, card in hand. She speared it on a vicious-looking metal spike near the phone.

I looked at her some more. She took the card off the spike and got up.

"I'll just put this on his desk," she said and clopped off again.

"Good plan," I said.

I went back to the motel and made some phone calls. Ruth, in Charlie Scorsoni's office, said that he was still out of town but she gave me the number of his hotel in Denver. I called but he wasn't in, so I left my number at the message desk. I called Nikki and brought her up to date and then I checked with my answering service. There were no messages. I put on my jogging clothes and drove down to the beach to run. Things did not seem to be falling into place very fast. So far, I felt like I had a lapful of confetti and the notion of piecing it all together to make a picture seemed very remote indeed. Time had shredded the facts like a big machine, leaving only slender paper threads with which to reconstruct reality. I felt clumsy and irritable and I needed to blow off steam.

I parked near the Santa Monica pier and jogged south along the promenade, a stretch of asphalt walk that parallels the beach. I trotted past the old men bent over their chess games, past thin black boys roller-skating with incredible grace, boogeying to the secret music of their padded headphones, past guitar players, dopers, and loiterers whose eyes followed me with scorn. This stretch of pavement is the last remnant of the sixties' drug culture—the barefoot, sag-eyed, and scruffy young, some looking thirty-seven now instead of seventeen, still mystical and remote. A dog took up company with me, running along beside me, his tongue hanging out, eyes rolling up at me now and then happily. His coat was thick and bristly, the color of caramel corn, and his tail curled up like a party favor. He was one of those mutant breeds with a large head, short body, and little bitty short legs, but he seemed quite self-possessed. Together, we trotted beyond the promenade, past Ozone, Dudley, Paloma, Sunset, Thornton, and Park; by the time we reached Wave Crest, he'd lost interest, veering off to participate in a game of Frisbee out on the beach. The last I saw of him, he had made an incredible leap, catching a Frisbee midflight, mouth turned up in a grin. I smiled back. He was one of the few dogs I'd met in years that I really liked.

At Venice Boulevard I turned back, running most of the way and then slowing to a walk as I reached the pier again. The ocean breeze served as a damper to my body heat. I found myself winded but not sweating much. My mouth felt dry and my cheeks were aflame. It hadn't been a long run but I'd pushed myself a little harder than I normally did and my lungs were burning: liquid combustion in my chest. I run for the same reasons I learned to drive a car with a stick shift and drink my coffee black, imagining that a day might come when some amazing emergency would require such a test. This run was for "good measure," too, since I'd already decided to take a day off for good behavior. Too much virtue has a corrupt-

ing effect. I got back in my car when I'd cooled down and I
drove east on Wilshire, back to my motel.

As I unlocked the door to my room, the phone began to
ring. It was my Las Vegas buddy with Sharon Napier's address.

"Fantastic," I said. "I really appreciate this. Let me know
how to get in touch when I get down there and I'll pay you for
your time."

"General delivery is fine. I never know where I'll be."

"You got it. How much?"

"Fifty bucks. A discount. For you. She's strictly unlisted and
it wasn't easy."

"Let me know when I can return the service," I said, knowing full well that he would.

"Oh, and Kinsey," he said, "she's dealing blackjack at the
Fremont but she's also hustling some on the side, so I hear. I
watched her operate last night. She's very sharp but she's not
fooling anyone."

"Is she stepping on someone's toes?"

"Not quite, but she's comin' close. You know, in this town no
one cares what you do as long as you don't cheat. She shouldn't
call attention to herself."

"Thanks for the information," I said.

"For sure," he said and hung up.

I showered and put on a pair of slacks and a shirt, then
went across the street and ate fried clams drowned in ketchup
with an order of french fries on the side. I got two cups of
coffee to go and went back to my room. As soon as the door
shut behind me, the phone began to ring. This time it was
Charlie Scorsoni.

"How's Denver?" I asked as soon as he identified himself.

"Not bad. How's L.A.?"

"Fair. I'm driving up to Las Vegas tonight."

"Gambling fever?"

"Not a bit. I got a line on Sharon."

"Terrific. Tell her to pay me back my six hundred bucks."

"Yeah. Right. With interest. I'm trying to find out what she knows about a murder and you want me to hassle her about a bad debt."

"*I'll* never have occasion to, that's for sure. When will you be back in Santa Teresa?"

"Maybe Saturday. When I come back through L.A. on Friday, I want to see some boxes that belong to Libby Glass. But I don't think it will take long. What makes you ask?"

"I want to buy you a drink," he said. "I'm leaving Denver day after tomorrow, so I'll be in town before you. Will you call me when you get back?"

I hesitated ever so slightly. "Okay."

"I mean, don't put yourself out, Millhone," he said wryly.

I laughed. "I'll call. I swear."

"Great. See you then."

After I hung up, I could feel a silly smile linger on my face long after it should have. What was it about that man?

LAS Vegas is about six hours from L.A. and I decided I might as well hit the road. It was just after 7:00 and not dark yet, so I threw my things in the backseat of my car and told Arlette I'd be gone for a couple of days.

"You want me to refer calls or what?" she said.

"I'll call you when I get there and let you know how I can be reached," I said.

I headed north on the San Diego Freeway, picking up the Ventura, which I followed east until it turned into the Colorado Freeway, one of the few benign roads in the whole of the

L.A. freeway system. The Colorado is broad and sparsely traveled, cutting across the northern boundary of metropolitan Los Angeles. It is possible to change lanes on the Colorado without having an anxiety attack and the sturdy concrete divider that separates east- and westbound traffic is a comforting assurance that cars will not wantonly drift over and crash into your vehicle head-on. From the Colorado, I doglegged south, picking up the San Bernardino Freeway, taking 15 northeast on a long irregular diagonal toward Las Vegas. With any luck, I could talk to Sharon Napier and then head south to the Salton Sea, where Greg Fife was living. I could complete the circuit with a swing up to Claremont on my way back for a brief chat with his sister, Diane. At this point, I wasn't sure what the journey would net me but I needed to complete the basics of my investigation. And Sharon Napier was bound to prove interesting.

I LIKE driving at night. I'm not a sightseer at heart and in travels across the country, I'm never tempted by detours to scenic wonders. I'm not interested in hundred-foot rocks shaped like crookneck squash. I'm not keen on staring down into gullies formed by rivers now defunct and I do not marvel at great holes in the ground where meteors once fell to earth. Driving anywhere looks much the same to me. I stare at the concrete roadway. I watch the yellow line. I keep track of large trucks and passenger vehicles with little children asleep in the backseat and I keep my foot pressed flat to the floor until I reach my destination.

12

BY THE TIME LAS VEGAS LOOMED UP, TWINKLING ON THE horizon, it was well after midnight and I felt stiff. I was anxious to avoid the Strip. I would have avoided the whole town if I could. I don't gamble, having no instincts for the sport and even less curiosity. Life in Las Vegas exactly suits my notion of some eventual life in cities under the sea. Day and night mean nothing. People ebb and surge aimlessly as though pulled by invisible thermal currents that are swift and disagreeably close. Everything is made of plaster of paris, imitative, larger than life, profoundly impersonal. The whole town smells of $1.89 fried shrimp dinners.

I found a motel near the airport, on the outskirts of town. The Bagdad looked like a foreign legion post made of marzipan. The night manager was dressed in a gold satin vest and an orange satin shirt with full puffed sleeves. He wore a fez with a tassel. His breathing had a raspy quality that made me want to clear my throat.

"Are you an out-of-state married couple?" he asked, not looking up.

"No."

"There's fifty dollars' worth of coupons with a double if you're an out-of-state married couple. I'll put it down. Nobody checks."

I gave him my credit card, which he ran off while I filled out the registration form. He gave me my key and a small paper cup full of nickels for the slot machines near the door. I left them on the counter.

I parked in the space outside my door and left the car, taking a cab into town through the artificial daylight of Glitter Gulch. I paid the cabbie and took a moment to orient myself. There was a constant stream of traffic on East Fremont, the sidewalks crowded with tourists, hot yellow signs, and flashing lights—THE MINT, THE FOUR QUEENS—illuminating a complete catalogue of hustlers: pimps and prostitutes, pickpockets, corn-fed con artists from the Midwest who flock to Vegas with the conviction that the system can be beaten with sufficient cunning and industry. I went into the Fremont.

I could smell the Chinese food from the coffee shop and the odor of chicken chow mein mingled oddly with the perfumed jet trail left by a woman who passed me in a royal blue polyester print pantsuit that made her look like a piece of walking wallpaper. I watched idly as she began to feed quarters into a slot machine in the lobby. The blackjack tables were off to my left. I asked one of the pit bosses about Sharon Napier and was told she'd be in at 11:00 in the morning. I hadn't really expected to run into her that night, but I wanted to get a feel for the place.

The casino hummed, the croupiers at the craps tables shoveling chips back and forth with a stick like some kind of table-top shuffleboard with rules of its own. I once made a tour of the Nevada Dice Company, watching with something close to reverence as the sixty-pound cellulose nitrate slabs, an inch thick, were cured and cut into cubes, slightly bigger than the finished size, hardened, buffed and drilled on all sides, a white resinous compound applied to the sunken dots with special brushes. The dice, in process, looked like tiny squares of cherry Jell-O that might have been served up like some sort of low-cal dessert. I watched people place their bets. The Pass line, the Don't Pass line, Come, Don't Come, the Field, the Big 6 and the Big 8 were mysteries of another kind and I couldn't, for the life of me, penetrate the catechism of wins, losses, numbers being rattled out in a low chant of intense concentration and surprise. Over it all there hung a pale cloud of cigarette smoke, infused with the smell of spilled Scotch. The darkened mirrors above the tables must have been scanned by countless pairs of eyes, restlessly raking the patrons below for telltale signs of chicanery. Nothing could escape notice. The atmosphere was that of a crowded Wool-worth's at Christmas, where the throngs of frantic shoppers couldn't be trusted not to lift an item now and then. Even the employees might lie, cheat, and steal, and nothing could be left to chance. I felt a fleeting respect for the whole system of checks and balances that keeps so much money flowing freely and allows so little to slip back into the individual pockets from which it has been coaxed. A sudden feeling of exhaustion came over me. I walked back out to the street again and found a cab.

THE "Middle Eastern" decor of the Bagdad halted abruptly at the door to my room. The carpet was dark green cotton shag, the wallpaper lime-green foil in a pattern of overlapping palms, flocked with small clumps that might have been dates or clusters of fruit bats. I locked the door, kicked off my shoes, and pulled down the chenille spread, crawling under the covers with relief. I put a quick call through to my answering service and another to a groggy Arlette, leaving my latest location with the number where I could be reached.

I woke up at 10:00 A.M., feeling the first faint stages of a headache—as though I had a hangover in the making before I'd even had a drink. Vegas tends to affect me that way, some combination of tension and dread to which my body responds with all the symptoms of incipient flu. I took two Tylenols and showered for a long time, trying to wash away the roiling whisper of nausea. I felt like I'd eaten a pound of cold buttered popcorn and washed it down with bulk saccharin.

I stepped out of my motel room, the light causing me to squint. The air, at least, was fresh and there was, by day, the sense of a town subdued and shrunken, flattened out again to its true proportions. The desert stretched away behind the motel in a haze of pale gray, fading to mauve at the horizon. The wind was mild and dry, the promise of summer heat only hinted at in the distant shimmering sunlight that sat on the desert floor in flat pools, evaporating on approach. Occasional patches of sagebrush, nearly silver with dust, broke up the long low lines of treeless wasteland fenced in by distant hills.

I stopped off at the post office and left a fifty-dollar money order for my friend and then I checked out the address he had

given me. Sharon Napier lived in a two-story apartment complex on the far side of town, salmon-pink stucco eroding
around the edges as though animals had crept up in the night
to gnaw the corners away. The roof was nearly flat, peppered
with rocks, the iron railings sending streaks of rust down the
sides of the building. The landscaping was rock and yucca and
cactus plants. There were only twenty units, arranged around
a kidney-shaped pool that was separated from the parking area
by a dun-colored cinder-block wall. A couple of young kids
were splashing about in the pool and a middle-aged woman
was standing in front of her apartment up on the landing, a
grocery bag wedged between her hip and the door as she let
herself in. A Chicano boy hosed down the walks. The buildings on either side of the complex were single-family dwell-
ings. There was a vacant lot across the street in back.

Sharon's apartment was on the ground floor, her name was
neatly embossed on the mailbox on a white plastic strip. Her
drapes were drawn, but some of the hooks had come loose at
the top, causing the lined fabric to bow inward and sag, forming a gap through which I could see a beige Formica table and
two beige upholstered plastic kitchen chairs. The telephone sat
on one corner of the table, resting on a pile of papers. Beside
it was a coffee cup with a waxy crescent of hot-pink lipstick on
the rim. A cigarette, also rimmed with pink, had been extin-
guished in the saucer. I glanced around. No one seemed to be
paying any particular attention to me. I walked quickly
through a passageway that connected the courtyard to the rear
of the apartment building.

Sharon's apartment number was marked on the rear door,
too, and there were four other back doors at intervals, the
rear entrances emptying into little rectangles surrounded by
shoulder-high cinder-block walls designed, I suspected, to

create the illusion of small patios. The trash containers were lined up on the walkway outside the wall. Her kitchen curtains were drawn. I eased onto her little patio. She had arranged six geraniums in pots along the back step. There were two aluminum folding chairs stacked against the wall, a pile of old newspapers by the back door. There was a small window up on the right and a larger window beyond that. I couldn't judge whether it might be her bedroom or her neighbor's. I looked out across the vacant lot and then eased out of the patio, turning left along the walk, which opened out onto the street again. I got back in my car and headed for the Fremont.

I felt as if I'd never left. The lady in royal blue was still pasted to the quarter slot machine, her hair sculpted into a glossy mahogany scrollwork on top of her head. The same crowd seemed to be pressed to the craps table as though by magnetic force, the croupier pushing chips back and forth with his little stick as if it were a flat-bottomed broom and someone had made an expensive mess. Waitresses circulated with drinks and a heavyset man, whom I guessed to be plainclothes security, wandered about trying to look like a tourist whose luck had gone bad. I could hear the sounds of a female vocalist in the Carnival Lounge, singing a slightly flat but lusty medley of Broadway show tunes. I caught a glimpse of her, emoting to a half-deserted room, her face a bright powder pink under the spotlight.

Sharon Napier was not hard to find. She was tall, maybe five ten or better in her high-heeled shoes. She was the sort of woman you noticed from the ground up: long shapely legs looking slender in black mesh hose, a short black skirt flaring slightly at the tops of her thighs. She had narrow hips, a flat stomach, and her breasts were pushed together to form pronounced mounds. The bodice of her black outfit was tight and low-cut, her name stitched above her left breast. Her hair was an ashen blonde, pallid under the houselights; her eyes an eerie green, a luminous shade I guessed to be from tinted contact lenses. Her skin was pale and unblemished, the oval of her face as white as eggshell and as finely textured. Her lips were full and wide, the bright pink lipstick emphasizing their generous proportions. It was a mouth built for unnatural acts. Something about her demeanor promised cool improvisational sex for the right price and it would not be cheap.

She dealt cards mechanically, with remarkable speed. Three men were perched on stools ranged around the table where she worked. No one said a word. The communication was by the slightest lift of a hand, cards turned over or placed under substantial bets, a shoulder shrugged as the up card showed. Two down, one up. Flick, flick. One man scraped the edge of his up card against the surface of the table, asking for a hit. On the second round, one man turned up a blackjack and she paid off—two hundred and fifty dollars' worth of chips. I could see his eyes take her in as she flicked the cards back, shuffling quickly, dealing out cards again. He was thin, with a narrow balding head and a dark mustache, shirt sleeves rolled up, underarms stained with sweat. His gaze drifted down across her body and back up again to the immaculate face, cold and clean, the green eyes blazing. She paid no particular attention to him, but I had the feeling the two of them might do some private business later on. I retreated to another table, watching her from an easy distance. At 1:30, she took a break. Another dealer took her place and she crossed the casino, heading toward the Fiesta Room, where she ordered a Coke and lit up a cigarette. I followed.

"Are you Sharon Napier?" I asked.

She looked up. Her eyes were rimmed with dark lashes, the green taking on an almost turquoise hue in the fluorescent light overhead.

"I don't think we've met," she said.

"I'm Kinsey Millhone," I said. "May I sit down?"

She shrugged by way of consent. She took a compact out of her pocket and checked her eye makeup, removing a slight smudge of shadow from her upper lid. Her lashes were clearly false, but the effect was flashy, giving her eyes an exotic slant. She applied fresh lip gloss, using her little finger, which she dipped into a tiny pot of pink. "What can I do for you?" she asked, glancing up briefly from her compact mirror.

"I'm looking into the death of Laurence Fife."

That stopped her. She paused, her whole body going still. If I'd been taking a picture, it would have been the perfect pose. A second passed and she was in motion again. She snapped the compact shut and tucked it away, taking up her cigarette. She took a long drag, watching me all the while. She flicked an ash. "He was a real shitheel," she said brusquely, smoke wafting out with each word.

"So I've heard," I said. "Did you work for him long?"

She smiled. "Well, you've done your homework at any rate. I bet you even know the answer to that."

"More or less," I said. "But there's lots I don't know. Want to fill me in?"

"On what?"

I shrugged. "What it was like to work for him? How you felt about his death . . ."

"He was a prick to work for. I felt terrific about his death," she said. "I hated secretarial work in case you haven't guessed."

"This must suit you better," I said.

"Look, I got nothing to discuss with you," she said flatly. "Who sent you up here anyway?"

I took a flyer on that one. "Nikki."

She seemed startled. "She's still in prison. Isn't she?"

I shook my head. "She's out."

She took a moment to calculate and then her manner became somewhat more gracious. "She's got bucks, right?"

"She's not hurting, if that's what you mean."

She stubbed out her cigarette, bending the live ember under and mashing it flat. "I'm off at seven. Why don't you come out to my place and we can chat."

"Anything you'd care to mention now?"

"Not here," she said.

She rattled out her address and I dutifully jotted it down in my notebook. She glanced off to the left and I thought at first she was lifting a hand to greet a friend. Her smile flashed and then faltered and she glanced back at me with uncertainty, turning slightly so that my line of sight was blocked. I peered back over her shoulder automatically but she distracted my attention, touching the back of my hand with a fingernail. I looked at her. She towered over me, her expression remote.

"That was the pit boss. End of my break."

She told lies the way I do, with a certain breezy insolence that dares the listener to refute or contradict.

"I'll see you at seven then," I said.

"Make it seven forty-five," she said easily. "I need time to unwind from work."

I wrote out my name and the name of my motel, tearing a sheet from my notebook. She made a sharp crease and tucked the slip into her cigarette pack under the cellophane wrapper. She walked away without a backward glance, hips swaying gracefully.

The mashed butt of her cigarette was still sending up a drift of smoke and my stomach emitted a little message of protest. I was tempted to hang around, just to keep an eye on her, but my hands were feeling clammy and I longed to lie down. I didn't feel good at all and I was beginning to think that my flu symptoms might be more real than reactionary. The headache was creeping up again from the back of my neck. I walked out through the lobby. Fresh air helped me some but only momentarily.

I drove back to the Bagdad and bought a 7Up from the vending machine. I needed to eat but I wasn't sure anything would stay down. It was early afternoon and I didn't have to be anywhere until well after suppertime. I put the Do Not Disturb sign on my door and crawled back into my unmade bed, pulling the covers around me tightly. My bones had begun to ache. It was a long time before I got warm.

THE TELEPHONE RANG WITH STARTLING SHRILLNESS AND I awoke with a jolt. The room was dark. I had no idea what time it was, no idea what bed I was in. I groped for the phone, feeling flushed and hot, shoving the covers away from me as I propped myself up on one elbow. I flicked on the light, shading my eyes from the sudden harsh glare.

"Hello?"

"Kinsey, this is Sharon. Did you forget about me?"

I looked at my watch. It was 8:30. Shit. "God, I'm sorry," I said. "I fell asleep. Will you be there for a while? I can be right over."

"All right," she said coolly, as though she had better plans. "Oh, hang on. There's someone at my door."

She put the phone down with a clack and I pictured it resting on the hard Formica surface of the tabletop. I listened idly, waiting for her to come back. I couldn't believe I'd overslept and I was kicking myself for my stupidity. I heard the door open and her muffled exclamation of surprise. And then I heard a brief, nearly hollow report.

I squinted, sitting up abruptly. I pressed my ear to the phone, pressing my hand over the receiver. What was going on? The receiver was picked up on her end. I expected to hear her voice and I nearly spoke her name but some impulse made me clamp my mouth shut. There was the sound of breathing in my ear, the sexless hushed tones of someone slightly winded. There was a whispered "hello" that chilled me. I closed my eyes, willing myself to silence; an alarm had spread through my body in a rush that made my heart pound in my ears. There was a small breathy chuckle and then the line went dead. I slammed the phone down and reached for my shoes, grabbing my jacket as I left the room.

The jolt of adrenaline had washed my body clean of pain. My hands were shaking but at least I was in motion. I locked the door and went out to the car, my keys jingling as I tried to hit the ignition switch. I started the car and backed out rapidly, heading toward Sharon's apartment. I reached for the flashlight in my glove compartment, checking it. The light was strong. I drove, anxiety mounting. She was either playing games or dead, and I suspected I knew which.

I pulled up across the street. The building showed no particular signs of activity. No one was moving about. There were no crowds gathered, no police cars parked at the street, no sirens wailing an approach. There were numerous cars parked in the slots, and the lights in the building had been turned on in almost every apartment that I could see. I reached around in the backseat, removing a pair of rubber gloves from my locked briefcase. My hand touched the short barrel of my little automatic and I desperately longed to tuck that in my windbreaker pocket. I wasn't sure what I'd find in her apartment, wasn't sure who might be waiting for me, but the notion of being discovered there in possession of a loaded gun wouldn't do at all if she was dead. I left the gun where it was and got out, locking my car, tucking the keys into my jeans.

I moved into the front courtyard. It was dark, but several outdoor spots were placed strategically along the walk, six more green and yellow spots shooting upward along the cactus plants. The effect was more gaudy than illuminating. Sharon's apartment was dark and the gap in the drapes had been pulled tight. I tapped at the door. "Sharon?" I kept my voice low, scanning the front of the place for any signs of lights coming on. I pulled on the rubber gloves and tried the knob. Locked. I tapped again, repeating her name. There was no sound from inside. What was I going to do if someone was in there?

I moved along the short stretch of walk that led around the building to the rear. I could hear a stereo playing somewhere in one of the upstairs apartments. The small of my back ached and my cheeks felt as hot as if I'd just gotten back from a run, though whether it was from flu or fear I couldn't say. I moved quickly and silently along the rear walkway. Sharon's kitchen was the only one of the five that was dark. There was an outside bulb burning above each back door, casting a shallow but clear light onto each small patio. I tried the back door. Locked. I tapped on the glass.

"Sharon?" I strained for sounds inside the apartment. All was quiet. I scanned the rear entrance. If she had an extra set of keys outside, they would be hidden someplace close. I glanced back at the small panes of glass in her back door. If all else failed, I could always break one out. I slid my fingers along the top of the doorframe. Too narrow for keys. All the flowerpots seemed straight and a quick search revealed nothing tucked down in the dirt. There was no doormat. I lifted the pile of old newspapers, giving them a little riff, but no keys clattered out. The surrounding cinder-block patio wall was made of one-foot square decorative "bricks," each design of sufficient intricacy to provide an ample, if not original, hiding place for a key. I hoped I wasn't going to have to check every single one. I glanced back at the small panes of glass, wondering if it might not be more to the point to pop one out with a padded fist. I looked down. There was a green plastic watering can and a trowel in one corner right up against the wall. I crouched, sliding my right hand into each of the decorative whorls of concrete. There was a key in one.

I reached up and gave the bulb above her back door a quick twist to the left. The patio was immersed in shadow. I fitted the key into the knob lock and opened the door a crack. "Sharon!" I whispered hoarsely. I was tempted to leave the apartment in darkness but I had to know if I was alone. I held the flashlight like a club, groping to my right until I found a switch. The recessed light above the sink went on. I saw the switch to the overhead kitchen light on the opposite wall. I crossed the room and flipped it on, ducking down and out of sight. I hunkered, holding my breath, my back against the refrigerator. I listened intently. Nothing. I hoped like hell I wasn't making a colossal fool of myself. For all I knew, the noise I'd heard was the popping of a champagne cork and Sharon was in the darkened bedroom performing illicit sexual acts with a little show dog and a whip.

I peered into the living room. Sharon was sprawled out on

the living-room floor in a kelly green velour robe. She was either dead or sound asleep and I still didn't know who else might be in that apartment with me. I crossed to the living room in two steps and pressed myself up against the wall, waiting a moment before I peered back out into the darkened hallway. I couldn't see shit. I found a light switch just to my left and flipped it on. The hall was ablaze with light and the portion of the bedroom I could see seemed unoccupied. I felt for the bedroom switch and flipped it on, peering around quickly. I guessed the open doorway off to my right was the bathroom. There was no indication that the place had been ransacked. The sliding closet doors were shut and I didn't like that. From the bathroom, there was a faint metallic sound. I froze. My heart gave a thud and a half and I crouched. Me and my flashlight. I wished like hell I'd brought the gun. The little metallic squeak picked up again, assuming a rhythm that suddenly took on a familiar tone. I crept over to the door and flashed the light in. There was a goddamn little mouse going round and round in an exercise wheel. The cage sat on the bathroom counter. I flipped the light on. The bathroom was empty.

I crossed to the closet doors and slid one open, half waiting to get my head bashed in. Both sides of the closet were empty of anything but clothing. I let out the long breath I'd been holding and then did a second quick search of the place. I made sure the back door was locked, pulling the kitchen curtains across the window above the sink. And then I went back to Sharon. I flipped on the lamp in the living room and knelt down beside her. She had a bullet hole at the base of her throat, looking like a little locket filled with raw flesh instead of a photograph. Blood had soaked into the carpet under her head and it had darkened now to the color of uncooked chicken liver. There were small slivers of bone in her hair. I guessed that her spine had been shattered by the bullet on impact. Nice for her. No pain. She seemed to have been knocked straight back, arms flung out on either side of her body, her hips turned slightly. Her eyes were half open, the luminous green color looking sour now. Her blonde hair looked gray in death. If I'd gotten there when I was supposed to, she might not be dead, and I wanted to apologize for my bad manners, for the delay, for being sick, for being too late. I wanted to hold her hand and coax her back to life again but there was no way and I knew, in a quick flash, that if I'd been there on time, I might be dead myself.

I ran my gaze around the room with care. The carpeting was a high-low, matted with wear, so there were no shoe prints. I crossed to the front window and readjusted the drapes, making sure no crack appeared to afford a view from outside now that the lights were turned on. I made a brief tour again, taking in details this time. The bed was unmade. The bathroom was littered with damp towels. Dirty clothing bulged out of the hamper. An ashtray sat on the rim of the tub with several cigarette butts stubbed out, folded over and mashed flat in the manner I'd seen her use. The apartment was basically only those three rooms—living room with the dining table near the front windows, kitchen, and bedroom. The furniture looked as if it had been ordered by the boxcarload, and I assumed that little of it was actually hers. Whatever the disorder on the premises, it seemed to be of her own making—dishes in the sink, trash unemptied. I glanced down at the papers under the phone, a collection of past-due notices and bills. Apparently her penchant for financial chaos hadn't changed since her days in Santa Teresa. I picked up the whole batch and shoved them into my jacket pocket.

I could hear the little metallic squeak again and I went back to the bathroom, staring down at that foolish little creature.

He was small and brown, with bright red eyes, patiently making his way around and around, going nowhere. "I'm sorry," I whispered, and tears stung my lips briefly. I shook my head. It was misplaced sentiment and I knew it. His water bottle was full but the plastic food dish was empty. I filled it with little green pellets and then I went back to the phone and dialed the operator, asking for the Las Vegas police. Con Dolan's warning sounded dully in my memory. All I needed was the LVPD holding me for questioning. One of those gravelly officious voices came on the line after two rings.

"Oh hello," I said. My voice had a tremor in it and I had to clear my throat quickly. "I, uh, heard some noise in my neighbor's apartment a little while ago and now I can't seem to get her to answer my knock. I'm worried that she's hurt herself. Is there any way you could check that out?"

He sounded irritated and bored, but he took down Sharon's address and said he'd send someone.

I checked my watch. I'd been in the apartment less than thirty minutes, but it was time to get out of there. I didn't want the phone to ring. I didn't want somebody knocking at the door unexpectedly. I moved toward the back, turning out lights as I went, unconsciously listening for sounds of someone approaching. I didn't have a lot of time to spare.

I glanced back at Sharon. I didn't like to leave her that way but I couldn't see the point in waiting it out. I didn't want to be linked to her death and I didn't want to hang around Las Vegas waiting for the coroner's inquest. And I certainly didn't want Con Dolan to find out I'd been here. Maybe the Mafia had killed her, or maybe some pimp, or maybe the man at the casino who'd looked at her with such hunger when she counted out his two hundred and fifty bucks. Or maybe she knew something about Laurence Fife that she wasn't supposed to tell.

I moved past her. Her fingers were relaxed in death, looking graceful, each tipped with a long rose-polished nail. I caught my breath. She had taken the slip with my name and motel jotted on it and had tucked it into her cigarette pack. But where was it? I looked around quickly, heart racing. I didn't see it on the Formica tabletop, though there was a cigarette that had apparently burned down to nothing, leaving only a perfect column of ash. There was no cigarette pack on the arm of the couch, none on the counter. I checked the bathroom again, listening acutely for sounds of the police. I could have sworn I heard a siren some distance off and I felt a ripple of alarm. Shit. I had to find that note. The bathroom trash was full of Kleenex and a soap wrapper, old cigarette butts. No cigarette pack on the bedtable. None on the dresser top. I went back to the living room and looked down at her with distaste. There were two generous side pockets in the green velour robe. I gritted my teeth, feeling gingerly. The pack was on the right-hand side, with maybe six cigarettes left, the sharply creased slip of paper bearing my name still visible under the cellophane. I tucked it hastily into my jacket.

I turned out the remaining lights and slipped to the back door, opening it a crack. I could hear voices remarkably close. A garbage can lid clattered near the apartment to my right.

"You better tell the manager her light's burned out," a woman commented. She sounded as if she was standing right next to me.

"Why don't you tell *her*?" came the slightly annoyed reply.

"I don't think she's home. Her lights are off."

"Yes she is. I just saw the lights on a minute ago."

"Sherman, they're off. The whole place is dark. She must have gone out the front," the woman said. The wailing siren was very loud, its tone winding down like a phonograph.

My heart was pounding so hard it was making my chest burn. I eased out onto the darkened patio, pausing to tuck the keys back into the little crevice behind the plastic watering can. I hoped like hell it wasn't my car keys I was hiding there. I slipped out of the patio, turning left, moving toward the street again. I had to force myself to walk casually past the patrol car that was now parked out front. I unlocked my car and got in, pushing the lock down hastily as though someone were in pursuit. I stripped off the rubber gloves. My head was aching fiercely and I felt a flash of clammy sweat, bile rising up in my throat. I had to get out of there. I swallowed convulsively. The nausea welled up and I fought an almost irresistible urge to heave. My hands were shaking so badly I could hardly get my car started but I managed, finally, and pulled away from the curb with care.

As I drove past the entranceway, I could see a uniformed patrolman move around to the back of Sharon's apartment, hand on the gun at his hip. It seemed somewhat theatrical for a simple domestic complaint and I wondered, with a chill, if someone else had placed a call with a message more explicit than mine. Half a minute more and I'd have been trapped in that apartment with a lot of explaining to do. I didn't like that idea at all.

I went back to the Bagdad and packed, cleaning the place of fingerprints. I felt as if I were running a low-grade fever. All I really wanted to do was roll up in a blanket and go back to sleep. Head throbbing, I went into the office. The manager's wife was there this time, looking like a Turkish harem girl—if the word "girl" applied. She was probably sixty-five, with a finely wrinkled face, like something that had been left in the dryer too long. She wore a pale satin pillbox perched on her gray hair, veils draped provocatively over her ears.

"I'll be on the road at five in the morning and I thought I'd get my bill squared away tonight," I said.

I gave her my room number and she sorted through the upright file, coming up with my ledger card. I was feeling restless, anxious, and sick, and I wanted to be out on the road. Instead, I had to force myself, brightly, casually, to deal with this woman who moved in slow motion.

"Where you headed?" she asked idly, toting up the charges on the adding machine. She made a mistake and had to do it all over again.

"Reno," I said, lying automatically.

"Any luck?"

"What?"

"You win much?"

"Oh yeah, I'm doing pretty good," I said. "I really surprised myself."

"Better than most folk," she remarked. "You won't be making any long-distance calls before you leave?" She gave me a sharp look.

I shook my head. "I'm going to hit the sack."

"You look like you could use some sleep," she said. She filled out the credit-card charge slip, which I signed, taking my copy.

"I didn't use the fifty dollars' worth of coupons," I said. "You might as well have those back."

She put the unused coupons in the drawer without a word.

Within minutes, miraculously, I was out on Highway 93, heading southeast toward Boulder City, where I took 95 south. I got as far as Needles and then I had to have relief. I found a cheap motel and checked in, crawled under the covers again, and slept for ten hours straight. Even that far down in oblivion, I felt an awesome dread of what had been set in motion and a pointless, aching sense of apology to Sharon Napier for whatever part I'd played in her death.

14

In the morning, I felt whole again. I ate a big breakfast in a little diner across the road from the motel, washing down bacon, scrambled eggs, and rye toast with fresh orange juice and three cups of coffee. I had the car filled up with gas, the oil checked, and then hit the road again. After Las Vegas, the desert drive was a pleasure. The land was spare, the colors subdued: a mild very pale lavender overlaid with fine dust. The sky was a stark, cloudless blue, the mountain ridges like crushed velvet, wrinkled dark gray along the face. There was something appealing about all that country unconquered yet, miles and miles of terrain without neon signs. The population was reduced to races of kangaroo rat and ground squirrel, the rocky canyons inhabited by kit fox and desert lynx. At fifty-five miles an hour, no wildlife was visible but I had heard the cries of tree frogs even in my sleep and I pictured now, from my speeding car, the clay and gravel washes filled with buff-colored lizards and millipedes, creatures whose adaption to their environment include the husbanding of moisture and an aversion to hot sun. There are parasol ants in the desert that cut off leaves and carry them as sunshades over their backs, storing them later like beach umbrellas in the subterranean chambers where they live. The idea made me smile, and I kept my mind resolutely from the recollection of Sharon Napier's death.

I found Greg Fife in a little gray humpbacked camper outside Durmid on the eastern shore of the Salton Sea. It had taken me a while to track him down. Gwen had said that he lived on his boat but the boat had been pulled out of the water for paint and repair and Greg was temporarily lodged in an aluminum trailer that looked like a roly-poly bug. The interior was compact with a folding table hooked flat against the wall, a padded bench that became a single bed, a canvas chair that completely blocked passage to the sink, a chemical toilet, and a hot plate. He opened two bottles of beer, which he'd taken from a refrigerator the size of a cardboard box, located under the sink.

He offered me the padded bench, unfolding the small table between us. A single leg flopped down to give it support. I was effectively hemmed in and could only get comfortable by turning sideways. Greg took the canvas chair, tilting back so he could study me while I studied him. He looked a lot like Laurence Fife—lank dark-brown hair, a square-cut smooth face that was clean-shaven, dark eyes, bold dark brows, square chin.

He looked younger than twenty-five but his smile had the same touch of arrogance that I remembered from his father. He was darkly tanned, cheekbones tinted with sunburn. His shoulders were wide, his body lean, his feet bare. He wore a red cotton turtleneck and cutoffs that were ragged at the bottom, nearly ruffled with bleached threads. He took a sip of beer.

"You think I look like him?"

"Yes," I said. "Does that suit you?"

Greg shrugged. "Doesn't matter much at this point," he said. "We weren't anything alike."

"How so?"

"God," he said facetiously, "let's just skip over the preliminaries and get right down to the personal stuff, why don't we."

I smiled. "I'm not very polite."

"Neither am I," he said.

"So what do you want to talk about first? The weather?"

"Skip it," he said. "I know what you're here for so get to the point."

"You remember much about that time in your life?"

"Not if I can help it."

"Except for shrinks," I suggested.

"I did that to please my mom," he said and then smiled briefly as though he recognized the fact that the phrase "my mom" sounded too boyish for him, at his age.

"I worked for your father a couple of times," I said.

He began to peel a strip of label with his thumbnail, feigning disinterest. I wondered what he'd heard about his father and I decided, on impulse, not to give Laurence Fife any posthumous pats lest I sound condescending or insincere.

I said, "I've heard he was a real bastard."

"No shit," Greg said.

I shrugged. "I didn't think he was that bad myself. He was

straight with me. I suspect he was a complicated man and I
don't think many people got close to him."

"Did you?"

"No," I said. I shifted slightly in my seat. "How'd you feel
about Nikki?"

"Not that good."

I smiled. "Try to keep your answers short so I can get 'em
on one line," I said. He didn't bite. I drank beer for a while,
then rested my chin on my fist. Sometimes I just really do get
sick of trying to coax information out of people who aren't in
the mood. "Why don't you fold up the table and we'll go outside," I said.

"What for?"

"So I can get some fresh air, fucker, what do you think?"

He chuckled suddenly and moved his long legs out of my
way as I slid out of the seat.

I'd surprised myself, getting snappish with him, but I get
tired of people being cute or sullen or cautious or tight-
lipped. I wanted straight answers and a lot of them too. And I
wanted a relationship based, just once, on some sort of mutual
exchange instead of me always having to connive and manipulate. I walked aimlessly, Greg at my heels, trying to cool myself down. It wasn't his fault, I knew, and I'm suspicious of
myself anyway when I'm feeling righteous and misunderstood.

"Sorry I snapped at you," I said.

The trailer was about two hundred yards from the water's
edge. There were several larger trailers nearby, all facing the
sea, like a queer band of animals that had crept down to the
water to drink. I pulled off my tennis shoes and tied the laces
together, hanging them around my neck. The Salton Sea has
a mild to nonexistent surf, like an ocean that has been totally
tamed. There is no vegetation visible in the water and few if

any fish. It gives the shore a curious air, as though the tides had been brought to heel, becalmed, the life forms leeched away. What remains is familiar but subtly changed, like a glimpse into the future where certain laws of nature have been altered by the passage of time. I placed a drop of water on my tongue. The taste of salt was fierce. "Is this ocean water?"

Greg smiled, apparently unperturbed by my former outburst. In fact he seemed friendlier. "You want a lesson in geology," he said, "I'll give you one." It was the first time his voice had contained any sign of enthusiasm.

"Sure, why not?"

He picked up a rock, using it like a piece of chalk as he drew a crude map in the wet sand. "This is the California coastline and this is Baja. Over here is Mexico. Right at the tip of the Gulf of California is Yuma—southeast of here, more or less. This is us here," he said, pointing. "The Colorado River curves right up through here and then up past Las Vegas. That's Hoover Dam. Then it goes up here and over into Utah and then to Colorado, but we can skip that part. Now," he said, tossing the rock aside. He began to draw with his fingertip, glancing up at me to see if I was listening. "This area in here is called the Salton Sink. Two hundred and seventy-three feet below sea level—something like that. If it weren't for the Colorado River forming a kind of natural dam right here, all this water from the Gulf of California would have spilled into the Salton Sink years ago—all the way up to Indio. God, that gives me the willies when I think of it. Anyway, the Salton Sea came from the Colorado River itself, so it was originally fresh water. Overflowed in 1905—the river did, billions of gallons of water pouring in over a two-year period. It was finally controlled with rock and brush dams. The salt, which has been gradually saturating the water, was probably from prehistoric times when all of this area was submerged." He stood up, brushing wet sand off his hands, apparently satisfied with his summary.

We began to walk—he on the beach side, me scuffling my bare feet through the shallows. He tucked his hands in his back pockets. "Sorry if I was a pissant before," he said lightly. "I've been in a bad mood with my boat out of the water. I was never meant to be on land."

"You sure snapped out of it quick enough," I remarked.

"Because you said 'fuck.' I always get tickled when women say that. Especially you. It was the last thing I expected to come out of your mouth."

"What do you do down here?" I asked. "Fish?"

"Some. Mostly sail. Read. Drink beer. Hang out."

"I'd go nuts."

Greg shrugged. "I started out nuts so I'm getting sane."

"Not really 'nuts,' " I said.

"Not certifiable, no."

"What kind then?"

"Don't make me tell all that stuff," he said mildly. "I get bored with myself. Ask me something else. Three questions. Like magic wishes."

"If I have to limit myself to three questions, I might as well go home," I said, but basically I was willing to play the game. I looked over at him. He was looking less like his father and more like himself. "What do you remember from the period just before he died?"

"You asked me that before."

"Yeah, and that's just about the time you turned all surly on me. I'll tell you why I'm asking. Maybe that will help. I'd like to reconstruct the events just before his death. Maybe as far back as the last six months before he was killed. I mean, maybe he was involved in some kind of legal hassle—a personal feud.

Maybe he fought with a neighbor over a property line. Somebody did it, and there had to be a sequence of events."

"I wouldn't know about that stuff," he said. "I can tell you just family events, but the other I wouldn't know."

"That's okay."

"We came down here that fall. That's one of the reasons I came back."

I wanted to prompt him with another question but I was afraid he'd count it as one of my three so I kept my mouth shut. He went on.

"I was seventeen. God, I was such a jerk and I thought my father was so impossibly perfect. I didn't know what he expected of me but I figured I'd never measure up, so I was a pissant. He was supercritical and he hurt my feelings a lot, but I'd just stonewall him. Half the time I hung on his every word and the rest of the time I hated his guts. So when he died, I lost the chance to square myself with him. I mean, for all time, you know? That's it. I've got no way to take care of any old business with him, so I'm stuck. I figured if I was stuck in time, I might as well be stuck in place, too, so that's why I came here. We were out on the beach once—and he had to go back to the car for something and I remember watching him walk. Just looking at him. He had his head bent and he was probably thinking about anything but me. I felt like I should call him back, really tell him how much I loved him, but of course I didn't. So that's the way I remember him. That whole business really screwed me up."

"It was just the two of you?"

"What? No, the whole family. Except Diane. She got sick and stayed with Mom. It was Labor Day weekend. We drove to Palm Springs first, just for the day, and then came on down here."

"How'd you feel about Colin?"

"Okay I guess, but I didn't see why the whole family had to revolve around him. The kid had a handicap and I felt bad about that, but I didn't want my life to focus on his infirmity, you know? I mean, Jesus, I would have had to develop a terminal disease to compete with him. This is me at seventeen, you understand. Now I'm a little more compassionate, but back then, I couldn't cope with that stuff. I didn't see why I should. Dad and I were never bosom buddies, but I needed time with him too. I used to have these fantasies of what it would be like. I'd really tell him something important and he'd really listen to me. Instead, all we talked about was bullshit—just *bull*shit. So six weeks later he's dead."

He glanced at me and then shook his head, smiling sheepishly.

"Shakespeare should have done a play about this stuff," he said. "I could have done the monologue."

"So he never talked to you about his personal life?"

"That's number three, you know," he remarked. "You sneaked in that little question about whether it was just Dad and me down here. But the answer is no. He never talked to me about anything. I told you I couldn't be much help. Let's knock it off for a while, okay?"

I smiled and tossed my shoes up on the beach, starting to jog.

"Do you jog?" I called back over my shoulder.

"Yeah, some," he said, catching up. He began to trot at my side.

"What happens if I work up a sweat?" I asked. "Can we get cleaned up?"

"The neighbors let me use their shower."

"Great," I said and picked up the pace.

WE RAN, not exchanging a word, just taking in sun and sand and dry heat. The whole time, the same question came up over and over again. How could Sharon Napier fit into this scheme? What could she possibly have known that she didn't live long enough to tell? So far, none of it made sense. Not Fife's death, not Libby's, not Sharon's death eight years later. Unless she was blackmailing someone. I glanced back at the little trailer, still visible, looking remarkably close in the odd perspective of the flat desert landscape. There was no one else around. No sign of vehicles, no boogeymen on foot. I smiled at Greg. He wasn't even panting yet.

"You're in good shape," I said.

"So are you. How long do we keep this up?"

"Thirty minutes. Forty-five."

We chunked along for a while, the sand causing mild pains in my calves.

"How about I ask you three?" he said.

"Okay."

"How'd you get along with your old man?"

"Oh great," I said. "He died when I was five. Both of them did. In a car wreck. Up near Lompoc. Big rock rolled down the mountain and smashed the windshield. Took them six hours to pry me out of the back. My mother cried for a while and then she stopped. I still hear it sometimes in my sleep. Not the sobs. The silence after that. I was raised by my aunt. Her sister."

He digested that. "You married?"

"Was." I held up two fingers.

He smiled. "Is that for 'twice' or question number two?"

I laughed. "That's number three."

"Hey come on. You cheat."

"All right. One more. But make it count."

"You ever kill anyone?"

I glanced over at him with curiosity. It seemed like a strange follow-up. "Let's put it this way," I said. "I did my first homicide investigation when I was twenty-six. A job I did for the public defender's office. A woman accused of killing her own kids. Three of them. Girls. All under five. Taped their mouths, hands, and feet, then put them in garbage cans and let them suffocate. I had to look at the glossy eight-by-ten police photographs. I got cured of any homicidal urges. Also any desire for motherhood."

"Jesus," he said. "And she really did it?"

"Oh sure. She got off, of course. Pleaded temporary insanity. She might be back on the streets again for all I know."

"How do you keep from getting cynical?" he asked.

"Who says I'm not?"

WHILE I showered in the trailer next door, I tried to think what else I might learn from Greg. I was feeling restless, anxious to be on the road again. If I could get to Claremont by dark, I could talk to Diane first thing in the morning and then drive back to Los Angeles after lunch. I toweled my hair dry and dressed. Greg had opened another beer for me, which I sipped while I waited for him to get cleaned up. I glanced at my watch. It was 3:15. Greg came into the trailer, leaving the door open, sliding the screen door shut. His dark hair was still damp and he smelled of soap.

"You look poised for flight," he said, getting himself a beer. He popped the cap.

"I'm thinking I should try to get to Claremont before dark," I said. "You have any messages for your sister?"

"She knows where I am. We talk now and then, often enough to keep caught up," he said. He sat down in the canvas chair, propping his feet up on the padded bench next to me. "Anything else you want to ask?"

"Couple of things if you don't mind," I said.

"Fire away."

"What do you remember about your father's allergies?"

"Dogs, cat dander, sometimes hay fever but I don't know what that consisted of exactly."

"He wasn't allergic to any kind of food? Eggs? Wheat?"

Greg shook his head. "Not that I ever heard. Just stuff in the air—pollens, things like that."

"Did he have his allergy capsules with him when the family came down here that weekend?"

"I don't remember that. I would guess no. He knew we'd be out in the desert and the air down here is usually pretty clear even in late summer, early fall. The dog wasn't with us. We left him at home, so Dad wouldn't have needed the allergy medication for that, and I don't think there was anything else he needed it for."

"I thought the dog got killed. I thought Nikki told me that," I said.

"Yeah, he was. While we were gone as a matter of fact."

I felt a sudden chill. There was something odd about that, something off. "How'd you find out about it?"

Greg shrugged. "When we got home," he said, apparently not attaching much to the fact. "Mom had taken Diane over to the house to pick something up. Sunday morning I guess. We didn't get back until Monday night. Anyway, they found Bruno lying out on the side of the road. I guess he was pretty badly mangled. Mom wouldn't even let Diane see him up close. She called the animal-shelter people and they came and picked him up. He'd been dead awhile. All of us felt bad about it. He was a great beast."

"Good watchdog?"

"The best," he said.

"What about Mrs. Voss, the housekeeper? What was she like?"

"Nice enough, I guess. She seemed to get along with everybody," he said. "I wish I knew more but that's about it as far as I can tell."

I finished my beer and got up, holding out my hand to him. "Thanks, Greg. I may need to talk to you again if that's okay."

He kissed the back of my hand, pretending to clown but meaning something else, I was almost sure. "Godspeed," he said softly.

I smiled with unexpected pleasure. "Did you ever see *Young Bess*? Jean Simmons and Stewart Granger? That's what he says to her. He was doomed, I think, or maybe she was—I forget. Ripped my heart out. You ought to watch for it on the late movie some night. It killed me when I was a kid."

"You're only five or six years older than me," he said.

"Seven," I replied.

"Same smell."

"I'll let you know what I find out," I said.

"Good luck."

As I pulled away, I glanced back out of the car window. Greg was standing in the trailer doorway, the screen creating the ghostly illusion of Laurence Fife again.

I reached Claremont at 6:00, driving through Ontario, Montclair, and Pomona: all townships without real towns, a peculiar California phenomenon in which a series of shopping malls and acres of tract houses acquire a zip code and become realities on the map. Claremont is an oddity in that it resembles a trim little midwestern hamlet with elms and picket fences. The annual Fourth of July parade is composed of kazoo bands, platoons of children on crepe-paper-decorated bikes, and a self-satirizing team of husbands dressed in Bermuda shorts, black socks, and business shoes doing close-order drills with power mowers.

Except for the smog, Claremont could even be considered "picturesque" with Mount Baldy forming a raw backdrop.

I pulled into a gas station and called the number Gwen had given me for Diane. She was out, but her roommate said she'd be home at 8:00. I headed up Indian Hill Boulevard, turning left onto Baughman. My friends Gideon and Nell live two doors down in a house with two kids, three cats, and a hot tub. Nell I've known since my college days. She's a creature of high intellect and wry humor who's learned never to be too amazed by my appearances on her doorstep. She seemed pleased to see me nevertheless and I sat in her kitchen, watching her make soup while we talked. I called Diane again after supper and she agreed to meet me for lunch. After that, Nell and I stripped down and soaked in the hot tub out on the deck, with icy white wine and a lot more catching up to do. Gideon graciously kept the children at bay. I slept on the couch that night with a cat curled up on my chest, wondering if there was any way I could have such a life for myself.

I MET Diane at one of those brown-bread-and-sprout restaurants that all look the same: lots of natural varnished wood and healthy hanging plants, macramé and leaded-glass windows and waiters who don't smoke cigarettes but would probably toke on anything else you've got. Ours was thin with receding hair and a dark mustache, which he stroked incessantly, taking our order with an earnestness that I don't think any sandwich ever deserved. Mine was avocado and bacon. Hers was a "vegetarian delite" stuffed in pita bread.

"Greg says he really treated you like shit when you first got down there," she said and laughed. Some sort of dressing was leaking out through a crack in her pita bread and she lapped it off.

"When did you talk to him? Last night?"

"Sure." She took another unwieldy mouthful and I watched her lick her fingers and wipe her chin. She had Greg's clean good looks but she carried more weight, wide rump packed into a pair of faded jeans, and an unexpected powdering of freckles on her face. Her dark hair was parted in the center and pulled up on top with a broad leather band, pierced through with a wooden skewer.

"Did you know Nikki was out on parole?" I asked.

"That's what Mom said. Is Colin back?"

"Nikki was just on her way up to get him when I talked to her a couple of days ago," I said. I was struggling to keep my sandwich intact, thick bread breaking with every bite, but I caught the look in her eye. Colin interested her. Nikki did not.

"Did you meet Mom?"

"Yes. I liked her a lot."

Diane flashed a quick, proud smile. "Daddy was really an asshole to dump her for Nikki if you ask me. I mean, Nikki's okay, but she's kind of cold, don't you think?"

I murmured something noncommittal. Diane didn't seem to be listening anyway. "Your mother said you went into therapy right after your father died," I said.

Diane rolled her eyes, taking a sip of peppermint tea. "I've been in therapy half my life and my head's still not on straight. It's really a drag. The shrink I got now thinks I should go into analysis but nobody does that anymore. He says I need to go into my 'dark' side. He's into this real Freudian horseshit. All those old guys are. You know, they want you to lie there and tell 'em all your dreams and kinky fantasies so they can whack off mentally at your expense. I did Reichian before that but I got sick of huffing and puffing and pulling on towels. That just felt dumb to me."

I took a big bite of sandwich, nodding as if I knew what she was talking about. "I've never been in therapy," I murmured.

"Not even *group*?"

I shook my head.

"God, you must really be neurotic," she said respectfully.

"Well I don't bite my nails or wet the bed."

"You're probably the compulsive type, avoiding commitments and shit like that. Daddy was like that some."

"Like how?" I said, skipping right over the reference to my character. After all, it was just a wild guess.

"Oh. You know. Fucking around all the time. Greg and I still compare notes on that. My shrink says he was just warding off pain. My granny used to manipulate the shit out of him so he turned around and manipulated everyone else, including Greg and me. And Mom. And Nikki, and I don't even know who else. I don't think he ever loved anybody in his life except Colin maybe. Too threatening."

She finished her sandwich and spent a few minutes wiping her face and hands. Then she folded the paper napkin carefully.

"Greg told me you missed the trip to Salton Sea," I said.

"What, before Daddy died? Yeah I did. I had the flu, really grisly stuff, so I stayed with Mom. She was great, really poured on the TLC. I never slept so much in my life."

"How did the dog get out?"

She put her hands in her lap. "What?"

"Bruno. Greg said he got hit by a car. I just wondered who let him out. Was Mrs. Voss staying at the house while the family was gone?"

Diane looked at me with care and then away. "I don't think so. She was on vacation, I think." Her eyes strayed to the clock on the wall behind me. "I've got a class," she said. Her face was suffused with pink.

"Are you okay?"

"Sure. Fine," she said, casually gathering up her purse and books. She seemed relieved to have something to do. "Oh, I nearly forgot. I've got something for Colin if you're going to see him." She held out a paper bag. "It's an album I put together for him. We had all those pictures in a box." She was all business now, her manner distracted, her attention disengaged. She gave me a brief smile. "I'm sorry I don't have any more time. How much is my part of the lunch?"

"I'll take care of it," I said. "Can I drop you someplace?"

"I've got a car," she said. All the animation had left her face.

"Diane, what's going on?" I said.

She sat down again abruptly, staring straight ahead. Her voice had dropped about six notes. "I let the dog out myself," she said, "the day they left. Nikki said to let him have a run before Mom picked me up so I did but I just felt like shit. I lay down on the couch in the living room to wait for Mom and when she honked, I just grabbed my stuff and went out the front. I never even thought about the dog. He must have been running around for two days before I remembered. That's why Mom and I drove over there. To feed him and let him in."

Her eyes finally met mine and she seemed close to tears. "That poor thing," she whispered. The guilt seemed to take possession of her totally. "It was my fault. That's why he got hit. Because I forgot." She put a trembling hand against her mouth, blinking. "I felt awful about it but I never told anyone except Mom and nobody ever asked. You won't tell, will you? They were so upset that he got killed that nobody ever even asked me how he got out and I never said a word. I couldn't. Nikki would have hated me."

"Nikki's not going to hate you because the dog got killed,

Diane," I said. "That was years ago. What difference does it make now?"

Her eyes took on a haunted look and I had to lean forward to hear what she was saying. "Because someone got in. While the dog was out. Someone got into the house and switched the medication. And that's why Daddy died," she said. She fumbled in her purse for a Kleenex, her sobs sounding like a series of gasps, involuntary, quick, her shoulders hunching helplessly.

Two guys from the next table looked over at her with curiosity.

"Oh God, oh God," she whispered, her voice hoarse with grief.

"Let's get out of here," I said, grabbing up her belongings. I left too much money on the table for the check. I took her by the arm, propelling her toward the door.

By the time we got out to the parking lot, she was almost in control of herself. "God, I'm sorry. I can't believe I did that," she said. "I never fall apart that way."

"That's okay," I said. "I had no idea I'd set you off like that. It was just something that stuck in my mind after Greg mentioned it. I didn't mean to *accuse* you of anything."

"I couldn't believe you said it," she said, tears rising again. She looked at me earnestly. "I thought you knew. I thought you must have found out. I never would have admitted it otherwise. I've felt so awful about that for so long."

"How can you blame yourself? If someone wanted to get into the house, he would have let the dog loose anyway. Or killed it and made it look like an accident. I mean, who's going to get upstairs with a goddamn German shepherd barking and snarling?" I said.

"I don't know. Maybe so. It could be, I guess. I mean, he *was* a good watchdog. If he'd been in, nobody could have done anything."

She let out a deep breath, blowing her nose again on the damp twisted Kleenex. "I was so irresponsible in those days. They were always on my case, which just made things worse. I couldn't tell 'em. And nobody seemed to make the connection when Daddy died except me and I *couldn't* admit it then."

"Hey it's over," I said, "it's done. You can't beat yourself to death with it. It's not as if you did it deliberately."

"I know, I know. But the result was the same, you know?" Her voice lifted up and her eyes squeezed shut again, tears running down her cheeks. "He was such a shit and I loved him so much. I know Greg hated his guts, but I just thought he was great. I didn't care if he screwed around. That wasn't his fault. He was just so messed up all his life. He really was."

She wiped her eyes with the wad of Kleenex and then took another deep breath. She reached in her purse for a compact.

"Why don't you skip your class and go home?" I said.

"Maybe I will," she said. She looked at herself in the mirror. "God, I'm a wreck. I can't go anywhere looking like this."

"I'm sorry I triggered this. I think I feel worse than you," I said sheepishly.

"No, that's all right. It's not your fault. It's mine. I guess I'll even have to tell my shrink now. He'll think it's cathartic. He loves that shit. I guess everyone will know now. God, that's all I need."

"Hey, I may or may not have to mention it. I really don't know yet, but I don't think it matters now. If someone was determined to kill your father, it would have been done one way or the other. That's just a fact."

"I guess so. Anyway, it's nice of you to say that. I feel better. Really. I didn't even know it was still weighing on me, but it must have been."

"You're sure you're okay now?"

She nodded, giving me a little smile.

We said our good-byes, which took a few minutes more, and then she walked to her car. I watched while she drove off and then I tossed the album for Colin in the backseat of my car and pulled out. Actually, though I hated to admit it, she was probably right. If the dog had been in the house, no one could have messed with anything. With the dog in or out, dead or alive, it certainly wouldn't have protected Libby Glass. And at least one piece of the puzzle now fit. It didn't seem to mean much, but it did seem to establish the approximate date of entry to the house, if that's how the killer had effected the switch. It felt like the first blank I'd really filled in. Small progress but it made me feel good. I drove back to the San Bernardino Freeway and headed for L.A.

16

When I got back to the Hacienda, I went into the office to check for telephone messages. Arlette had four, but three of them turned out to be from Charlie Scorsoni. She leaned an elbow on the counter, munching on something sticky and dark brown enclosed in cookie dough.

"What is that thing?"

"Trimline Diet Snack Bar," she said. "Six calories each." Some of the filling seemed to be stuck to her teeth like dental putty and she ran a finger along her gums, popping goo into her mouth again. "Look at this label. I bet there's not one natural ingredient in this entire piece of food. Milk powder, hydrogenated fat, powdered egg, and a whole list of chemicals and additives. But you know what? I've noticed real food doesn't taste as good as fake. Have you noticed that? It's just a fact of life. Real food is bland, watered-down-tasting. You take a supermarket tomato. Now it's pathetic what that tastes like," she said and shuddered. I was trying to sort through my messages but she was making it hard.

"I bet this isn't even real flour in this thing," she said. "I mean, I've heard people say junk food just has empty calories, but who needs full ones? I like 'em empty. That way I figure I can't gain any more weight. That Charlie Scorsoni sure kept in touch, didn't he? He called once from Denver and then he called from Tucson and last night from Santa Teresa. Wonder what he wants. He sounded cute."

"I'll be in my room," I said.

"Well all right. Good enough. You want to return those calls, you just give me a buzz up here and I'll put you through."

"Thanks," I said.

"Oh yeah, and I gave your telephone number in Las Vegas to a couple of people who didn't want to leave messages. I hope that's okay. You didn't say I couldn't refer calls."

"No, that's fine," I said. "Any idea who it might have been?"

"Male and female, one each," she said airily.

WHEN I got to my room, I kicked my shoes off and called Charlie Scorsoni's office and talked to Ruth.

"He was supposed to get back last night," she said. "But he didn't plan to come in to the office. You might try him at home."

"Well, if I don't get him there, will you tell him I'm back in Los Angeles? He knows where to reach me here."

"Will do," she said.

The other message was a bonus. Apparently Garry Steinberg, the accountant at Haycraft and McNiece, had come back from New York a few days early and was willing to talk to me on Friday afternoon, which was today. I called and talked to him briefly, telling him I'd be there within the hour. Then I called Mrs. Glass and told her I should be out at her place shortly after supper. There was one more call I felt I should make, though I dreaded the necessity. I sat for a moment on the edge of the bed, staring at the phone and then I said to hell with it and dialed my friend in Las Vegas.

"Jesus, Kinsey," he said through his teeth. "I wish you wouldn't do this to me. I get you the lowdown on Sharon Napier and next thing I know she's dead."

I gave him the situation as succinctly as I could but it didn't seem to ease his anxieties. Or mine. "It could have been anyone," I said. "We don't *know* that she was shot because of me."

"Yeah, but I got to cover myself anyway. Somebody remembers that I was asking around after this lady and then she's found with a bullet in her throat. I mean, how does that look?"

I apologized profusely and told him to let me know anything he found out. He didn't seem that eager to keep in touch. I changed clothes, putting on a skirt, hose, and heels, and then I drove to the Avco Embassy building and took the elevator to the tenth floor. I was feeling bad about Sharon Napier all over again, guilt sitting in my gut like a low-level colic. How could I have missed that appointment? How could that have happened to me? She knew *something* and if I'd gotten there on time, I might be wrapping this investigation up instead of being where I was—which was nowhere in particular. I made my way back into the imitation barnyard of Haycraft and McNiece, staring at the dried corn on the wall while I whipped myself some more.

GARRY Steinberg turned out to be a very nice man. I guessed him to be in his early thirties, with dark curly hair, dark eyes, and a small gap between his front teeth. He was probably five feet, ten inches and his body looked soft, his waist puffing out like rising bread dough.

"You're noticing my waist, am I right?" he asked.

I shrugged somewhat sheepishly, wondering if he did or did not want me to comment. He motioned me into a chair and then sat down behind his desk.

"Let me show you something," he said, lifting a finger. He opened his top desk drawer and took out a snapshot, which he handed to me. I glanced at it.

"Who's this?"

"Perfect," he said. "That was the perfect response. That's me. When I weighed three hundred and ten pounds. Now I weigh two-sixteen."

"My God," I said and looked at the picture again. Actually I could see now that in the old days he had looked a bit like Arlette might if she decided to cross-dress. I'm crazy about "before-and-after" shots, an avid fan of all those magazine ads showing women pumped up like tires and then magically thin, one foot arranged in front of the other, as though weight loss also involved the upsurge of charm and modeling skills. I wondered if there was anyone left in California not obsessed with self-image.

"How'd you do it?" I asked, handing the snapshot back.

"Scarsdale," he said. "It was a real honest-to-God bitch but I did it. I only cheated once—well, twice. Once was when I turned thirty-five. I figured I was entitled to a bagel and cream cheese with a birthday candle. And one night I binged because my girl friend got mad at me and kicked me out. I mean, lookit, when I was three-ten I never even had a girl. Now I'm having fits when she throws me out. We made up again though, so that turned out all right. I've got twenty-five pounds to lose yet but I'm giving myself a break. Strictly maintenance. Have you ever done Scarsdale?"

I shook my head apologetically. I was beginning to feel I'd never done anything. No Scarsdale, no therapy.

"No alcohol," he said. "That's the hard part. On the maintenance diet, you can have like a small glass of white wine now and then, but that's it. I figure the first fifty pounds I lost was from that. Giving up booze. You'd be surprised how much weight that adds."

"Sounds a lot better for you," I said.

"I feel good about myself," he said. "That's the important thing. So. Enough of that. What do you want to know about Libby Glass? The receptionist says you came about her."

I explained what I was up to and how I came to be involved in the matter of her death. He took it all in, asking occasional questions. "What can I tell you?" he said, finally.

"How long had she handled Laurence Fife's account?"

"I'm glad you asked me that because that's one thing I looked up when I knew you were coming over. We handled his personal finances first for about a year. The law firm of Fife and Scorsoni had only been with us six months. Actually a little less. We were just putting in our own computer system and Libby was trying to get all the records straightened out for the changeover. She was a very good accountant by the way. Real conscientious and real smart."

"Were you a good friend of hers?"

"Pretty good. I was El Blimpo back then but I had a crush

on her and we kind of had this brother-sister relationship—
platonic. We didn't date. Just had lunch together once a week,
something like that. Sometimes a drink after work."

"How many accounts did she handle?"

"All together? I'd say twenty-five, maybe thirty. She was a
very ambitious girl and she really knocked herself out . . . for
all the good it did."

"Meaning what?"

He got up and closed the door to his office, pointing sig-
nificantly to the wall of the office next door.

"Listen, old man Haycraft was a petty tyrant, the original
male chauvinist pig. Libby thought if she worked hard, she'd
get a promotion and a raise, but no such thing. And these guys
aren't much better. You want to know how I get a raise? I
threaten to quit. Libby didn't even do that."

"How much was she paid?"

"I don't know. I could maybe look that up. Not enough to
suit her, I can tell you that. Fife and Scorsoni was a big
account—not the biggest, but big. She didn't feel it was fair."

"She did more work for Fife than Scorsoni, I assume."

"At first. After that, it was half and half. A lot of the purpose
of our taking over their business management was to keep
track of all the estate work. That was a big part of their ongoing business from what she said. The dead guy, Fife, did a lot
of messy divorce work, which paid big fees but didn't require
that much in the way of bookkeeping. Also, we did accounts
receivable for them, paid their office bills, kept track of profits
from the firm, and made suggestions about investments. Well,
at that point, we weren't doing much in the way of investment
counseling because they hadn't been with us that long but that
was the object of the exercise eventually. We like to hold off
some until we see where our clients stand. Anyway, I can't go

into details on that but I can probably answer any other general questions you might have."

"Do you know anything about where the money from Fife's estate went?"

"The kids. It was divided equally among them. I never saw the will but I helped settle the estate in terms of disbursements after probate."

"You don't happen to represent Scorsoni's new law firm, do you?"

"Nope," Garry said. "I met him a couple of times after Fife died. He seemed like a nice man."

"Is there any way I could look at the old books?"

"Nope," he said. "You could do it if I had Scorsoni's written permission but I don't know what good that would do you anyway unless you're an accountant yourself. Our system isn't that complicated, but I don't think it'd make sense to you."

"Probably not," I said, trying to think what else I wanted to ask him about.

"You want coffee? I'm sorry, I should have asked you sooner."

"No thanks. I'm fine," I said. "What about Libby's personal affairs. Is there any chance that she was sleeping with Laurence Fife?"

Garry laughed. "Now that I don't know. She'd been going with some creepy little guy ever since high school, and I knew she'd broken up with him. On my advice, I might add."

"How come?"

"He came in to apply for a job here. I was in charge of screening all applicants. He was just supposed to messenger stuff back and forth but he didn't even look that smart. He was belligerent, too, and if you want my honest opinion, he was high."

"You wouldn't still have his application on file, would you?" I asked, feeling a faint surge of excitement.

Garry looked at me. "We're not having this conversation, am I right?"

"Right."

"I'll see what I can find," he said promptly. "It wouldn't be here. It'd be over in the warehouse. We have all the old records stored there. Accountants are real pack rats. We never throw anything away and everything gets written down."

"Thanks, Garry," I said. "I can't tell you how much I appreciate this."

He smiled happily. "And maybe I'll look for the old Fife files as long as I'm over there. It won't hurt to take a peek. And to answer your question about Libby, my guess would be no. I don't think she was having an affair with Laurence Fife." He glanced at his watch. "I got a meeting."

I shook his hand across the desk, feeling good. "Thanks again," I said.

"No problem. Stop by again. Anytime."

I got back to my hotel room at 3:30. I put a pillow on the plastic chair, set my typewriter up on the wobbly desk, and spent an hour and a half typing up my notes. It had been a long time since I sat down to do paperwork but it had to be caught up. By the time I pecked my way through the last paragraph, I had a pain in my lower back and another one right between my shoulder blades. I changed into my running clothes, my body heat resurrecting the smell of old sweat and car fumes. I was going to have to find a Laundromat soon. I jogged south on Wilshire, just for variety, cutting across to San Vicente at Twenty-sixth Street. Once I got on the wide grassy divider, I could feel myself hit stride. Running always hurts—I don't care what they say—but it does acquaint one with all of one's body parts. This time I could feel my thighs protest and I noticed a mild aching in my shins, which I ignored, plodding on gamely. For my bravery, I netted a few rude remarks from two guys in a pickup truck. When I got back to the motel, I showered and got back into my jeans and then I stopped by McDonald's and had a Quarter Pounder with cheese, fries, and a medium Coke. By then, it was 6:45. I filled up the car with gas and headed over the hill into Sherman Oaks.

17

MRS. GLASS ANSWERED THE DOOR AFTER HALF A BUZZ. This time the living room had been picked up to some extent, her sewing confined now to a neatly folded pile of fabric on the arm of the couch. Raymond was nowhere in sight.

"He had a bad day," she said to me. "Lyle stopped by on his way home from work and we put him to bed."

Even the television set was turned off, and I wondered what she did with herself in the evenings.

"Elizabeth's things are in the basement," she murmured. "I'll just get the key to the storage bin."

She returned a moment later and I followed her out into the corridor. We turned left, past the stairway back to the basement door which was set into the right-hand wall. The door was locked and after she opened it, she flipped the light switch at the top of the stairs. I could already smell the dry musty scent of old window screens and half-empty cans of latex paint. I was about two steps behind her as we made our way down the narrow passageway, wooden stairs taking a sharp right-hand turn. At the landing, I caught a glimpse of concrete floor with bins of wooden lathing reaching to the low ceiling. Something wasn't right but the oddity didn't really register before the blast rang out. The light bulb on the landing shattered, spraying us both with thin flakes of glass and the basement was instantly blanketed in darkness. Grace shrieked and I grabbed her, pulling her back up the stairs. I lost my balance and she stumbled over me. There must have been an outside exit because I heard a wrenching of wood, a bang, and then someone taking the concrete steps outside two at a time. I struggled out from under Grace, jerking her up the stairs with me and then I left her in the corridor, racing out through the front and around the side of the building. Someone had left an old power mower in the driveway and I tripped in the darkness, sprawling forward on my hands and knees, cursing savagely as I scrambled back to my feet again. I reached the rear of the building, keeping low, my heart pounding in my ears. It was black-dark, my eyes just beginning to adjust. A vehicle started up one street over and I could hear it chirp out with a quick shift of gears. I ducked back, leaning against the building then, hearing nothing but the fading roar of a vehicle being driven away at high speed. My mouth was dry. I was drenched in sweat and belatedly I felt a shudder go through me. Both my palms stung where the gravel had bitten into the flesh. I trotted back to my car and got out my flashlight, tucking the little automatic into my windbreaker pocket. I didn't think there was anyone left to shoot but I was tired of being surprised.

GRACE was sitting on the doorsill, her head hanging down between her knees. She was shaking from head to foot and she'd started to weep. I helped her to her feet, easing open the apartment door.

"Lyle knew I was picking the stuff up, right?" I snapped at her. She gave me a haunted, pleading look.

"It couldn't have been him. He wouldn't have done that to me," she whimpered.

"Your faith is touching," I said. "Now sit. I'll be back in a minute."

I went back to the basement stairs. The beam from the flashlight cut through the blackness. There was a second bulb at the bottom of the stairs and I pulled the chain. A flat dull light from the swinging bulb threw out a yellow arc that slowed to a halt. I turned off the flashlight. I knew which bin belonged to Mrs. Glass. It had been smashed open, the padlock dangling ineffectually where the lathing had been broken through. Cardboard boxes had been torn open, the contents strewn about in haste, forming an ankle-deep mess through which I picked my way. The emptied boxes all bore the name "Elizabeth," obligingly rendered in bold Magic Marker strokes. I wondered if we'd interrupted the intruder before or after he'd found what he was looking for. I heard a sound behind me and I whirled, raising the flashlight instantly like a club.

A man stood there staring at me with bewilderment.

"Got a problem down here?"

"Oh fuck. Who are you?"

He was middle-aged, hands in his pockets, his expression sheepish. "Frank Isenberg from apartment three," he said apologetically. "Did somebody break in? You want me to call the police?"

"No, don't do that yet. Let me check upstairs with Grace. This looks like the only bin that's been damaged. Maybe it was just kids," I said, heart still thudding. "You didn't have to sneak up on me."

"Sorry. I just thought you might need some help."

"Yeah, well thanks anyway. I'll let you know if I need anything."

He stood there surveying the chaos for a moment and then he shrugged and went back upstairs.

I checked the basement door at the rear. The glass had been broken out and someone had pulled back the bolt by reaching through. The door was wide open of course. I shut it, pushing the bolt back into place. When I turned around, Grace was creeping timidly down the stairs, her face still pale. She clung to the railing. "Elizabeth's things," she whispered. "They spoiled all of her boxes, all the things I saved."

She sank down on the steps, rubbing her temples. Her large dark eyes looked injured, perplexed, with a touch of something else that I could have sworn was guilt.

"Maybe we should call the police," I said, feeling mean, wondering just how protective of Lyle she intended to be.

"Do you really think?" she said. Her gaze flitted back and forth indecisively and she took out a handkerchief, pressing it against her forehead as though to remove beads of sweat. "Nothing might be missing," she said hopefully. "Maybe nothing's gone."

"Or maybe we won't know the difference," I said.

She pulled herself up and moved over to the bin, taking in

the disastrous piles of papers, stuffed animals, cosmetics, underwear. She stopped, picking up papers randomly, trying to make stacks. Her hands still trembled but I didn't think she was afraid. Startled perhaps, and thinking rapidly.

"I take it Raymond is still asleep," I said.

She nodded, tears welling up as the extent of the vandalism became more and more apparent. I could feel myself relent. Even if Lyle had done it, it was mean-spirited, a violation of something precious to Grace. She had already suffered enough without this. I set the flashlight aside and began to pile papers back into the boxes: costume jewelry, lingerie, old issues of *Seventeen* and *Vogue*, patterns for clothing that Libby had probably never made. "Do you mind if I take these boxes with me and go through them tonight?" I asked. "I can have them back to you by morning."

"All right. I suppose. I can't see what harm it would do now anyway," she murmured, not looking at me.

It seemed hopeless to me. In this jumble, who knew what might be missing? I'd have to go through the boxes and see if I could spot anything, but the chances weren't good. Lyle couldn't have been down there long—if it had been him. He knew I was coming back for the stuff and when he'd been there earlier, Grace probably told him exactly what time I expected to arrive. He'd had to wait until dark and he probably thought we'd spend more time upstairs before coming down. Still, he was cutting it close—unless he simply didn't care. And why didn't he break in during the three days I was gone? I thought back to his insolence and I suspected that he might take a certain satisfaction in thwarting me, even if he was caught at it.

Grace helped me cart the boxes to the car, six of them. I should have taken the stuff the first time I was there, I thought, but I couldn't picture driving to Vegas with the entire backseat filled with cardboard boxes. Still, the boxes would have been intact. It was my own damn fault, I thought sourly.

I told Grace I'd be back first thing in the morning and then I pulled out. It was going to be a long night.

I BOUGHT two containers of black coffee across the street, locked the door to my motel room, and closed the drapes. I emptied the first carton onto the bed and then I started making stacks. School papers in one pile. Personal letters. Magazines. Stuffed animals. Clothing. Cosmetics. Bills and receipts. Grace had apparently saved every article Elizabeth had touched since kindergarten. Report cards. School projects. Really, six cartons seemed modest when I realized how much there was. Blue books from college. Copies of applications for work. Tax returns. The accumulation of an entire life and it was really only so much trash. Who would ever need to refer to any of this again? The original energy and spirit had all seeped away. I did feel for her. I did get some sense of that young girl, whose gropings and triumphs and little failures were piled together now in a drab motel room. I didn't even know what I was looking for. I flipped through a diary from the fifth grade—the handwriting round and dutiful, the entries dull. I tried to imagine myself dead, someone sorting carelessly through my belongings. What was there really of my life? Canceled checks. Reports all typewritten and filed. Everything of value reduced to terse prose. I didn't keep much myself, didn't hoard or save. Two divorce decrees. That was about the sum of it for me. I collected more information about other people's lives than I did about my own, as though, perhaps, in poring over the facts about other people, I could discover something about myself. My own mystery, unplumbed, undetected, was sorted into files that were neatly labeled but really didn't say much. I picked through the last of Elizabeth's boxes but there was nothing of interest. It was 4:00 in the morning when I finished. Nothing. If there had been anything there, it was gone now and I was irritated with myself again, berating myself for my own poor judgment. This was the second time I'd arrived too late—the second time some vital piece of information had slipped away from me.

I began to repack boxes, automatically rechecking as I went, sorting. Clothes in one box, stuffed animals tucked into the spaces along the sides. School papers, diaries, blue books in the next box. Back it all went, neatly catalogued this time, compulsively arranged, as though I owed Elizabeth Glass some kind of order after I'd pried into the hidden crevices of her abandoned life. I riffed through magazines, held textbooks by the spine, letting the pages fly loose. The stacks on the bed diminished. There weren't that many personal letters and I felt guilty reading them, but I did. Some from an aunt in Arizona. Some from a girl named Judy whom Libby must have known in high school. No one seemed to refer to anything intimate in her life and I had to conclude that she confided little or else that she had no tales to tell. The disappointment was acute. I was down to the last pile of books, mostly paperbacks. Such taste. Leon Uris and Irving Stone, Victoria Holt, Georgette Heyer, a few more exotic samples that I guessed had been from some literature survey course in college. The letter slipped out of the pages of a dog-eared copy of *Pride and Prejudice*. I nearly tossed it in the box with the rest of the stuff. The handwriting was a tightly stroked cursive on two sides in dark blue ink. No date. No envelope. No postmark. I picked it up by one corner and read it, feeling a cold pinching sensation begin at the base of my spine.

Darling Elizabeth . . . I'm writing this so you'll have something when you get back. I know these separations are hard for you and I wish there were some way I could ease your pain. You are so much more honest than I am, so much more open about what you feel than I allow myself to be, but I do love you and I don't want you to have any doubts about that. You're right when you say that I'm conservative. I'm guilty as charged, your Honor, but I'm not immune to suffering and as often as I've been accused of being selfish, I'm not as reckless of others as you might think. I would like to take our time about this and be sure that it's something we both want. What we have now is very dear to me and I'm not saying—please believe me— that I wouldn't turn my life around for you if it comes to that. On the other hand, I think we should both be sure that we can survive the day-to-day absurdities of being together. Right now, the intensity dazzles and it seems simple enough for us both to chuck it all and make some kind of life, but we haven't known each other that long or that well. I can't afford to risk wife, kids, and career in the heat of the moment though you know it tempts me. Please let's move slowly on this. I love you more than I can say and I don't want to lose you—which is selfish enough, I suppose, in itself. You're right to push, but please don't lose sight of what's at stake, for you as well as me. Tolerate my caution if you can. I love you. Laurence

I didn't know what to make of it. I realized, in a flash, that it wasn't just that I hadn't believed in an affair between Laurence and Elizabeth. I hadn't *wanted* to believe. I wasn't sure I believed it yet but why the resistance? It was so neat. So convenient. It fit in so nicely with what I knew of the facts and still I stared at the letter, holding it gingerly by one corner as I read it again. I leaned back against the bed. What was the matter with me? I was exhausted and I knew I'd been through too much in the last few days but something nagged at me and I wasn't sure it had so much to do with the letter as it did with myself, with something in my nature—some little niggling piece of self-illumination that I was fighting hard not to recognize. Either the letter was real or it was not, and there were ways to verify that. I pulled myself together wearily. I found a large envelope and slipped the letter inside, being careful not to smudge fingerprints, already thinking ahead to Con Dolan, who would love it since it confirmed all his nastiest suspicions about what had been going on back then. Was this what Sharon Napier had figured out? Was this what she could have corroborated if she'd lived long enough?

I lay on the bed fully dressed, body tense, brain wired. Who could she have hoped to blackmail with this information if she'd known? It had to be what she was up to. It had to be why she'd been killed. Someone had followed me to Las Vegas, knowing that I would see her, knowing that she might confirm what I hadn't wanted to believe. I couldn't prove it, of course, but I wondered if I was getting close enough to the truth to be in danger myself. I wanted to go home. I wanted to retreat to the safety of my small room. I wasn't thinking clearly yet, but I was getting close. For eight years, nothing happened and now it was all beginning again. If Nikki was innocent, then someone had been sitting pretty all this time, someone in danger of exposure now.

I saw, for an instant, the look that had flashed in Nikki's eyes, unreasoning malevolence, a harsh irrational rage. She had set this all in motion. I had to consider the possibility that Sharon Napier was blackmailing *her*, that Sharon knew something that could link Nikki to Libby's death. If Sharon had dropped out of sight, it was possible that Nikki had hired me to flush her out and that Nikki had then eliminated any threat with one quick shot. She might also have followed me back to Sherman Oaks for a frantic search through Libby's belongings for anything that might have linked Libby to Laurence Fife. There were pieces missing yet but they would fall into place and then maybe the whole of it would make sense. Assuming I lived long enough myself to figure it out . . .

I DRAGGED MYSELF OUT OF BED AT 6:00 A.M. I HADN'T SLEPT at all. My mouth felt stale and I brushed my teeth. I showered and dressed. I longed to run but I felt too vulnerable to jog down the middle of San Vicente at that hour. I packed, closing up my type-writer, shoving the pages of my report into my briefcase. I loaded the boxes into my car again, along with my suitcase. The lights in the office were on and I could see Arlette taking jelly doughnuts out of a bakery box, putting them on a plastic plate with a clear dome lid. Water was already heating for that awful, flat instant coffee. She was licking powdered sugar from her fingers when I went in.

"God, you're up awful early," she said. "You want breakfast?"

I shook my head. Even with my penchant for junk food, I wouldn't eat a jelly doughnut. "No, but thanks," I said. "I'm checking out."

"Right now?"

I nodded, almost too tired to talk. She finally seemed to sense that this was the wrong time to chat. She got my bill ready and I signed it, not even bothering to add up the charges. She usually made a mistake but I didn't care.

I got in my car and headed for Sherman Oaks. There was a light on in Grace's kitchen, which I approached from around the side of the building. I tapped on the window and after a moment, she came into the service porch and opened the side door. She looked small and precise this morning in an A-line corduroy skirt and a coffee-colored cotton turtleneck. She kept her voice low.

"Raymond's not awake yet but there's coffee if you like," she said.

"Thanks, but I've got a breakfast meeting at eight," I said, lying without much thought. Whatever I said would be passed on to Lyle and my whereabouts were none of his business—or hers. "I just wanted to drop the boxes off."

"Did you find anything?" she asked. Her gaze met mine briefly and then she blinked, glancing first at the floor and then off to my left.

"Too late," I said, trying to ignore the flush of relief that tinted her cheeks.

"That's unfortunate," she murmured, placing a hand against her throat. "I'm . . . uh . . . sure it wasn't Lyle . . ."

"It doesn't matter much anyway," I said. I felt sorry for her in spite of myself. "I packed everything back as neatly as I could. I'll just stack the boxes in the basement near the bin.

You'll probably want to have that repaired when you get the basement door fixed."

She nodded. She moved to close the door and I stepped back, watching her pad back into the kitchen in her soft-soled slippers. I felt as if I'd personally violated her life somehow, that everything was ending on a bad note. She'd been as helpful as she knew how and she'd gotten little in return. I had to shrug. There was nothing I could do at this point. I unloaded the car, making several trips, stacking boxes just inside the damaged bin. Unconsciously, I listened for Lyle. The light in the basement was cold and gray by day, but aside from the splintered lathework and the shattered window, there was no other evidence of the intruder. I went out the back way on the last trip up from the basement, checking idly for smashed cigarette butts, bloody fingerprints, a small printed business card perhaps, dropped by whoever broke in. I came up the concrete stairs outside, looking off to the right at the path the intruder had taken—across the patchy grass in the backyard, over a sagging wire fence, and through a tangle of bushes. I could see through to the next street where the car must have been parked. It was early morning yet and the sunlight was flat and still. I could hear heavy traffic on the Ventura Freeway, which was visible in glimpses through the clumps of trees off to the right. The ground wasn't even soft enough to absorb footprints. I moved around the building to the driveway on my left, noting with interest that the power mower had now been pulled off to one side. My palms were still ripped up in places, two-inch tracks where I'd skidded across the gravel on my hands. I hadn't even thought to use Bactine and I hoped I wouldn't be subject to raging gangrene, perilous infections, or blood poisoning—dangers my aunt had warned me about every time I skinned my knee.

I got back in my car and headed for Santa Teresa, stopping in Thousand Oaks for breakfast. I was home by 10:00 in the morning. I wrapped myself up in a quilt on the couch and slept for most of the day.

AT 4:00, I drove out to Nikki's beach house. I had called to say I was back in town and she invited me out for a drink. I wasn't sure yet how much I would tell her or how much, if anything, I would hold back, but after my recent gnawing suspicions about her, I wanted to test my perceptions. There are moments in every investigation when my speculations about what's possible cloud and confuse any lingering sense I have of what's actually true. I wanted to check out my intuitions.

The house was situated on a bluff overlooking the ocean. The lot was small, irregular in shape, surrounded by eucalyptus trees. The house was tucked into the landscaping—laurel and yew, with pink and red geraniums planted along the path—its exterior made of cedar shingles, still a raw-looking wood brown, the roofline undulating like an ocean swell. There was a large oval window in the front, flanked by two bow windows, all undraped. The lawn was a pale green, tender blades of grass looking almost edible, curls of eucalyptus bark intermingled like wood shavings. White and yellow daisies grew in careless patches. The whole effect was of subtle neglect, a refined wilderness untended but subdued, curiously appealing with the thick scent of ocean overlaid and the dull thunder of waves crashing down below. The air was moist and smelled of salt, wind buffeting the ragged grass. Where the house in Montebello was boxy, substantial, conventional, plain, this was a whimsical cottage, all wide angles, windows, and unpainted wood. The front door had a tall oval leaded-glass window in it, filled with tulip shapes, and the doorbell sounded like wind chimes.

Nikki appeared at once. She was wearing a celery-green caftan, its bodice embroidered with mirrors the size of dimes, the sleeves wide. Her hair was pulled up and away from her face, tied with a pale green velvet ribbon. She seemed relaxed, her wide forehead unlined, the gray eyes looking light and clear, her mouth faintly tinted with pink, curving upward as though from some secret merriment. The languidness in her manner was gone and she was animated, energetic. I had brought the photograph album Diane had given me and I handed it to her as she closed the door behind me.

"What's this?" she asked.

"Diane put it together for Colin," I said.

"Come see him," she said. "We're making bread."

I followed her through the house. There were no square rooms at all. The spaces flowed into one another, connected by gleaming pale wood floors and bright shag rugs. There were windows everywhere, plants, skylights. A free-form fireplace in the living room looked as if it had been constructed from buff-colored boulders, piled up randomly like the entrance to a cave. On the far wall, a crude ladder led up to a loft that overlooked the ocean. Nikki smiled back at me happily, placing the album on the glass coffee table as she passed.

The kitchen was a semicircle, wood and white Formica and luscious healthy houseplants, windows on three sides looking onto a deck with the ocean stretching out beyond, wide and gray in the late afternoon. Colin was kneading bread, his back to me, his concentration complete. His hair was the same pale no-color shade as Nikki's, silky like hers where it curled down on his neck. His arms looked wiry and strong, his hands capable, fingers long. He gathered the edges of the dough, pressing inward, turning it over again. He looked like he was just on the verge of adolescence, beginning to shoot up in height but not awkward yet. Nikki touched him and he turned quickly, his gaze sliding over to me at once. I was startled. His eyes were large, tilted slightly, an army-fatigue green, his lashes thick and dark. His face was narrow, chin pointed, ears coming to a delicate point, a pixie effect with the fine hair forming a point on his forehead. The two of them looked like an illustration from a fairy book—fragile and beautiful and strange. His eyes were peaceful, empty, glowing with acute intelligence. I have seen the same look in cats, their eyes wise, aloof, grave.

When I spoke to Nikki, he watched our lips, his own lips parting breathlessly, so that the effect was oddly sexual.

"I think I just fell in love," I said and laughed. Nikki smiled, signing to Colin, her fingers graceful, succinct. Colin flashed a smile at me, much older than his years. I felt myself flush.

"I hope you didn't tell him that," I said. "We'd probably have to run off together."

"I told him you were my first friend after prison. I told him you needed a drink," she said, still signing, eyes resting on Colin's face. "Most of the time we don't sign this much. I'm just brushing up."

While Nikki opened a bottle of wine, I watched Colin work the bread dough. He offered to let me help and I shook my head, preferring to watch his agile hands, the dough developing a smooth skin almost magically as he worked. He made gruff, unintelligible sounds now and then without seeming aware of it.

Nikki gave me chilled white wine in a glass with a thin stem while she drank Perrier. "Here's to parole," she said.

"You look much more relaxed," I said.

"Oh I am. I feel great. It's so good to have him here. I follow him everywhere. I feel like a puppy dog. He gets no peace."

Her hands were moving automatically and I could see that she was translating for him simultaneously with her comments to me. It made me feel rude and clumsy that I couldn't sign too. I felt as if there were things I wanted to say to him myself, questions I wanted to ask about the silence in his head. It was like charades of some kind, Nikki using body, arms, face, her whole self totally involved, Colin signing back to her casually. He seemed to speak much more quickly than she, without deliberation. Sometimes Nikki would halt, struggling for a word, remembering, laughing at herself as she relayed to him her own forgetfulness. His smile in those moments was indulgent, full of affection, and I envied them this special world of secrets, of self-mockery, wherein Colin was the master and Nikki the apprentice. I couldn't imagine Nikki with any other kind of child.

Colin placed the smooth dough in the bowl, turning it once to coat its pale surface with butter, covering it carefully then with a clean white towel. Nikki motioned him into the living room, where she showed him the photo album. Colin settled on the edge of the couch, leaning forward, elbows on his knees, the album open on the coffee table in front of him. His face was still but his eyes took in everything and he was already engrossed in the snapshots.

Nikki and I went out onto the deck. It was getting late but there was still enough sunlight to create the illusion of warmth. She stood at the railing, staring out at the ocean that rumbled below us. I could see tangles of kelp just under the surface in places, dark strands undulating in waves of paler green.

"Nikki, did you talk to anyone about where I was and what I was up to?" I asked.

"Not at all," she said, startled. "What makes you ask?"

I filled her in on the events of the last few days—Sharon Napier's death, my talks with Greg and Diane, the letter I'd found among Libby Glass's effects. My trust in her was instinctive.

"Would you recognize his handwriting?"

"Sure."

I took the manila envelope out of my purse, carefully removing the letter, which I unfolded for her. She glanced at it briefly.

"That's him," she said.

"I'd like you to read it," I said. "I want to see if it coincides with your intuitions about what was going on."

Reluctantly her gaze dropped back to the pale blue pages. When she finished, she seemed almost embarrassed. "I wouldn't have guessed it was that serious. His other affairs weren't."

"What about Charlotte Mercer?"

"She's a bitch. She's an alcoholic. She called me once. I hated her. And she hated him. You should have heard what she said."

I folded the letter carefully. "I didn't get it. From Charlotte Mercer to Libby Glass. That's quite a leap. I assumed he was a man of taste."

Nikki shrugged. "He was easily seduced. It was his own vanity. Charlotte *is* beautiful . . . in her own way."

"Was she in the process of divorcing? Is that how they met?"

Nikki shook her head. "We socialized with them. Judge Mercer was a sort of mentor of Laurence's at one point. I don't imagine he ever found out about the affair—it would have killed him, I think. He's the only decent judge we've got anyway. You know what the rest are like."

"I only talked to her a short time," I said, "but I can't see how she could be involved. It had to be somebody who knew where I was and how could she have come by that kind of information? Somebody had to have followed me up to Las Vegas. Sharon's murder was too closely timed to have been coincidence."

Colin appeared at Nikki's side, placing the open photograph album up on the railing. He pointed to one of the snapshots, saying something I couldn't understand at all, an indistinct blur of vowels. It was the first time I'd heard him speak. His voice was deeper than I would have imagined for a twelve-year-old.

"That's Diane's junior-high-school graduation," Nikki said to him. Colin looked at her for a moment and then pointed again more emphatically. He put his index finger in front of his mouth and moved it up and down rapidly. Nikki frowned.

" 'Who' what, honey?"

Colin placed his finger on the picture of a group of people.

"That's Diane and Greg and Diane's friend, Terri, and Diane's mother," she said to him, enunciating carefully and signing at the same time.

A puzzled smile formed on Colin's face. Colin spread his hands out, putting his thumb against his forehead and then his chin.

Nikki laughed this time, her expression as puzzled as his.

"No, *that's* Nana," she said, pointing to a snapshot one page back. "This is *Diane's* mother, not Daddy's. The mother of Greg and Diane. Don't you remember Nana? Oh God, how could he," she flashed at me. "She died when he was a year old." She looked back at him.

Colin made some guttural sounds, something negative and frustrated. I wondered what would happen to his temper when puberty really caught up with him. Again the thumb against the forehead, then the chin. Nikki shot me another look. "He keeps saying 'Daddy's mother' for Gwen. How do you explain 'ex-wife'?" She signed again patiently.

Colin shook his head slightly, suddenly unsure of himself. He watched her for a moment more as though some other explanation might be forthcoming. He took the album and backed away, eyes still fixed on Nikki's face. He signed once more, flushing uncomfortably. Apparently, he didn't want to look foolish in front of me.

"We'll go through those together in a minute," she signed to him, translating for me.

Colin moved slowly back through the sliding glass doors, pushing the screen door shut.

"Sorry for the interruption," she said briefly.

"That's all right, I've got to go anyway," I said.

"You can stay for supper if you like. I've made a big pot of beef bourguignon. It's great with Colin's bread."

"Thanks but I've got all kinds of things to do," I said.

Nikki walked me to the door, signing our final chitchat without even being aware of it.

I got in my car and sat for a moment, puzzled by Colin's puzzlement over Gwen. That was odd. Very odd.

WHEN I GOT BACK TO MY APARTMENT, CHARLIE SCORSONI was sitting on my doorstep. I felt grubby and unprepared and I realized with embarrassment that I'd been entertaining a fantasy of how we'd meet again and it wasn't like this.

"God, don't get all excited, Millhone," he said when he saw the expression on my face.

I got out my key. "I'm sorry," I said, "but you catch me at the worst possible times."

"You have a date," he said.

"No, I don't have a date. I look like shit." I unlocked the

door and flipped on the desk lamp, letting him follow me in.

"At least I caught you in a good mood," he said, making himself at home. He sauntered out to the kitchen and got out the last beer. The familiarity in his manner made me cross.

"Look, I've got laundry to do. I haven't been to the grocery store for a week. My mail is piled up, the whole place is covered with dust. I haven't even shaved my legs since I saw you last."

"You need a haircut too," he said.

"No I don't. It always looks like this."

He smiled, shaking his head. "Get dressed. We'll go out."

"I don't want to go out. I want to get my life in shape."

"You can do that tomorrow. It's Sunday. I bet you always do shit like that on Sunday anyway."

I stared at him. It was true. "Wait a minute. Here's how it's supposed to go," I said patiently. "I get home. I do all my chores, get a good night's sleep, which I could sorely use, then tomorrow I call you and we see each other tomorrow night."

"I gotta be at the office tomorrow night. I have a client coming in."

"On Sunday night?"

"We've got a court appearance first thing Monday morning and this is the only thing we could work out. I just got back into town myself Thursday night and I'm up to my ass."

I stared at him some more, wavering. "Where would we go? Would I have to dress up?"

"Well I'm not going to take you anywhere looking like *that*," he said.

I glanced down. I was still wearing jeans and the shirt I'd slept in but I wasn't ready to back down yet. "What's wrong with this?" I asked perversely.

"Take a shower and change clothes. I'll pick up some stuff at the grocery store if you give me a list. By the time I get that done, you'll be ready, yes?"

"I like to shop for my own stuff. Anyway, all I need is milk and beer."

"Then I'll take you to a supermarket after we eat," he said, emphasizing every single word.

WE DROVE down to the Ranch House in Ojai, one of those elegant restaurants where the waiter stands at your table and recites the menu like a narrative poem.

"Shall I order for us or would that offend your feminine sensibilities?"

"Go ahead," I said, feeling oddly relieved, "I'd like that." While he and the waiter conferred, I studied Charlie's face surreptitiously. It was strong and square, good jawline, visible dent in his chin, full mouth. His nose looked like it might have been broken once but mended skillfully, leaving only the slightest trace just below the bridge. His glasses had large lenses, tinted a blue-gray, and behind them, his blue eyes were as clear as sky. Sandy lashes, sandy brows, his thick sandy hair only beginning to recede. He had big hands, big bones in his wrists, and I could see a feathering of sandy hair at the cuff. There was something else about him, too, smoldering and opaque, the same sense I'd had before of sexuality that surfaced now and then. Sometimes he seemed to emit an almost audible hum, like a line of power stations marching inexorably across a hillside, ominous and marked with danger signs. I was afraid of him.

The waiter was nodding and moving away. Charlie turned back to me, obscurely amused. I felt myself go mute, but he pretended not to notice and I felt dimly grateful, faintly flushed. I was overcome with the same self-consciousness I'd felt once at a birthday party in the sixth grade when I realized that all the other little girls had worn nylon stockings and I was still wearing stupid white ankle socks.

The waiter returned with a bottle of wine and Charlie went through the usual ritual. When our glasses were filled, he touched his rim to mine, his eyes on my face. I sipped, startled by the delicacy of the wine, which was pale and cool.

"So how's the investigation going?" he asked when the waiter had left.

I shook my head, taking a moment to orient myself. "I don't want to talk about it," I said shortly and then caught myself. "I don't mean to be rude," I said in a softened tone. "I just don't think talking about it will help. It's not going well."

"I'm sorry to hear that," he said. "It's bound to improve."

I shrugged and watched while he lit a cigarette and snapped the lighter shut. "I didn't know you smoked," I said.

"Now and then," he said. He offered me the pack and I shook my head again. He seemed relaxed, in possession of himself, a man of sophistication and grace. I felt doltish and tongue-tied, but he didn't seem to expect anything of me, talking on about inconsequential things. He seemed to operate at half speed, taking his own time about everything. It made me aware of the usual tension with which I live, that keyed-up state of raw nerve that makes me grind my teeth in my sleep. Sometimes I get so wired that I forget to eat at all, only remembering at night, even then not being hungry but wolfing down food anyway as though the speed and quantity of consumption might atone for the infrequency. With Charlie, I could feel my time clock readjust, my pace slowing to match his. When I finished the second glass of wine, I heaved a sigh and only then did I realize that I'd been holding myself tensely, like a joke snake ready to jump out of a box.

"Feel better?" he said.

"Yes."

"Good. Then we'll eat."

The meal that followed was one of the most sensual I ever experienced: fresh, tender bread with a crust of flaky layers, spread with a buttery pâté, Boston lettuce with a delicate vinaigrette, sand dabs sautéed in butter and served with succulent green grapes. There were fresh raspberries for dessert with a dollop of tart cream, and all the time Charlie's face across the table from me, shadowed by that suggestion of caution, that hint of something stark and fearful held back, pulling me forward even while I felt myself kept in check.

"How'd you end up in law school?" I asked him when coffee arrived.

"Accident I guess. My father was a drunk and a bum, a real shit. Knocked me around a lot. Not seriously. More like a piece of furniture that got in his way. He beat my mother too."

"Doesn't do much for your self-esteem," I ventured.

Charlie shrugged. "It was good for me actually. Made me tough. Let me know I couldn't depend on anyone but myself, which is a lesson you might as well learn when you're ten. I took care of me."

"You worked your way through school?"

"Every nickel's worth. I picked up money ghosting papers for jocks, sitting in on tests, writing C minus answers so no one would suspect. You'd be surprised how tricky it is to miss just enough questions to look genuine. I had regular jobs, too, but after I watched half a fraternity get into law school on my smarts, I figured I might as well try it myself."

"What'd your father do when he didn't drink?"

"Construction till his health broke down. He finally died of cancer. Took him six years. Bad stuff. I didn't give a shit and he knew it. All that pain. Served him right," he said and shook his head. "My mother died four months after he did. I thought she'd be relieved he was gone. Turns out she was dependent on the abuse."

"Why do estate law? That doesn't seem like you. I picture you doing criminal law, something like that."

"Listen, my father pissed away everything he had. I ended up with nothing—less than nothing. It took me years to pay off his hospital bills and his fucking debts. I had to pay for my mother's death, too, which at least was quick, God bless her, but hardly cheap. So now I show people how to outwit the government even in death. A lot of my clients are dead so we get along very well and I make sure their greedy heirs get more than they deserve. Also when you're executor for somebody's estate, you get paid on time and nobody calls you up about your bill."

"Not a bad deal," I said.

"Not at all," he agreed.

"Have you ever been married?"

"Nope. I never had time for that. I work. That's the only thing that interests me. I don't like the idea of giving someone else the right to make demands. In exchange for what?"

I had to laugh. I felt the same way myself. His tone throughout was ironic and the look he laid on me then was oddly sexual, full of strange, compelling male heat as though money and power and sexuality were all somehow tangled up for him and fed on one another. There was really nothing open or loose or free about him, however candid he might seem, but I knew that it was precisely his opacity that appealed to me. Did he know that I was attracted to him? He gave little indication of his own feelings one way or the other.

When we finished our coffee, he signaled for the waiter without a word and paid the check. Conversation between us was dwindling anyway and I let it lie, feeling watchful, quiet, even wary of him again. We moved through the restaurant, our bodies close but our behavior polite, circumspect. He opened the door for me. I passed through. He'd made no gesture toward me, verbally or otherwise, and I was suddenly disconcerted, lest my sense of his pull turned out to be something generated in me and not reciprocal. Charlie took my arm briefly, guiding me up a shallow step, but as soon as we were on smooth pavement again, he dropped his hand. We went around to my side of the car. He opened the door and I got in. I didn't think I'd said anything flirtatious and I was glad of that, curious still about his intentions toward me. He was so matter-of-fact, so removed.

We drove back to Santa Teresa, saying little. I was feeling mute again, not uncomfortable but languid. As we approached the outskirts of town, he reached over and took my hand noncommittally. It felt like a low-voltage current was suffusing my left side. He kept his left hand on the steering wheel. With his right hand, he was carelessly, casually rubbing my fingers, his attitude inattentive. I was trying to be as casual as he, trying to pretend there might be some other way to interpret those smoldering sexual signals that made the air crackle between us and caused my mouth to go dry. What if I was wrong, I thought. What if I fell on the man like a dog on a bone only to discover that his meaning was merely friendly, absentminded, or impersonal? I couldn't think about anything because there was no sound between us, nothing said, not anything I could react to or fix on—no way to divert myself. He was making it hard to breathe. I felt like a glass rod being rubbed on silk. Out of the corner of my eye, I thought I saw his face turn toward me. I glanced at him.

"Hey," he said softly. "Guess what we're going to do?"

Charlie shifted in his seat slightly and pressed my hand between his legs. A charge shot through me and I groaned involuntarily. Charlie laughed, a low excited sound, and then he looked back at the road.

MAKING love with Charlie was like being taken into a big warm machine. Nothing was required of me. Everything was attended to with such ease, such fluidity. There were no awkward moments. There was no holding back, no self-consciousness, no hesitation, no heed. It was as though a channel had been opened between us, sexual energy flowing back and forth without impediment. We made love more than once. At first, there was too much hunger, too much heat. We came at each other with a clash, an intensity that admitted of no tenderness. We crashed against one other like waves on a breakwater, surges of pleasure driving straight up, curling back again. All of the emotional images were of pounding assault, sensations of boom and buffet and battering ram until he had broken through to me, rolling down again and over me until all my walls were reduced to rubble and ash. He raised himself up on his elbow then and kissed me long and sweet and it began all over again, only this time at his pace, half speed, agonizingly slow like the gradual ripening of a peach on a limb. I could feel myself go all rosy, turn to honey and oil—a mellowing ease filtering through me like a sedative. We lay there afterward, laughing and sweaty and out of breath and then he encompassed me in sleep, the weight of his big arms pinning me to the bed. But far from feeling trapped, I felt comforted and safe, as though nothing could ever harm me as long as I stayed in the shadow of this man, this sheltering cave of flesh, where I was tucked away until morning without waking once.

At 7:00, I felt him kiss me lightly on the forehead, and after that the door closed softly. By the time I'd stirred myself awake, he was gone.

20

I GOT UP AT 9:00 AND SPENT SUNDAY TAKING CARE OF personal chores. I cleaned my place, did laundry, went to the supermarket, and had a nice visit in the afternoon with my land-lord, who was sunning himself in the backyard. For a man of eighty-one, Henry Pitts has an amazing set of legs. He also has a wonderful beaky nose, a thin aristocratic face, shocking white hair, and eyes that are periwinkle blue. The overall effect is very sexy, electric, and the photographs I've seen of him in his youth don't even half compare. At twenty and thirty and forty, Henry's face seems too full, too unformed. As the decades pass, the pictures begin to reveal a man growing lean and fierce, until now he seems totally concentrated, like a basic stock boiled down to a rich elixir.

"Listen, Henry," I said, plunking down on the grass near his chaise. "You live entirely too idle a life."

"Sin and degradation," he said complacently, not even bothering to open his eyes. "You had company last night."

"A sleep-over date. Just like our mamas warned us about."

"How was it?"

"I'm not telling," I said. "What kind of crossword puzzle did you concoct this week?"

"An easy one. All doubles. Prefixes—'bi,' 'di,' 'bis,' 'dis.' Twin. Twain. Binary. Things like that. Try this one: six letters, 'double impression.' "

"Already, I give up."

" 'Mackle.' It's a printer's term. Kind of a cheat but the fit was so nice. Try this. 'Double meaning.' Nine letters."

"Henry, would you *quit* that?"

" 'Ambiguity.' I'll leave it on your doorstep."

"No, don't. I get those things in my head and I can't get 'em out."

He smiled. "You run yet?"

"No, but I'm on my way," I said, hopping up again. I crossed the grass, glancing back at him with a grin. He was putting suntan oil on his knees, which were already a gorgeous shade of caramel. I wondered how much it really mattered that there was a fifty-year difference in our ages. But then again, I had Charlie Scorsoni to think about. I changed clothes and did my run. And thought about him.

MONDAY morning, I went in to see Con Dolan at Homicide. He was talking on the phone when I got there, so I sat down at his desk. He was tipped back in his chair, feet jammed against the edge of the desk, the receiver laid loosely against his ear. He was saying, "uh-huh, uh-huh, uh-huh," looking bored. He scanned me with care, taking in every detail of my face, as though he were memorizing me all over again, running me through a computer file of known felons, looking for a match. I stared back at him. In moments, I could see the young man in his face, which was sagging now and worn, pouches beneath his eyes, hair slicked down, cheeks turning soft at the jawline as though the flesh were beginning to warm and melt. The skin on his neck had collapsed into a series of fine folds, reddened and bulging slightly over his starched shirt collar. I feel an ornery kind of kinship with him, which I never can quite identify. He's tough, emotionless, withdrawn, calculating, harsh. I've heard he's mean, too, but what I see in him is the overriding competence. He knows his business and he takes no guff and despite the fact he gives me a hard time whenever he can, I know he likes me, though grudgingly. I saw his attention sharpen. He focused on what was being said to him and it made his temper climb.

"All right now, you listen here, Mitch, because I've said all I intend to say. We're getting down to the short strokes on this and I don't want you fuckin' up my case. Yeah, I know that. Yeah, that's what you said. I just want it clear between us. I gave your boy all the breaks I mean to give so either he cooperates or we can put him right back where he was. Yeah, well you talk to him again!"

Con dropped the phone down from a height, not exactly slamming it but making his point. He was done. He looked at me through a haze of irritation. I put the manila envelope on his desk. He put his feet on the floor.

"What *is* this?" he said snappishly. He peered in through

the flap, removing the letter I'd found in Libby Glass's effects. Even without knowing what it was, he held it by the edges, his eyes raking the contents once and then going back again with caution. He glanced up at me sharply. He tucked it back in the envelope.

"Where'd you get it?"

"Libby Glass's mother kept all her stuff. It was shoved in a paperback book. I picked it up Friday. Can you have it checked for fingerprints?"

The look he gave me was cold. "Why don't we talk about Sharon Napier first?"

I felt a spurt of fear, but I didn't hesitate. "She's dead," I said, reaching for the envelope. He smacked his fist down on it and I drew my hand back. We locked eyes. "A friend of mine in Vegas told me," I said. "That's how I knew."

"Horseshit. You drove up there."

"Wrong."

"God damn it, don't lie to me," he snapped.

I could feel my temper flare. "You want to read me my rights, Lieutenant Dolan? You want to hand me a certification of notification of my constitutional rights? Because I'll read it and sign it if you like. And then I'll call my attorney, and when he gets down here, we can chat. How's that?"

"You've been on this business two weeks and somebody shows up dead. You cross me up and I'll have your ass. Now you give it to me straight. I told you to keep out of this."

"Uh-uh. You told me to keep out of trouble, which I did. You said you'd like a little help making the connection between Libby Glass and Laurence Fife and I gave you that," I said, indicating the manila envelope.

He picked it up and tossed it in the trash. I knew it was just for effect. I tried another tack.

"Come on, Con," I said. "I had nothing to do with Sharon Napier's death. Not in any way, shape, or form. What do you think? That I'd run up there and kill somebody who might be of help? You're crazy! I never even went to Vegas. I was down at the Salton Sea talking to Greg Fife and if you doubt my word, call *him*!" I shut my mouth then and stared at him hotly, letting this bold admixture of truth and utter falsehood penetrate his darkened face.

"How'd you know where she was?"

"Because I spent a day and a half on a trace through a Nevada P.I. named Bob Dietz. I was going to drive to Vegas after I talked to Greg. I put a call through first and found out somebody'd put a bullet in her. How do you think *I* feel about that? She might have filled in a few blanks for me. I've got it tough enough as it is. This goddamn case is eight years old, now give me a break!"

"Who knew you intended to talk to her?"

"I don't know that. If you're implying that somebody killed her to keep her from talking to me, I think you're wrong but I couldn't swear to that. She was stepping on a lot of toes up there from what I hear. And don't ask me the particulars because I don't know. I just hear she was treading on somebody's turf."

He sat and stared at me then and I guessed that I must have hit a vein. The rumors my friend in Vegas had passed on must have lined up with whatever the Las Vegas Police Department had turned up. I was personally convinced that she'd been killed to shut her mouth, that someone had followed me and had gotten to her just in time, but I was damned if I was going to have a finger pointed at me. I couldn't see what purpose it would serve and it would only prevent me from getting on with my own inquiries. I still wasn't entirely easy about the fact that someone else had probably tipped off the Las Vegas

PD about the shooting. One more minute in her apartment and I'd have been in a real jam, which might have closed down my investigation for good. Whatever regret I felt for my involvement with her death wasn't going to be expiated by my being caught up in the aftermath.

"What else have you found out about Libby Glass?" he asked me then, his tone shifting slightly along with the subject.

"Not a lot. Right now, I'm still trying to make a few pieces fall into place, and so far I'm not having much luck. If that letter really was written by Laurence Fife, then at least we can nail that down. Frankly, I hope it wasn't, but Nikki seems to think the writing is his. There's something about it that doesn't sit well with me. Can you let me know if the prints match?"

Con pushed impatiently at a stack of files on his desk. "I'll think about that," he said. "I don't want us to get buddy-buddy over this."

"Believe me, we will never be close friends," I said, and for some reason his expression softened slightly and I almost thought he might smile.

"Get out of here," he said gruffly.

I went.

I GOT in my car and left the downtown area, taking a left on Anaconda down to the beach. It was a gorgeous day— sunny and cool, with fat clouds squatting on the horizon. There were sailboats here and there, probably planted by the Chamber of Commerce to look picturesque for the tourists who straggled along the sidewalk taking snapshots of other tourists who were sitting in the grass.

At Ludlow Beach, I followed the hill upward and then branched off onto the steep side street where Marcia Threadgill lived. I parked and got out my binoculars, scanning her patio. All of her plants were present and accounted for and they were all looking healthier than I liked. There was no sign of Marcia or the neighbor she feuded with. I wished she would move so I could take pictures of her lugging fifty-pound cartons of books down to a U-Haul van. I'd even settle for a glimpse of her coming back from the grocery store with a big double bag of canned goods ripping across the bottom from the weight. I focused in on her patio again and noticed for the first time that there were actually four plant hooks screwed into the wooden overhang of the patio above. On the hook at the near corner was the mammoth plant I'd seen before, but the other three hooks were empty.

I put the binoculars away and went into the building, pausing at the landing between the second and third floors. I peered down through the stair railing. If I situated myself correctly, I'd be able to focus my camera at just the right angle to pick up a nice view of Marcia's front door. Having ascertained that much, I went out to my car again and drove to the Gateway supermarket. I hefted a few houseplants potted in plastic and found one that was just right for my purposes—twenty-five pounds of sturdy trunk with a series of vicious swordlike leaves protruding at intervals. I picked up some prettied gift ribbons in a fire-engine red and a get-well card with a sentimental verse. All of this was taking up precious time that I would have preferred devoting to Nikki Fife's business, but I have my rent to account for and I felt like I owed California Fidelity for at least half a month.

I went back to Marcia's apartment and parked in front. I checked my camera, tore open the packaged ribbons, and stuck several of them to the plastic pot in a jaunty fashion and then tucked the card down inside with a signature scrawled on it that even I couldn't read. I hoisted plant, camera, and myself with a slightly thudding heart up the steep concrete stairs, into the building, and up to the second floor. I set the plant down near Marcia's doorsill and then went up to the landing, where I checked my light meter, set up the camera, and adjusted the focus on the lens. Nice angle, I thought. This was going to be a work of art. I trotted back down, took a deep breath and rang Ms. Threadgill's bell, racing back up the stairs again at breakneck speed. I picked up the camera and checked the focus again. My timing was perfect.

Marcia Threadgill opened her front door and stared down with surprise and puzzlement. She was wearing shorts and a crocheted halter and in the background the voice of Olivia Newton-John boomed out like an audible lollipop. I hesitated a moment and then peered over the rail. Marcia was leaning over to extract the card. She read it, turned it over, and then studied its face again, shrugging with bewilderment. She glanced down the stairwell as though she might catch sight of the delivery person. I began to click off pictures, the whir of the thirty-five-millimeter camera obscured by the record being played too loudly. Marcia padded back to her doorsill and bent casually from the waist, picking up twenty-five pounds of plant without even bothering to bend her knees as we've all been instructed to in the exercise manuals. As soon as she'd trucked the plant inside, I raced back down the stairs and out to the street, focusing again from the sidewalk below just as she appeared on the patio and placed the plant up on the rail. She disappeared. I backed up several yards, attaching the telephoto lens, waiting then with my breath held.

Back she came with what must have been a kitchen chair. I clicked off some nice shots of her climbing up. Sure enough, she picked up the plant by the wire, heaving it up to shoulder height, muscles straining until she caught the wire loop on the overhead hook. The effort was such that her halter hiked up and I got a nice shot of Marcia Threadgill's quite large bosom peeping out. I turned away just in time, I suspect, catching only the inkling of her quick look around to see if anyone else had spotted her exposure. When I glanced back casually she was gone.

I dropped the film off to be developed, making sure it was properly dated and identified. Still photographs were not going to be much good to us, especially without a witness to corroborate my testimony as to the date, time, and circumstance, but the pictures might at least persuade the claims manager at California Fidelity to pursue the case, which was the best I could hope for at this point. With his authorization, I could go back with a video outfit and a real photographer and pick up some footage that would stand up in court.

I SHOULD have known he wouldn't see it that way. Andy Motycka is in his early forties and he still bites his nails. He was working on his right hand that day, trying to gnaw off what remained of his thumb. It made me nervous just to look at him. I kept expecting him to rip loose a big triangle of flesh at the corner of his cuticle. I could feel my face set with distaste and I had to stare just over his shoulder to the left. Before I was even halfway through my explanation, he was shaking his head.

"Can't do it," he said bluntly. "This chick doesn't even have an attorney. We're supposed to get a signed release from the doctor next week. No deal. I don't want to mess this one up. Forty-eight hundred dollars is chicken feed. It'd cost us ten grand to go into court. You know that."

"Well, I know, but—"

"But nothing. The risk is too great. I don't even know why

Mac had you check this one out. Look, I know it frosts your ass, but so what? You set her off and she'll go straight out and hire a lawyer and next thing you know, she'll sue us for a million bucks. Forget it."

"She'll just do it again somewhere else," I said.

Andy shrugged.

"Why do I waste my time on this shit," I said, voice rising with frustration.

"Beats me," he said conversationally. "Let me see the pix, though, when you get 'em back. Her tits are huge."

"Screw you," I said and moved on into my office.

THERE WERE TWO MESSAGES ON MY ANSWERING SERVICE.
The first was from Garry Steinberg. I called him back.

"Hey, Kinsey," he said when I'd been put through.

"Hi, Garry. How are you?"

"Not bad. I've got a little piece of information for you," he said. I could tell from his tone that he was feeling satisfied with himself, but what he said next still took me by surprise.

"I looked up that job application on Lyle Abernathy this morning. Apparently he worked for a while as an apprentice to a locksmith. Some old guy named Fears."

"A locksmith?"

"That's right. I called the guy this morning. You'd have loved it. I said Abernathy had applied for a job as a security guard and I was doing a background check. Fears hemmed and hawed some and finally said he'd had to fire the kid. Fears was getting a lot of complaints about missing cash on jobs where Lyle had worked and he began to suspect he was involved in petty thievery. He never could prove it, but he couldn't afford to take the chance, so he let Lyle go."

"Oh God, that's great," I said. "That means Lyle could have gotten into the Fifes' house anytime he wanted to. Libby's too."

"It looks that way. He worked for Fears for eight months and he sure picked up enough information to give it a try, judging from what Fears said. Unless they had burglar alarms or something like that."

"Listen, the only security system they had in effect was a big German shepherd that got hit by a car six weeks before Laurence Fife died. He and his wife and kids were away when the dog was killed."

"Nice," Garry said. "Nothing you could prove after all this time, but it might put you on the right track at any rate. What about the application? You want a copy?"

"I'd love it. What about Fife's accounts?"

"I've got those at my place and I'll look at 'em when I can. It's a lot of stuff. In the meantime, I just thought you might want to know about that locksmith stint."

"I appreciate your help. Jesus, what a shmuck that guy is."

"I'll say. Hey, I got another call coming in. I'll be in touch." He gave me his home phone in case I needed him.

"You're terrific. Thanks."

The second message was from Gwen at K-9 Korners. One

of her assistants answered and I listened to assorted dogs bark and whine while Gwen came to the phone.

"Kinsey?"

"Yeah, it's me. I got your call. What's happening?"

"Are you free for lunch?"

"Just a minute. I'll check my appointment book," I said. I put my palm against the mouth of the receiver and looked at my watch. It was 1:45. Had I *eaten* lunch? Had I even eaten breakfast today? "Yes, I'm free."

"Good. I'll meet you at the Palm Garden in fifteen minutes if that's okay for you."

"Sure. Fine. See you shortly."

MY GLASS of white wine had just arrived when I glanced up to see Gwen approaching from across the courtyard: tall and lean, her gray hair slicked away from her face. The blouse she wore was a gray silk, long full sleeves nipped in at the wrist, the dark gray skirt emphasizing her trim waist and hips. She was stylish, confident—like Nikki in that—and I could see where both women must have appealed to Laurence Fife. I guessed that once upon a time Charlotte Mercer fit the same mold: a woman of stature, a woman of taste. I wondered idly if Libby Glass would have aged as well had she lived. She must have been much less secure at twenty-four, but bright—someone whose freshness and ambition might have appealed to Laurence as he neared the age of forty. God save us all from the consequences of male menopause, I thought.

"Hello. How are you," Gwen said briskly, sitting down. She removed the napkin beside her plate and ordered wine as the waitress passed. Close up, her image softened, the angularity of her cheekbones offset by the large brown eyes, the purposeful mouth tinted with soft pink. Most of all, there was her manner: amused, intelligent, feminine, refined.

"How are all the dogs?" I said.

She laughed. "Filthy. Thank God. We're swamped today, but I wanted to talk to you. You've been out of town."

"I just got back Saturday. Have you been trying to get in touch?"

She nodded. "I called the office on Tuesday, I think. Your answering service said you were in Los Angeles so I tried to reach you there. Some total nitwit answered—"

"Arlette."

"Well, whoever it was, she got my name wrong twice so I hung up."

The waitress arrived with Gwen's wine.

"Have you ordered yet?"

I shook my head. "I was waiting for you."

The waitress got out her order card, glancing at me.

"I'll have the chef's salad," I said.

"Make that two."

"Dressing?"

"Blue cheese," I said.

"I'll have oil and vinegar," Gwen said and then handed both menus to the waitress, who moved away. Gwen turned her attention to me.

"I've decided I should level with you."

"About what?"

"My old lover," she said. Her cheeks had flushed mildly. "I realized that if I didn't tell you who he was, you'd be off on some wild-goose chase, wasting a lot of time trying to find out his name. It really amounts to more mystery than it's worth."

"How so?"

"He died a few months ago of a heart attack," she said, her manner turning brisk again. "After I talked to you, I tried tracking him down myself. His name was David Ray. He was a schoolteacher. Greg's, as a matter of fact, which is how we met. I thought he should know that you were asking questions about Laurence's death, or at any rate that your curiosity might lead you to him."

"How'd you find him?"

"I'd heard that he and his wife had moved to San Francisco. Apparently he was living in the Bay Area, where he was a principal of one of the Oakland public schools."

"Why not tell me before?"

She shrugged. "Misplaced loyalty. Protectiveness. That was a very important relationship and I didn't want him involved at this late date."

She looked at me and she must have read the skepticism in my face. The flush in her cheeks deepened almost imperceptibly.

"I know how it looks," she said. "First I refuse to give you his name and then he's dead and out of reach, but that's exactly the point. If he were still alive, I don't know that I'd be telling you this."

I thought that was probably true, but there was something else going on and I wasn't sure what it was. The waitress arrived with our salads and there was a merciful few minutes in which we busied ourselves with melba rounds. Gwen was rearranging her lettuce but she wasn't eating much. I was curious to hear what else she had to say and too hungry to worry about it much until I'd eaten some.

"Did you know he had heart trouble?" I asked finally.

"I had no idea, but I gather he was ill for years."

"Did he break off the relationship or did you?"

Gwen smiled bitterly. "Laurence did that but I wonder now

if David might have engineered it to some extent. The whole affair must have complicated his life unbearably."

"He'd told his wife?"

"I think so. She was very gracious on the phone. I told her that Greg had asked me to get in touch and she played right along. When she told me that David was dead, I was . . . I didn't even know what to say to her but of course, I had to babble right on—how sorry, how sad . . . like some disinterested bystander making the right noises somehow. It was awful. Terrible."

"She didn't mention your relationship herself?"

"Oh no. She was much too cool for that, but she did know exactly who I was. Anyway, I'm sorry I didn't tell you to begin with."

"No harm done," I said.

"How's it going otherwise?" she asked.

I felt myself hesitate. "Bits and pieces. Nothing concrete."

"Do you really expect to turn up anything after all this time?"

I smiled. "You never know. People get careless when they're feeling safe."

"I guess that's true."

We talked briefly about Greg and Diane and my visits with them, which I edited heavily. At 2:50 Gwen glanced at her watch.

"I've got to get back," she said, fishing in her purse for her billfold. She took out a five-dollar bill. "Will you keep in touch?"

"Sure," I said. I took a sip of wine, watching her get up. "When did you last see Colin?"

She focused abruptly on my face. "Colin?"

"I just met him Saturday," I said as though that explained

it. "I thought maybe Diane might like to know he's back. She's fond of him."

"Yes, she is," Gwen said. "I don't know when I saw him last myself. Diane's graduation, I guess. Her junior-high-school graduation. What makes you ask?"

I shrugged. "Just curious," I said. I gave her what I hoped was my blandest look. A mild pink patch had appeared on her neck and I wondered if that could be introduced in court as a lie-detecting device. "I'll take care of the tip," I said.

"Let me know how it goes," she said, all casual again. She tucked the money under her plate and moved off at the same efficient pace that had brought her in. I watched her departure, thinking that something vital had gone unsaid. She could have told me about David Ray on the phone. And I wasn't entirely convinced she hadn't known about his death to begin with. Colin popped into my head.

I walked the two blocks to Charlie's office. Ruth was typing from a Dictaphone, fingers moving lightly across the keyboard. She was very fast.

"Is he in?"

She smiled and nodded me on back, not missing a word, gaze turned inward as she translated sound to paper with no lag time in between.

I stuck my head into his office. He was sitting at his desk, coat off, a law book open in front of him. Beige shirt, dark brown vest. When he saw me, a slow smile formed and he leaned back, tucking an arm up over the back of his swivel chair. He tossed the pencil on his desk.

"Are you free for dinner?" I said.

"What's up?"

"Nothing's up. It's a proposition," I said.

"Six-fifteen."

"I'll be back," I said and closed his office door again, still thinking about that pale shirt and the dark brown vest. Now *that* was sexy. A man in a nylon bikini, with that little knot sticking out in front, isn't half as interesting as a man in a good-looking business suit. Charlie's outfit reminded me of a Reese's Peanut Butter Cup with a bite taken out and I wanted the rest.

I DROVE out to Nikki's beach house.

22

NIKKI ANSWERED THE DOOR IN AN OLD GRAY SWEATSHIRT and a pair of faded jeans. She was barefoot, hair loose, a paintbrush in one hand, her fingers stained the color of pecan shells.

"Oh hi, Kinsey. Come on in," she said. She was already moving back toward the deck and I followed her through the house. On the other side of the sliding glass doors, I could see Colin, shirtless, in a pair of bib overalls sitting cross-legged in front of a chest of drawers, which the two were apparently refinishing. The drawers were out, leaning upright along the balcony, hardware removed. The air smelled of stripper and turpentine, which mingled not incompatibly with the smell of eucalyptus bark. Several sheets of fine sandpaper were folded and tossed aside, creases worn white with wood dust, looking soft from hard use. The sun was hot on the railings and newspapers were spread out under the chest to protect the deck.

Colin glanced up at me and smiled as I came out. His nose and cheeks were faintly pink with sunburn, his eyes green as sea water, bare arms rosy, there wasn't even a whisper of facial hair yet. He went back to his work.

"I want to ask Colin something but I thought I'd try it out on you first," I said to Nikki.

"Sure, fire away," she replied. I leaned against the railing while she dipped the tip of her brush back into a small can of stain, easing the excess off along the edge. Colin seemed more interested in the painting than he was in our exchange. I imagined that it was a bit of a strain to try to follow a conversation even if his lip-reading skills were good or maybe he thought adults were a bore.

"Can you remember offhand if you were out of town for any length of time in the four to six months before Laurence died?"

Nikki looked at me with surprise and blinked, apparently not expecting that. "I was gone once for a week. My father had a heart attack that June and I flew back to Connecticut," she said. She paused then and shook her head. "That was the only time, I think. What are you getting at?"

"I'm not sure. I mean, this is going to seem farfetched, but I've been bothered by Colin's calling Gwen 'Daddy's mother.' Has he mentioned that since?"

"Nope. Not a word."

"Well, I'm wondering if he didn't have occasion to see Gwen at some point while you were gone. He's too smart to get her mixed up with his own grandmother unless somebody identified her to him that way."

Nikki gave me a skeptical look. "Boy, that *is* a stretch. He couldn't have been more than three and a half years old."

"Yeah, I know, but a little while ago I asked Gwen when she saw him last and she claims it was at Diane's junior-high-school graduation."

"That's probably true," Nikki said.

"Nikki, Colin must have been fourteen months old at the time. I saw those snapshots myself. He was still a babe in arms."

"So?"

"So why did he remember her at all?"

Nikki applied a band of stain, giving that some thought. "Maybe she saw him in a supermarket or ran into him with Diane. She could have seen him or he could easily have seen her without any particular significance attached to it."

"Maybe. But I think Gwen lied to me about it when I asked. If it was no big deal, why not just say so. Why cover up?"

Nikki gave me a long look. "Maybe she just forgot."

"Mind if I ask him?"

"No, go ahead."

"Where's the album?"

She gestured over her shoulder and I went back into the living room. The photograph album was sitting on the coffee table and I flipped through until I found the snapshot of Gwen. I slipped it out of the four little corners holding it down and went back out to the deck. I held it out to him.

"Ask him if he can remember what was happening when he saw her last," I said.

Nikki reached over and gave him a tap. He looked at her and then at the snapshot, eyes meeting mine inquisitively.

Nikki signed the question to him. His face closed up like a day lily when the sun goes down.

"Colin?"

He started to paint again, his face averted.

"The little shit," she said good-naturedly. She gave him a nudge and asked him again.

Colin shrugged her off. I studied his reaction with care.

"Ask him if she was here."

"Who, Gwen? Why would she be here?"

"I don't know. That's why we're asking him."

The look she gave me was half doubt, half disbelief. Reluctantly, she looked back at him. She signed to him, translating for my benefit. She didn't seem to like it much.

"Was Gwen ever here or at the other house?"

Colin watched her face, his own face a remarkable mirror of uncertainty and something else—uneasiness, secrecy, dismay.

"I don't know," he said aloud. The consonants blurred together like ink on a wet page, his tone conveying a sort of stubborn distrust.

His eyes slid over to me. I thought suddenly of the time in the sixth grade when I first heard the word *fuck*. One of my classmates told me I should go ask my aunt what it meant. I could sense the trap though I had no idea what it consisted of.

"Tell him it's okay," I said to her. "Tell him it doesn't matter to you."

"Well it certainly does," she snapped.

"Oh come on, Nikki. It's important and what difference does it make after all this time."

She got into a short discussion with him then, just the two of them, signing away like mad—a digital argument. "He doesn't want to talk about it," she said guardedly. "He made a mistake."

I didn't think so and I could feel excitement stir. He was watching us now, trying to get an emotional reading from our interchange.

"I know this sounds weird," I said to her tentatively, "but I wonder if Laurence told him that—that she was his mother."

"Why would he do that?"

I looked at her. "Maybe Colin caught them embracing or something like that."

Nikki's expression was blank for a moment and then she frowned. Colin waited uncertainly, looking from her to me. Nikki signed to him again. He seemed embarrassed now, head bent. She signed again more earnestly. Colin shook his head but the gesture seemed to come out of caution, not ignorance.

Nikki's expression underwent a change. "I just remembered something," she said. She blinked rapidly, color mounting in her face. "Laurence did come out here. He told me he brought Colin out the weekend I was back east. Greg and Diane stayed at the house with Mrs. Voss. Both had social plans or something, but Laurence said the two of them—he and Colin— came out to the beach to get away for a bit."

"Nice," I said with irony. "At three and a half, none of it would have made sense to him anyway. Let's just assume it's true. Let's assume she was out here—"

"I really don't care to go on with this."

"Just one more," I said. "Just ask him why he called her 'Daddy's mother.' Ask him why the 'Daddy's mother' bit."

She relayed the question to Colin reluctantly but his face brightened with relief. He signed back at once, grabbing his head.

"She had gray hair," she reported to me. "She *looked* like a grandmother to him when she was here."

I caught a glint of temper in her voice but she recovered herself, apparently for his sake. She tousled his hair affectionately.

"I love you," she said. "It's fine. It's okay."

Colin seemed to relax but the tension had darkened Nikki's eyes to a charcoal gray.

"Laurence hated her," she said. "He *couldn't* have—"

"I'm just making an educated guess," I said. "It might have been completely innocent. Maybe they met for drinks and talked about the kids' schoolwork. We really don't know anything for *sure*."

"My ass," she murmured. Her mood was sour.

"Don't get mad at me," I said. "I'm just trying to put this thing together so it makes some sense."

"Well I don't believe a word of it," she said tersely.

"You want to tell me he was too nice a man to do such a thing?"

She put the paintbrush on the paper and wiped her hands on a rag.

"Maybe I'd like to have a few illusions left."

"I don't blame you a bit," I said. "But I don't understand why it bothers you. Charlotte Mercer was the one who put it into my head. She said he was like a tomcat, always sniffing around the same back porch."

"All right, Kinsey. You've made your point."

"No, I don't think I have. You paid me five grand to find out what happened. You don't like the answers, I can give you your money back."

"No, never mind. Just skip it. You're right," she said.

"You want me to pursue it or not?"

"Yes," she said flatly, but she didn't really look at me again. I made my excuses and left soon after that, feeling almost depressed. She still cared about the man and I didn't know what to make of that. Except that nothing's ever cut-and-dried—especially where men and women are concerned. So why did I feel guilty for doing my job?

I WENT into Charlie's office building. He was waiting at the top of the stairs, coat over one shoulder, tie loose.

"What happened to you?" he said when he saw my face.

"Don't ask," I said. "I'm going to try to get a scholarship to secretarial school. Something simple and nice. Something nine-to-five."

I came up level with him, tilting my face slightly to look at him. It was as though I had suddenly entered a magnetic field like those two little dog-magnets when I was a kid—one black, one white. At the positive poles, if you held them half an inch apart, they would suck together with a little click. His face was solemn, so close, eyes resting on my mouth as though he might will me forward. For a full ten seconds we seemed caught and then I pulled back slightly, unprepared for the intensity.

"Jesus," he said, almost with surprise, and then he chuckled, a sound I knew well.

"I need a drink," I said.

"That's not all you need," he said mildly.

I smiled, ignoring him. "I hope you know how to cook because I don't."

"Hey listen, there is one slight kink," he said. "I'm house-sitting for my partner. He's out of town and I've got his dogs to feed. We can grab a bite to eat out there."

"Fine with me," I said.

He locked the office then and we went down the back stairs to the small parking lot adjacent to his office building. He opened his car door but I was already moving toward mine, which was parked out on the street.

"Don't you trust me to drive?"

"I'm courting a ticket if I stay parked out here. I'll follow you. I don't like to be stuck without my own wheels."

" 'Wheels'? Like in the sixties, you refer to your car as *'wheels'*?"

"Yeah, I read that in a book," I said dryly.

He rolled his eyes and smiled indulgently, apparently resigned. He got in his car and waited pointedly until I had reached mine. Then he pulled out, driving slowly so that I could follow him without getting lost. Once in a while, I could see him watching me in his rearview mirror.

"You sexy bastard," I said to him under my breath and then I shivered involuntarily. He had that effect.

We proceeded to John Powers's house at the beach, Charlie driving at a leisurely pace. As usual, he was operating at half speed. The road began to wind and finally his car slowed and he turned left down a steep drive, a place not far from Nikki's beach house, if my calculations were correct. I pulled my car in beside his, nose down, hoping my handbrake would hold. Powers's house was tucked up against the hill to the right, with a carport dead ahead and parking space for two cars. The carport itself had a white picket fence across it, the two halves forming a gate, locked shut, with what I guessed to be his car parked inside.

Charlie got out, waiting as I came around the front of my car. As with Nikki's property, this was up on the bluff, probably sixty or seventy feet above the beach. Through the carport, I could see a patchy apron of grass, a crescent of yard. We went along a narrow walkway behind the house and Charlie let us into the kitchen. John Powers's two dogs were of the kind I hate: the jumping, barking, slavering sort with toenails like sharks' teeth. They reeked of bad breath. One was black and the other was the color of moldering whale washed up on the beach for a month. Both were large and insisted on standing up on their hind legs to stare into my face. I kept my head back, lips shut lest wet, sloppy kisses be forthcoming.

"Charlie, could you help me with this?" I ventured through clenched teeth. One licked me right in the mouth as I spoke.

"Tootsie! Moe! Knock it off!" he snapped.

I wiped my lips. "Tootsie and Moe?"

Charlie laughed and dragged them both by neck chains to the utility room, where he shut them in. One began to howl while the other barked.

"Oh Jesus. Let 'em out," I said. He opened the door and both bounded out, tongues flapping like slivers of corned beef. One of the dogs galummoxed into the other room and came trotting back with a leash in its mouth. This was supposed to be cute. Charlie put leashes on both and they pranced, wetting the floor in spots.

"If I walk them, they calm down," Charlie remarked. "Sort of like you."

I made a face at him but there seemed to be no alternative but to follow him out the front. There were various dog lumps in the grass. A narrow wooden stairway angled down toward the beach, giving way in places to bare ground and rock. It was a hazardous descent, especially with two ninety-five-pound lunkheads doing leaps and pirouettes at every turn.

"John comes home at lunch to give 'em a run," Charlie said back over his shoulder.

"Good for him," I said, picking my way down the cliffside, concentrating on my feet. Fortunately, I was wearing tennis shoes, which provided no traction but at least didn't have heels that would catch in the rotting steps and pitch me headfirst into the Pacific.

The beach below was long and narrow, bounded by precipitous rocks. The dogs loped from one end to the other, the black one pausing to take a big steaming dump, backside hunched, eyes downcast modestly. Jesus, I thought, is that all dogs know how to do? I averted my gaze. Really, it was all so *rude*. I found a seat on a rock and tried to turn my brain off. I needed a break, a long stretch of time in which I didn't have to worry about anybody but myself. Charlie threw sticks, which the dogs invariably missed.

Finally, the dog romp at an end, we staggered back up the steps together. As soon as we were inside, the dogs flopped happily on a big oval rug in the living room and began to chew it to shreds. Charlie went into the kitchen and I could hear ice trays cracking.

"What do you want to drink?" he called.

I moved over to the kitchen doorway. "Wine if you have it."

"Great. There's some in the fridge."

"You do this often?" I asked, indicating the pups.

He shrugged, filling ice trays again. "Every three or four weeks. It depends," he said and then smiled over at me. "See? I'm a nicer guy than you thought."

I twirled an index finger in the air just to show how impressed I was, but I did, actually, think it was nice of him to sit the dogs. I couldn't imagine Powers finding a kennel to keep them. He'd have to take them to the zoo. Charlie handed me a glass of wine, pouring a bourbon on the rocks for himself. I leaned against the doorframe.

"Did you know that Laurence had an affair at one time with Sharon Napier's mother?"

He gave me a startled look. "You're making a joke."

"No I'm not. Apparently it happened some time before Sharon went to work for him. From what I gather, her 'em-

ployment' was a combination extortion and revenge. Which
might explain the way she treated him."

"Who told you this stuff?"

"What difference does that make?"

"Because it sounds like crap," he said. "The name Napier
never meant anything to me and I knew him for years."

I shrugged. "That's what you said about Libby Glass," I
replied.

Charlie's face began to fade. "Jesus, you don't forgive a thing,
do you?" He moved into the living room and I followed. He sat
down in a wicker chair, which creaked beneath his weight.

"Is that why you're here? To work?" he asked.

"Actually, it's not. Actually, it's just the opposite."

"Meaning what?"

"I came out here to get away from it," I said.

"Then why the questions? Why the third-degree? You know
how I feel about Laurence and I don't like to be used."

I felt my own smile fade, my face setting with embarrassment.

"Is that what you think?" I asked.

He looked down at his glass, speaking carefully. "I can appreciate the fact you have a job to do. That's fine with me and
I'm not complaining about that. I'll help you where I can, but
I can do without the interrogation at every step. I don't think
you have any idea what it's like. You ought to see the change
that comes over you when you start talking homicide."

"I'm sorry," I said stiffly. "I don't mean to do that to you. I
get information and I need to have it verified. I can't afford to
take things at face value."

"Not even me?"

"Why are you doing this?" I said, and my voice seemed to
have dropped to a hush.

"I'm just trying to get a few things clarified."

"Hey. You were the one who came after me. Remember that?"

"Saturday. Yes. And you were the one who came after me today. And now you're pumping me and I don't like that."

I stared down at the floor, feeling fragile and mortified. I didn't like being smacked down and it was pissing me off. A lot. I began to shake my head. "I had a hard day," I said. "I really don't need this shit."

"I had a hard day too," he said. "So what?"

I set my wineglass on the table and grabbed up my purse.

"Fuck off," I said mildly. "Just go fuck yourself."

I moved toward the kitchen. The dogs raised their heads and watched me pass. I was hot and they lowered their eyes meekly as though I had communicated that much at any rate. Charlie didn't move. I banged out the back door and got into my car, starting it up with energy, peeling back up the driveway with a chirp. As I backed out onto the road, I caught a glimpse of Charlie standing near the carport. I put the car into first and pulled away.

23

I'VE NEVER BEEN GOOD AT TAKING SHIT, ESPECIALLY FROM men. It was an hour after I got home before I cooled down. Eight o'clock and I still hadn't eaten anything. I poured myself a big glass of wine and sat down at my desk. I took out some blank index cards and began to work. At 10:00 I had dinner—a sliced hard-boiled-egg sandwich, which I ate hot on wheat bread with a lot of mayonnaise and salt, popping open a Pepsi and a package of corn chips. By then I'd consigned all the information I had to the index cards, which I'd tacked up on my bulletin board.

I sketched the story out, allowing myself to speculate. I mean, why not? I didn't have much else to go on at this point. It seemed likely that someone had broken into the Fifes' house the weekend the German shepherd was killed, while Nikki and Laurence were off at the Salton Sea with Colin and Greg. It also seemed likely that Sharon Napier had come up with something after Laurence died—which was (maybe) why she had gotten herself killed. I started making lists, systematizing the information I had, along with the half-formed ideas that were simmering at the back of my head. I typed up my sheets and arranged them in alphabetical order, starting with Lyle Abernathy and Gwen.

I didn't dismiss the idea that Diane and Greg were possibly involved, though I couldn't make any sense of the notion that either could have killed him, let alone Libby Glass. I included Charlotte Mercer on my list. She was spoiled and spiteful and I didn't think she would spare any energy or expense in seeing that the world was arranged exactly as she wanted it. She could have hired someone if she didn't want to go to the trouble of murdering him herself. And if she killed him, why not Libby Glass? Why not Sharon Napier, if Sharon had figured it out? I decided it might be smart to check with the airlines to see if her name appeared on any of the passenger lists for Las Vegas at the time Sharon died. That was one angle I hadn't thought of. I made a note to myself. Charlie Scorsoni was still on my list and the realization had a disturbing effect.

THERE was a knock at the door and I jerked involuntarily, adrenaline shooting through me. I glanced at my watch: 12:25. My heart was thumping so hard it made my hands shake. I crossed to the door and bent my head.

"Yes?"

"It's me," Charlie said. "Can I come in?"

I opened the door. Charlie was leaning against the frame. No jacket. No tie. Tennis shoes with no socks. His square handsome face looked solemn and subdued. He searched my face and then looked away. "I came down on you too hard and I'm sorry," he said.

I studied his face. "You had a legitimate complaint," I said. I knew that my tone of voice was unrelenting, regardless of the content, and I knew that my purpose was punitive. He only had time to look at me to guess my real attitude and it frosted him some.

"Jesus Christ, could we just talk?" he said.

I glanced at him briefly and then moved away from the door. He came in, closing it behind him. He leaned on the door, hands in his pockets, watching me prowl the room, circling back to my desk, where I began to take cards down, packing papers away.

"What do you want from me?" he said helplessly.

"What do you want from *me*?" I snapped back. I caught myself and raised a hand. "I'm sorry. I didn't mean to use that tone."

He stared down at the floor as though trying to figure out where to go next. I sat down in the upholstered chair near the couch, flinging my legs over the padded arm.

"Want a drink?" I asked.

He shook his head. He moved over to the couch and sat down heavily, leaning his head back. His face looked lined, his brow furrowed. His sandy hair looked as though he'd run a hand through it more than once. "I don't know what to do with you," he said.

"What's to do?" I asked. "I know I'm a bitch sometimes, but why not? I'm serious, Charlie. I'm too old to take any guff from anyone. And truly, in this case, I don't know who did what to whom. Did you generate that fight or did I?"

He smiled slightly. "Okay, so we're both touchy now and then. Is that fair enough?"

"I don't know from fair anymore. I don't know from any of this stuff."

"Haven't you ever heard of compromise?"

"Oh sure," I said. "That's when you give away half the things you want. That's when you give the other guy half of what's rightfully yours. I've done that lots of times. It sucks."

He shook his head, smiling wearily. I stared at him, feeling stubborn and belligerent. He'd already given more than I, and I still couldn't bend. He regarded me skeptically.

"Where do you go when you look at me that way?" he asked. I didn't know what to say so I kept my mouth shut. He reached over and waggled my bare foot as though to get my attention.

"You know you keep me at arm's length," he said.

"Really? Saturday night you think I did that?"

"Kinsey, sex was the only time you let me get close. What am I supposed to do with that? Chase around after you with my dick hanging out?"

I smiled inside, hoping it wouldn't show on my face. He read it anyway in my eyes. "Yeah, why not?" I said.

"I don't think you're used to men," he said, not making eye contact, and then he corrected himself. "Not men," he said. "I don't think you're used to having anyone in your life. I think you're used to being freewheeling. And that's okay. Essentially I live the same way, but this is different. I think we should be careful of this."

"This what?"

"This relationship," he said. "I don't want you shutting me out. You're not that hard to read. Sometimes you disappear like a shot and I can't cope with that. I will try to tread easy.

I'll try not to be a horse's ass myself, I promise you that. Just don't run off. Don't back away. You do this kind of knee-jerk retreat, like a clam—" He broke off then.

I softened, wondering if I'd misjudged him. I was too tough, too quick. I am hard on people and I know that.

"I'm sorry," I said. I had to clear my throat. "I'm sorry. I know I do that. I don't know who was at fault, but you ticked me off and I blew."

I held my hand out and he took it, squeezing my fingers. He looked at me for a long time. He took my fingertips and kissed them lightly, casually, looking at me the whole time. I felt like a switch was being turned on at the base of my spine. He turned my hand over and pressed his mouth into my palm. I didn't want him to do that but I noticed I wasn't pulling my hand away. I watched him, hypnotically, my senses dulled by the heat that was raging way down, way deep. It was like a pile of rags beginning to smolder, some dark part of me hidden away under the stairs, something firemen had warned us about in grade school. Paint cans, jars of gasoline—fumes in compression. All it needed was a spark, sometimes not even that. I could feel my eyes close, mouth coming open against my will. I sensed that Charlie was moving but I couldn't take that in and the next thing I was aware of, he was on his knees between mine, pulling the neck of my T-shirt down, his mouth on my bare breast. I clutched at him convulsively, slid down and forward against him and he half lifted me, hands cupped under my ass. I hadn't known how much I wanted him until then, until that point, but the sound I made was primitive and his response was fierce and immediate and after that, in the half-light, with the table pushed aside, we made love on the floor. He did things to me that I'd only read about in books, and at the end of it, legs trembling, heart thudding, I laughed and he buried his face against my belly, laughing too.

HE WAS gone again by 2:00 A.M. He had work to do the next day and so did I. Even so, I missed him as I brushed my teeth, smirking at my own reflection in the bathroom mirror. My chin was pink from whisker burn. My hair seemed to be standing straight up on end. There is nothing quite as smug as the self-congratulation that abounds when one has been thoroughly and proficiently screwed, but I was a little bit embarrassed with myself nevertheless. This was not good, not cool. As a rule, I scrupulously avoid personal contact with anyone connected with a case. My sexual wrangling with Charlie was foolish, unprofessional, and in theory, possibly dangerous. In some little nagging part of my head, it didn't feel right to me, but I did love his *moves*. I couldn't think when I'd last run into a man quite so inventive. My reaction to him was gut-level chemistry—like crystals of sodium flung in a swimming pool, throwing off sparks, dancing across the water like light. I had a friend once who said to me, "Wherever there is sex, we work to create a relationship that's worthy of it." I thought about that now, sensing that soon I would do that with him—start to bond, start to fantasize, start to throw out emotional tendrils like snow peas curling up a string. I was wary of it too. The sex was very good and very strong but the fact remained that I was still in the middle of an investigation and he still had not been crossed off my list. I didn't think our physical relationship had clouded my judgment about him, but how could I tell? I couldn't really afford to take the chance. Unless, of course, I was just rationalizing my own inclination to hold back. Was I *that* careful with myself these days? Was I really just sidestepping intimacy? Did I long to relegate him to the role of "possible suspect" in order to justify my own reluctance to take a risk? He was a nice man—smart, caring, responsible, attractive, perceptive. What in God's name did I want?

I turned the bathroom light out and made up my bed, which really just amounted to a quilt folded lengthways on the couch. I could have opened out the sofa bed and done it right—sheets, pillow case, a proper nightgown. Instead I'd pulled the same T-shirt over my head and tucked myself into the fold of the quilt. My body heat was making a sexual perfume waft up from between my legs. I turned out the lamp on the desk and smiled in the dark, shivering with the recollection of his mouth on me. Maybe this wasn't the time to get analytical, I thought. Maybe this was just a time to reflect and assimilate. I slept like the dead.

IN THE morning, I showered, skipping breakfast, reaching the office by 9:00. I let myself in and checked with the service. Con Dolan had called. I dialed the Santa Teresa Police Department and asked for him.

"What," he barked, already annoyed with the world.

"Kinsey Millhone here," I said.

"Oh yeah? What do you want?"

"Lieutenant, you called me!" I could hear him blink.

"Oh. Right. I got a report here from the lab on that letter. No prints. Just smudges, so that's no good."

"Rats. What about the handwriting? Does that match?"

"Enough to satisfy us," he said. "I had Jimmy go over it and he says it's legitimate. What else you got?"

"Nothing right now. I may come in and talk to you, though, in a couple of days if that's okay."

"Call first," he said.

"Trust me," I replied.

I went out on the balcony and stared down at the street. Something wasn't right. I'd been half convinced that letter was a fake but now it was confirmed and verified. I didn't like it. I went back in and sat down in my swivel chair, tipping back and forth slightly, listening to it creak. I shook my head. Couldn't figure it out. I glanced at the calendar. I'd been working for Nikki for two weeks. It felt like she'd hired me a minute ago and it felt like I'd been on the case all my life. I tilted forward and grabbed a scratch pad, totaling the time I'd put in, adding expenses on top of that. I typed it all up, made copies of my receipts, and stuck the whole batch in an envelope, which I mailed to her out at the beach. I went into the California Fidelity offices and shot the shit with Vera, who processes claims for them.

I skipped lunch and knocked off at 3:00. I stopped on the way home and picked up the eight-by-ten color photographs of Marcia Threadgill and I sat in my car for a moment to survey my handiwork. It isn't often that I have such a captivating spectacle of avarice and fraud. The best shot (which I might have called "Portrait of a Chiseler") was of Marcia standing up on her kitchen chair, shoulders strained by the weight of the plant as she lifted it up. Her boobs, in the crocheted halter top, sagged down like flesh melons bursting through the bottom of a string bag. The image was so clear that I could see where her mascara had left little black dots on her upper lids like tracks of some tiny beast. Such a jerk. I smiled to myself grimly. If that's the way the world works, then let me not forget. I was resigned by now to the fact that Ms. Threadgill would have her way. Cheaters win all the time. It wasn't big news but it was worth remembering. I slid all the pictures back into the manila envelope. I started the car and headed toward home. I didn't feel like running today. I wanted to sit and brood.

I PINNED THE PHOTOGRAPH OF MARCIA THREADGILL UP ON my bulletin board and stared at it. I kicked my shoes off and walked around. I'd been thinking all day and it was getting me nowhere, so I took out the crossword puzzle Henry had left on my doorstep. I stretched out on the couch, pencil in hand. I did manage to guess 6 Down—"disloyal," eight letters, which was "two-faced," and I got 14 Across, which was "double-reed instrument," four letters—"oboe." What a whiz. I got stuck on "double helix," three letters, which turned out later to be "DNA," a cheat if you ask me. At 7:05, I had an idea that jumped out of the dim recesses of my brain with a little jolt of electricity.

I looked up Charlotte Mercer's telephone number and dialed the house. The housekeeper answered and I asked for Charlotte.

"The judge and Mrs. Mercer are having dinner," she said disapprovingly.

"Well, would you mind interrupting please? I just have a quick question. I'm sure she won't mind."

"Who shall I say is calling?" she asked. I gave her my name.

"Just one moment." She put the receiver down.

I corrected her mentally. *Whom*, sweetheart. *Whom* shall I say is calling . . .

Charlotte answered, sounding drunk. "I don't appreciate this," she hissed.

"I'm sorry," I said. "But I need a piece of information."

"I told you what I know and I don't want you calling when the judge is here."

"All right. All right. Just one thing," I said hurriedly before she could hang up. "Do you happen to remember Mrs. Napier's first name?"

Silence. I could practically see her hold the receiver out to look at it.

"Elizabeth," she said and slammed down the phone.

I hung up. The piece I was looking for had just clicked into place. The letter wasn't written to Libby Glass at all. Laurence Fife had written it to Elizabeth Napier years ago. I was willing to bet on that. The real question now was how Libby Glass had gotten hold of it and who had wanted it back.

I took out my note cards and went back to work on my list. I had deliberately deleted Raymond and Grace Glass. I didn't believe either of them would have killed their own child, and if my guess about that letter could be verified, then it was possible that Libby and Laurence had never been romantically involved. Which meant that the reasons for their dying had to be something else. But what? Suppose, I said to myself, just suppose Laurence Fife and *Lyle* were involved in something. Maybe Libby stumbled on to it and Lyle killed them both to protect himself. Maybe Sharon got wind of it and he'd killed her too. It didn't quite make sense to me from that angle, but after eight years much of the real proof must have been lost or destroyed. Some of the obvious connections must have faded by now. I jotted down a couple of notes and checked the list.

When I came to Charlie Scorsoni's name, I felt the same uneasiness I'd felt before. I'd checked him out two weeks ago, before I'd even met with him and he was clean, but appearances are deceptive. As squeamish as it made me feel, I thought I'd better verify his whereabouts the night Sharon died. I knew he'd been in Denver because I'd called him there myself but I wasn't really sure where he'd gone after that. Arlette said he'd left messages from Tucson and again from Santa Teresa but she only had his word for that. When it came to Laurence Fife he did have opportunity. From the first, this had been a case where motive and alibi were oddly overlapped. Ordinarily, an alibi is an account of a suspect's whereabouts at the time a crime was committed and it's offered up as proof of innocence, but here it didn't matter where anyone was. With a poisoning, it only mattered if someone had *reason* to want someone else dead—access to the poison, access to the victim, and the intent to kill. That's what I was still sorting through. My impulse was simply to take Charlie off my list but I had to question myself on that. Did I really believe he was innocent or did I simply want to relieve myself of my own uneasiness? I tried to think about something else. I tried to move on, but my mind kept drifting back to the same point. I didn't think I was being smart. I wasn't sure I was being honest with myself. And suddenly, I didn't like the idea that my thinking might not be clear. The whole setup gave me a sick feeling down in my bones. I looked up his home phone number in the telephone book. I hesitated and then I shook myself free and dialed. I had to do it.

The phone rang four times. I thought he might be out at Powers's house at the beach but I didn't have that number. I was rooting for him to be out, gone. He picked up on the fifth ring and I felt my stomach churn. There was no point in putting it off.

"Hi, it's Kinsey," I said.

"Well hello," he said softly. The pleasure in his voice was audible and I could picture his face. "God, I was hoping I'd hear from you. Are you free?"

"No, actually I'm not. Uh, listen, Charlie. I'm thinking I shouldn't see you for a while. Until I get this wrapped up."

The silence was profound.

"All right," he said finally.

"Look, it's nothing personal," I said. "It's just a matter of policy."

"I'm not arguing," he said. "Do what you want. It's too bad you didn't think about 'policy' before."

"Charlie, it's not like that," I said desperately. "It may work out fine and it's no big deal, but it's been bothering me. A lot. I don't do this. It's been one of my cardinal rules. I can't keep on seeing you until I understand how this thing ties up."

"Babe, I understand," he said. "If it doesn't feel right to you, then it's no good anyway. Call me if you ever change your mind."

"Wait," I said. "God damn it, don't do that to me. I'm not rejecting you."

"Oh really," he said, his tone flat with disbelief.

"I just wanted you to know."

"Well. Now I know. I appreciate your honesty," he said.

"I'll be in touch when I can."

"Have a good life," he said and the phone clicked quietly in my ear.

I sat with a hand on the phone, doubts crowding in, wanting to call him back, wanting to erase everything I'd just said. I'd been looking for relief, looking for a way to escape the discomfort I felt. I think I'd even wanted him to give me a hard time so that I could resist and feel righteous. It was a question of my own integrity. Wasn't it? The injury in his voice had been awful after what we'd been through. And maybe he was right in his assumption that I was rejecting him. Maybe I was just being perverse, pushing him away because I needed space between me and the world. The job does provide such a perfect excuse. I meet most people in the course of my work and if I can't get emotionally involved there, then where else can I go? Private investigation is my whole life. It is why I get up in the morning and what puts me to bed at night. Most of the time I'm alone, but why not? I'm not unhappy and I'm not discontent. I had to free up until I knew what was going on. He would just have to misunderstand and to hell with him until I got this goddamn case nailed down and then maybe we could see where we stood—if it wasn't too late. Even if he was right, even if my breaking with him was an excess of conscience, a cover for something else—so what? There were no declarations between us, no commitments. I'd been to bed with him twice. What did I owe him? I don't know what love is about and I'm not sure I believe in it anyway. "Then why so defensive?" came a little voice in reply, but I ignored it.

I had to push on. There was no other way to get out of this now. I picked up the phone and called Gwen.

"Hello?"

"Gwen. This is Kinsey," I said, keeping my voice neutral. "Something's come up and I think we should talk."

"What is it?"

"I'd rather talk to you in person. Do you know where Rosie's is, down here at the beach?"

"Yes. I think I know the place," she said with uncertainty.

"Can you meet me there in half an hour? It's important."

"Well sure. Just let me get my shoes on. I'll be there as soon as I can."

"Thanks," I said.

I checked my watch. It was 7:45. I wanted her on my turf this time.

ROSIE'S was deserted, the lights dim, the whole place smelling of yesterday's cigarette smoke. I used to go to a movie theater when I was a kid and the ladies' rest room always smelled like that. Rosie was wearing a muumuu in a print fabric that depicted many flamingos standing on one leg. She was seated at the end of the bar, reading a newspaper by the light of a small television set, which she'd placed on the bar, sound off. She looked up as I came in and she set the paper aside.

"It's too late for dinner. The kitchen is closed. I gave myself the night off," she announced from across the room. "You want something to eat, you gotta fix it yourself at home. Ask Henry Pitts. He'll do you something good."

"I'm meeting someone for a drink," I said. "Big crowd you got."

She looked around as though maybe she'd missed someone. I went over to the bar. She looked as though she'd just redyed her hair because her scalp was faintly pink. She was using a Maybelline dark brown eyeliner pencil on her brows, which she seemed to draw closer together every time, coquettishly arched. Pretty soon, she could take care of the whole thing with one wavy line.

"You got a man yet?" she asked.

"Six or eight a week," I said. "Do you have any cold Chablis?"

"Just the crummy stuff. Help yourself."

I went around behind the bar and got a glass, taking the big gallon jug of white wine out of the refrigerator under the bar. I poured a tumblerful, adding ice. I went over to my favorite booth and sat down, preparing myself mentally like an actor about to go on stage. It was time to stop being polite.

Gwen arrived forty minutes later, looking crisp and capable. Her greeting to me was pleasant enough, but under it I thought I could detect the tension, as though she had some inkling of what I was about to say. Rosie shuffled over, giving Gwen a brief appraising look. She must have thought Gwen looked okay because she honored her with a direct question.

"You want something to drink?"

"Scotch on the rocks. And could I have a glass of water, too, please?"

Rosie shrugged. She didn't care what people drank. "You want to run a tab?" she said to me.

I shook my head. "I'll take care of it now," I said. Rosie moved off toward the bar. The look Gwen and I exchanged inadvertently indicated that both of us remembered her first reference to drinking Scotch in the days long past, when she was married to Laurence Fife and playing the perfect wife. I wondered what she was playing now.

"I revert now and then to the hard stuff," she said, picking up my thought.

"Why not?" I replied.

She studied me briefly. "What's up?"

The question was brave. I didn't think she really wanted to know, but she'd always struck me as the type to plunge right in. She probably whipped off big pieces of adhesive tape, too, with the same decisive thrust, just to get it over with.

"I talked to Colin," I said. "He remembered you."

The modification in her manner was slight and a look, not of apprehension, but of wariness flickered in her eyes.

"Well that's nice," she said. "I haven't seen him for years, of course. I told you that." She reached into her purse and took out a compact, checking her reflection quickly in the mirror, running a hand through her hair. Rosie came back with her Scotch and a glass of water. I paid the tab. Rosie tucked the money in the pocket of her muumuu and wandered back to the bar while Gwen took a sip of water. She seemed to be holding herself in check, not trusting herself to pick up the conversation where we'd left off. I bumped her along for the sake of surprise.

"You never mentioned that you had an affair with Laurence," I said.

A laugh burbled out. "Who, me? With him? You can't be *serious*."

I had to interrupt her merriment. "Colin saw you out at the beach house that weekend when Nikki was out of town. I don't know all the details, but I can make a guess."

I watched her compute that and shift gears. She was a very good little actress herself, but the slick cover she'd constructed was getting shabby from disuse. It had been a long time since she'd had to play this game and her timing was slightly off. She knew all the right lines, but the pretense was hard to sustain after an eight-year gap. She didn't seem to recognize the bluff and I kept my mouth shut. I could almost see what was happening inside her head. The terrible need to confess and be done with it, the pressure to spill it all out was too tempting to resist. She'd gone a few rounds with me and she'd pulled it off beautifully but only because I hadn't known which buttons to push.

"All right," she blurted out rebelliously, "I went to bed with him once. So what? I ran into him at the Palm Garden as a matter of fact. I nearly told you the other day. He was the one who told me Nikki was out of town. I was shocked that he'd even speak to me." She switched to the Scotch, taking a big drink.

She was fabricating as fast as she could and it sounded nice but it was like listening to a record album. I decided to skip the cuts I didn't want to hear. I bumped her again.

"It was more than once, Gwen," I said. "You had a full-blown affair with him. Charlotte Mercer was screwing his head off back then but he broke it off with her. She says he was into something very hush-hush. 'Very hot,' to quote her. I think it was you."

"What difference does it make if we had an affair. He'd been doing that for years."

I let a little time elapse and when I spoke I kept my voice low, leaning forward slightly just to give her the full effect.

"I think you killed him."

The animation drained out of her face as though a plug had been pulled. She started to say something but she couldn't get it out. I could see her mind working, but she couldn't put anything together quickly enough. She was struggling and I pressed.

"You want to tell me about it?" I said. My own heart was pounding and I could feel damp rings of sweat forming under my arms.

She shook her head but that was all she could manage. She seemed transfixed. Her face had changed, taking on that look people get in their sleep when all the guards are down. Her eyes were luminous and dark and two bright patches of pink appeared now in the pale of her cheeks, a clownish effect, as though she'd applied too much blusher in an artificial light. She blinked back tears then, propping her chin on her fist, looking off beyond me, fighting for self-control, but the last defense was breached and the guilt was pushing against that gorgeous facade. I'd seen it happen before. People can hold out just so long and then they fold. She was really an amateur at heart.

"You got pushed too hard and you broke," I said, hoping I wasn't overplaying my hand. "You waited until he and Nikki left town and then you used Diane's keys to get into the house. You put the oleander capsules in his little plastic vial, being careful to leave no prints, and then you left."

"I hated him," she said, mouth trembling. She blinked and a tear splashed on her shirt like a drop of rain. She took a deep breath, words coming out in a rush. "He ruined my life, took my kids, robbed me blind, insulted, abused—oh my God, you have no idea. The *venom* in that man . . ."

She snatched up a napkin and pressed it to her eyes. Amazingly, Rosie didn't seem to notice her distress. She sat at the bar, probably reading Ann Landers, thinking At Wit's End should have turned hubby in for the obscene calls he made, while a customer confessed to murder right under her nose. To her right, the little television set flickered a Muppets rerun.

Gwen sighed, staring down at the tabletop. She reached over and picked up her glass, taking in a big slug of Scotch, which made her shudder as it went down. "I didn't even feel bad about it, except for the kids. They took it hard and that surprised me. They were far better off with him gone."

"Why the affair?" I probed.

"I don't know," she said, folding and refolding the paper napkin. "I guess it was my revenge. He was such an egotist. I knew he couldn't resist. After all, I'd insulted the hell out of him by having an affair with someone else. He couldn't tolerate that. I knew he'd want his own back. It wasn't even that hard to engineer. He wanted to prove something to himself. He wanted to show me what I'd passed up. There was even a certain amount of jazz to the sex for once. The hostility was so close to the surface that it gave us both a sick charge. God, I loathed him. I really did. And I'll tell you something else," she said harshly. "Killing him once just wasn't enough. I wish I could kill him again."

She looked at me fully then and the enormity of what she was saying began to sink in.

"What about Nikki? What did she ever do to you?"

"I thought they'd acquit her," she said. "I never thought she'd go to jail, and when the sentence was handed down I wasn't going to stand up and take her place. By then it was too late."

"So what else?" I said and I noticed that my tone was getting sullen. "Did you kill the dog too?"

"I had nothing to do with that. He got hit Sunday morning. I drove Diane over there because she'd remembered that she'd left him out and she was upset. He was already lying in the street. My God, I wouldn't run over a *dog*," she said emphatically, as though I should appreciate the delicacy of her sentiments.

"And the rest just fell into place? The oleander in the yard? The capsules upstairs?"

"One capsule. I doctored *one*."

"Bullshit, Gwen. That's bullshit."

"It's not. I'm telling the truth. I swear to it. I'd thought about it for a long time but I couldn't see a way to make it work. I wasn't even sure it would kill him. Diane was a wreck about the dog anyway so I drove her to my place and put her to bed. As soon as she was asleep, I took her keys and went back and that's all it was." She spoke with an edge of defiance, as though having opened up this far there was no point in mincing words.

"What about the other two?" I snapped. "What about Sharon and Libby Glass?"

She blinked at me, pulling back. "I don't know what you're talking about."

"Oh the hell you don't," I said, getting up. "You've lied to me since the first minute we met. I can't believe a goddamn word you say and you know it."

She seemed startled by my energy. "What are you going to do?"

"Give the information to Nikki," I said. "She paid for it. We'll let her decide."

I moved away from the table, heading toward the door. Gwen grabbed her jacket and purse, keeping pace with me.

Out on the street, she snatched at my arm and I shook her off.

"Kinsey wait . . ." Her face was remarkably pale.

"Blow it out your ass," I said. "You'd better hire yourself a hot attorney, babe, because you're going to need one."

I moved off down the street, leaving Gwen behind.

I LOCKED THE DOOR TO MY PLACE AND TRIED DIALING Nikki out at the beach. The phone rang eight times and I hung up, pacing the room after that with an unsettled sensation in my chest. There was something off. There was something not right and I couldn't put my finger on what was bothering me. There was no feeling of closure. None. This should have been the end of it. The big climax. I'd been hired to find out who killed Laurence Fife and I had. The end. Finis. But I was left with half a case and a lot of loose ends. Gwen's killing of Laurence had been part premeditation and part impulse, but the rest of it didn't seem to fit. Why wasn't everything falling into place? I couldn't picture Gwen killing Libby Glass. Gwen had hated Laurence Fife for years, titillating herself perhaps with ways of killing him, maybe never even dreaming that she'd actually do it, never imagining that she could actually pull it off. She'd come up with the oleander scheme and suddenly she'd seen a way to make it work. A perfect opportunity had presented itself and she'd acted. Surely Libby Glass's death couldn't have been that easy to arrange. How did Gwen know about her? How did she know where she lived? How could she have gotten into that apartment? And how could she have counted on her taking medication of any kind? I couldn't picture Gwen driving to Vegas either. Couldn't imagine her shooting Sharon in cold blood. For what? What was the point? Killing Laurence had wiped out an old grudge, satisfied an ancient and bitter hatred between them, but why kill the other two? Blackmail? Threat of exposure? That might account for Sharon but why Libby Glass? Gwen had seemed truly self-righteous in her bewilderment. Like her denial of any responsibility for killing the dog. There was just that odd note of genuine outrage in her voice. It didn't make sense.

Unless there was someone else involved. Someone else who killed.

I felt a chill.

Oh my God. Lyle? Charlie? I sat down, blinking rapidly, hand across my mouth. I'd bought into the notion that one person killed all three, but maybe not. Maybe there was another possibility. I tried it out. Gwen had murdered Laurence Fife. Why couldn't someone else have spotted the opening and taken advantage of it? The timing was close, the method the same. Of course it was going to look like it was all part of the same setup.

I thought about Lyle. I thought about his face, the strange imperceptibly mismatched eyes: sullen, watchful, belligerent. He said he'd been with Libby three days before she died. I knew he'd heard about Laurence's death. He was not a man who possessed a giant intellect, but he could have managed that much, imitating the cunning of someone else—even stoned.

I called my answering service. "I'm going down to Los Angeles," I said. "If Nikki Fife calls, I want you to give her the telephone number of the Hacienda motel down there and tell her it's important that she get in touch. But no one else. I don't want it known that I'm out of town. I'll check in with you often enough to pick up whatever calls come in. Just say I'm tied up and you don't know where I am. You got that?"

"All right, Miss Millhone. Will do," she said cheerfully and then clicked off. God. If I'd said to her, "Hold the calls. I'm slitting my throat," she'd have responded with the same blank good will.

THE drive to Los Angeles was good for me—soothing, uneventful. It was after nine and there wasn't that much traffic on the darkened road south. On my left, hills swelled and rolled, covered with low vegetation—no trees, no rocks. On my right, the ocean rumbled, almost at arm's length, looking very black except for a ruffle of white here and there. I passed Summerland, Carpinteria, passed the oil derricks and the power plant, which was garlanded with tiny lights like a decorative display at Christmastime. There was something restful about having nothing to worry about except having a wreck and getting killed. It freed my mind for other things.

I had made a mistake, a false assumption, and I felt like a novice. On the other hand, I'd made the very assumption that everyone else had made: same M.O., same murderer. But now I didn't think that was true. Now it seemed to me the only explanation that made any sense was that someone else had killed Libby Glass—and Sharon too. I drove through Ventura, Oxnard, Camarillo, where the state mental asylum was located. I've heard that there is less tendency to violence among the institutionalized insane than there is in the citizenry at large and I believe that. I thought about Gwen without surprise or dismay, my mind jumping forward and back randomly. Somehow I was more offended by the minor crimes of a Marcia Threadgill who tried for less, without any motivation at all beyond greed. I wondered if Marcia Threadgill was the new standard of morality against which I would now judge all other sins. Hatred, I could understand—the need for revenge, the payment of old debts. That's what the notion of "justice" was all about anyway: settling up.

I went over the big hill into Thousand Oaks, with traffic picking up; tract housing stretched out on either side of the road, then shopping malls packed end to end. The night air was damp and I kept the windows rolled down. I felt over into the backseat for my briefcase and fumbled with the catch. I tucked my little automatic into my jacket pocket, encountering a wad of papers. I pulled them out and glanced down. Sharon Napier's bills. I'd stuck them in my windbreaker on the way out of her place and I hadn't thought about them since. I'd have to go through them. I tossed them on the passenger seat and looked at my watch by the icy wash of highway light. It was 10:10—forty-five minutes of driving left, maybe more given traffic on the surface roads once I got off the freeway. I thought about Charlie, wondering if I'd blown a perfectly nice relationship. He didn't seem like the type to forgive and forget, but who knew. He was a lot more yielding than I was, that was for sure. My thoughts rambled on disjunctively. Lyle had known I was driving to Vegas. I wasn't sure how Sharon connected, but I'd figure that out. Blackmail still seemed like the best bet. The letter I couldn't figure at all. How had Libby come by that? Or had she? Maybe Lyle and *Sharon* were in cahoots. Maybe Lyle got the letter from her. Maybe he was *planting* the letter among Libby's effects, not trying to take it away. It was certainly to his advantage to reinforce the idea of Libby's romantic tie to Laurence Fife. He had known I was stopping back through to pick up her boxes. He could have made it back to Los Angeles well in advance of me since I'd stopped for the night to see Diane. Maybe he had deliberately timed it closely to incite my curiosity about what might have been tucked away there. My mind veered off that and I thought about Lieutenant Dolan with a faint smile. He was so sure Nikki had killed her husband, so satisfied with that. I'd have to put a call through to him when I got back. I thought about Lyle again. I didn't intend to see him that night. He wasn't as smart as Gwen, but he might be dangerous. *If* it was him. I didn't think I should jump to conclusions again.

I checked into the Hacienda at 11:05, went straight to room #2, and put myself to bed. Arlette's mother was on the desk. She is twice as fat.

In the morning, I showered and got back into the same clothes, staggering out to the car to retrieve the overnight case I kept in the crowded backseat. I went back to my room and brushed my teeth—oh blessed relief—and ran a comb through my hair. I went down to a delicatessen on the corner of Wilshire and Bundy, where I ordered scrambled eggs, sausage links, a toasted bagel with cream cheese, coffee, and fresh orange juice. Whoever invented breakfast really did it good.

I walked back up to the Hacienda to find Arlette waving a massive arm out the office door for me. Her round face was flushed, her little cap of blonde curls in a flyaway state, her eyes squeezed almost to invisibility by the heavy cheeks. I wondered when she'd last seen her own neck. Still, I liked her, irksome as she was at times.

"There's someone on the phone for you and she sounds real upset. I told her you were out but I said I'd flag you down. Thank goodness you're back," she said to me, out of breath and wheezing hard.

I hadn't seen Arlette so excited since she found out that panty hose came in queen-size. I went into the office with Arlette hard on my heels, breathing heavily. The receiver was on the counter and I picked it up.

"Hello?"

"Kinsey, this is Nikki."

Why the dread in her voice, I thought automatically. "I tried calling you last night," I said. "What's the matter? Are you okay?"

"Gwen's dead."

"I just talked to her last night," I said blankly. Killed herself. She'd killed herself. Oh shit, I thought.

"It happened this morning. Hit-and-run driver. I just heard it on the news. She was jogging along Cabana Boulevard and someone ran her down and then skipped."

"I don't believe it. Are you sure?"

"Positive. I tried calling you and the service said you were out of town. What are you doing in L.A.?"

"I've got to check out something down here but I should be back tonight," I said, thinking fast. "Look, would you see if you can find out the details?"

"I can try."

"Call Lieutenant Dolan at Homicide. Tell him I told you to ask."

"Homicide," she said, startled.

"Nikki, he's a *cop*. He'll know what's going on. And it may not be an accident anyway, so see what he has to say and I'll call you as soon as I get back."

"Well, okay," she said dubiously, "I'll see what I can do."

"Thanks." I hung up the phone.

"Is someone dead?" Arlette asked. "Was it someone you knew?"

I looked right at her but I drew a blank. Why Gwen? What was happening?

She followed me out of the office and toward my room.

"Is there anything I can do to help? Do you need anything? You look awful, Kinsey. You're pale as a ghost."

I closed the door behind me. I thought about that last image of Gwen, standing on the street, her face white. *Could* it have been an accident? Coincidence? Things were moving too quickly. Someone was beginning to panic and for reasons I still couldn't quite understand.

A possibility flashed into my head and out. I stood stock-still, running it by me again like an old film clip. Maybe so. Maybe yes. It was all going to come together soon. It was all going to fit.

I threw everything into the backseat of my car, not even bothering to check out. I'd mail Arlette the damn twelve bucks.

THE drive to the Valley was a blur, the car moving automatically, though I paid no attention whatever to road, sun, traffic, smog. When I reached the house in Sherman Oaks where Lyle was laying brick, I saw his battered truck parked out front. I didn't have any more time to waste and I didn't want to play games. I locked the car and went up the drive, going around the side of the house to the back. I caught sight of Lyle before he caught sight of me. He was bending over a pile of two-by-fours: faded jeans, work boots, no shirt, a cigarette in the corner of his mouth.

"Lyle."

He turned around. I had the gun out and trained on him. I held it with two hands, legs apart, meaning business. He froze instantly where he stood, not saying a word.

I felt cold and my voice was tight, but the gun never wavered an inch. "I want some answers and I want them now," I said. I saw him glance to his right. There was a hammer lying on the ground but he made no move.

"Back up," I said, stepping forward slightly until I was between him and the hammer. He did as instructed, the pale blue eyes sliding back to mine, hands coming up.

"I don't want to shoot you, Lyle, but I will."

For once, he didn't look sullen or sly or arrogant. He stared straight at me with the first sign of respect I'd seen from him.

"You're the boss," he said.

"Don't fuckin' smart-mouth *me*," I snapped. "I'm not in the mood. Now sit down in the grass. Out there. And don't move a muscle unless I tell you to."

Obediently, he moved out to a small stretch of grass and sat down, eyes on me the whole time. It was quiet and I could hear birds chirping stupidly but we seemed to be alone and I liked it that way. I kept the gun pointed right at his chest, willing my hands not to shake. The sun was hot and it made him squint.

"Tell me about Libby Glass," I said.

"I didn't kill her," he shot back uneasily.

"That's not the point. I want to know what went on. I want to know what you haven't told me yet. When did you see her last?"

He shut his mouth.

"Tell me!"

He didn't have Gwen's poise and he didn't have her smarts. The sight of the gun seemed to help him make up his mind.

"Saturday."

"The day she died, right?"

"That's right, but I didn't do anything. I went over to see her and we had a big fight and she was upset."

"All right, all right. Skip the buildup. What else?"

He was silent.

"Lyle," I said warningly. The muscles in his face seemed to pull together like a drawstring purse and he started to weep. He put his hands up over his face pathetically. He'd kept it in for a long time. If I was wrong about this, I was wrong about everything. I couldn't let him off the hook.

"Just tell me," I said, tone dead, "I need to know."

I thought he was coughing but I knew what I heard were sobs. He might have been nine years old, looking squeezed up and frail and small.

"I gave her a *tranq*," he said with anguish. "She asked for one and I found this bottle in the medicine cabinet and gave it to her. God, I even gave her a glass of water. I loved her so much."

The first rush subsided and he dashed at the tears on his face with a grubby hand, leaving streaks of dirt. He hugged himself, rocking back and forth in misery, tears streaming down his bony cheeks again.

"Go on," I said.

"I left after that but I felt bad and I went back later and

that's when I found her dead on the bathroom floor. I was afraid they'd find my fingerprints and think I'd done something to her so I wiped the whole place down."

"And you took the tranquilizers with you when you left?"

He nodded, pressing his fingers into his eye sockets as though he could force the tears back. "I flushed 'em down the toilet when I got home. I smashed up the bottle and threw it away."

"How'd you know that's what it was?"

"I don't know. I just knew. I remembered that guy, the one up north and I knew he'd died that way. She might not have taken the goddamn thing if it weren't for me, but we had that screaming fight and she was so mad, she shook. I didn't even know she had any tranqs till she asked for one and I didn't see anything wrong with that. I went back to apologize." The worst of it seemed to be over with and he sighed deeply, his voice almost normal again.

"What else?"

"I don't know. The phone was unplugged. I plugged it back in and wiped that down too," he said woodenly. "I didn't mean any harm. I just had to protect myself. I wouldn't poison her. I wouldn't have done that to her, I swear to God. I didn't have anything to do with that or anything else except I cleaned the place. In case there were fingerprints. I didn't want anything pointing to me. And I took the bottle the pills were in. I did that."

"But you didn't break into the storage bin," I said.

He shook his head.

I lowered the gun. I'd half known but I had to be sure.

"Are you going to turn me in?"

"No. Not you."

I went back to the car and sat blankly, wondering in some

vague irrational way if I really would have used the gun. I didn't think so. Tough. I'm tough, scaring the shit out of some dumb kid. I shook my head, feeling tears of my own. I started the car and put it into gear, heading back over the hill toward West L.A. I had one more stop and then I could drive back to Santa Teresa and clean it up. I thought I knew now who it was.

26

I CAUGHT SIGHT OF MY REFLECTION IN ONE OF THE MIRRORED walls across from the entrance to Haycraft and McNiece. I looked like I was ready for the last round-up: seedy, disheveled, mouth grim. Even Allison, in her buckskin shirt with the fringes on the sleeves, seemed alarmed by the sight of me, and her prerehearsed receptionist's smile dropped from sixty watts to twenty-five.

"I have to talk to Garry Steinberg," I said, my tone apparently indicating that I wouldn't take much shit.

"He's back in his office," she said timidly. "Do you know which one it is?"

I nodded and pushed through the swinging doors. I caught sight of Garry walking down the narrow interior corridor toward his office, slapping a batch of unopened mail against his thigh.

"Garry?"

He turned, his face lighting up at the sight of me and then turning hesitant. "Where'd you come from? You look exhausted."

"I drove down last night. Can we talk?"

"Sure. Come on in."

He turned left into his office, gathering up a stack of files on the chair in front of his desk. "You want some coffee? Can I get you anything?" He tossed the mail on the file cabinet.

"No, I'm fine but I need to check out a hunch."

"Fire away," he said, sitting down.

"Didn't you tell me once upon a time—"

"Last week," he inserted.

"Yeah, I guess it was. You mentioned that Fife's accounts were being put on computer."

"Sure, we were converting everything. Makes it a hell of a lot easier on us and it's better for the client too. Especially at tax time."

"Well what if the books had been fiddled with?"

"You mean embezzlement?"

"In a word," I said with irony. "Wouldn't that have shown up pretty quickly?"

"Absolutely. You think Fife was milking his own accounts?"

"No," I said slowly, "I think Charlie Scorsoni was. That's part of what I need to ask you about. Could he have skimmed money out of the estates he was representing back then?"

"Sure. It can be done and it's not that hard," Garry said appreciatively, "but it might be a bitch to track. It really depends on how he did it." He thought for a moment, apparently warming to the idea. He shrugged. "For instance, he could have set up some kind of special account or an escrow account for all his estates—maybe two or three phony accounts within this overall account. A large dividend check comes in, he diverts a percentage of the check from the estate it's supposed to be credited to, and he credits it to a phony account instead."

"Could Libby have realized something was wrong?"

"She might have. She had a head for that kind of thing. She'd have had to trace the dividends through Moody's Dividend Book, which gives the amount of each dividend by company. Then if there was some kind of discrepancy, she might have asked for records or documentation—bank statements, canceled checks, stuff like that."

"Yeah, well Lyle told me last week that there were lots of phone calls back and forth, some attorney driving down for dinner. It finally occurred to me that Charlie might have engineered an affair with her in the hopes that she'd cover for him . . ."

"Or maybe he offered her a cut," Garry said.

"Oh God, would she have done that?"

Garry shrugged. "Hey, who knows? Would *he*?"

I stared down at his desk top. "Yeah, I think so," I said. "You know, everybody kept saying that she was involved with some Santa Teresa attorney and we all assumed it was Fife because both died the same way. But if I'm right about this embezzlement business then I need proof. Are the files still at your place?"

"No, I've got 'em right here as a matter of fact. I thought I'd take a look at 'em during my lunch hour. I've been having cottage cheese but I don't think that counts as food so I thought I'd do without. I brought 'em in yesterday and then I got tied up. Now that you mention it, I do think she was working on that account when she died, because the cops found her brief-case at her place," he said. He gave me a curious look. "How'd you fix on him?"

I shook my head. "I don't know. It just popped into my brain and it fit. Charlie told me that Fife made a trip to Los Angeles sometime in the week before he died, but I don't think that's true. I think probably Charlie made the trip himself and it would have been within a day or two after Laurence died. Libby had a bottle of tranqs and I think he doctored some—who knows, maybe all of 'em. We'll never know about that."

"Jesus. He killed Fife too?"

I shook my head. "No, I know who killed Fife. My guess is that Charlie saw a way to bail himself out. Maybe Libby wouldn't play ball with him or maybe she'd threatened to turn him in. Not that I've got any evidence one way or the other."

"Hey, it'll come," he said soothingly. "If it's there, we'll find it. I'll start on the files this afternoon."

"Good," I said, "I'd like that."

"Take care."

We shook hands across the desk.

I DROVE back to Santa Teresa, resolutely refusing to think of Gwen. Thinking about Charlie Scorsoni was depressing enough. I would have to check his whereabouts at the time Sharon died, but he could easily have checked out of the ho-tel in Denver and flown straight to Las Vegas, picking up my location from the answering service, finding my motel, and then following me to the Fremont. I thought about Sharon—that moment in the coffee shop when I thought she'd seen someone she knew. She'd said it was the pit boss signaling the end of her break, but I was sure she was lying. Charlie may have put in an appearance then, pulling back when he spotted me. Maybe she thought he had shown up to pay her off. I was relatively certain she'd been leaning on him for bucks, but then again, I'd have to pin that down. Sharon must have known that Fife was never involved with Libby Glass sexually. It was Charlie who'd been making the trips down to Los Angeles to discuss the accounts. Sharon must have kept her mouth shut during the trial, watching the whole tale unfold, biding her time, eventually cashing in on whatever information she had. It was also possible that Charlie Scorsoni hadn't known where she was—that I'd led him straight down the path to her door. I was aware, as I went over the sequence of events, that much of it sounded like a lot of fancy guesswork, but I felt I was headed in the right direction and I could probe now for corroborating evidence.

If Charlie had killed Gwen in that hit-and-run accident, there were bound to be ways to trace it back to him: hair and fibers on the fender of his car, which probably sustained some damage that would have to be repaired; paint flakes and glass fragments on Gwen's clothes. Maybe even a witness somewhere. It would have been much wiser if Charlie'd never made a move—just held tight and kept his mouth shut, lying low. It probably would have been impossible to put a case together against him after all these years. There was an arrogance in his behavior, a hint that he considered himself too smart and too slick to get caught. No one was *that* good. Especially at the rate he'd been operating these days. He had to be making mistakes.

And why not just go down for the count on the original embezzlement? He must have been desperately trying to cover for himself in Laurence Fife's eyes. But even if he'd been exposed, even if he'd been caught, I didn't believe Laurence would have turned him in. As sleazy as Fife had been in his personal life, I knew he was scrupulously honest in business matters. Still, Charlie was his best friend and the two went a long way back together. He might have warned Charlie off or smacked his hand—perhaps even dissolved the partnership. But I didn't think Charlie would have gone to jail or been disbarred from the practice of law. His life probably wouldn't have been ruined and he probably wouldn't have lost what he'd worked so hard to achieve. He would have lost Laurence Fife's good opinion and his trust perhaps, but he must have known that when he first put his hand in the cookie jar. The ludicrous fact of the matter is that in this day and age, a white-collar criminal can become a celebrity, a hero, can go on talk shows and write best-selling books. So what was there to sweat? Society will forgive just about anything except homicide. It was hard to shrug that one off, hard to rationalize that one away and whereas before, Charlie might have come out somewhat tarnished but intact, he was in big trouble now and things just seemed to be getting worse.

I didn't even address myself to the matter of his relationship to me. He'd played me for a sucker, just as he'd done with Libby Glass, and she, in her innocence, at least had a better excuse for the tumble than I did. It had been too long since I'd cared about anyone, too long since I'd taken that risk and I'd already invested too much. I just had to slam the gate shut emotionally and move on, but it didn't sit well with me.

WHEN I reached Santa Teresa, I went straight to the office, taking with me the sheaf of bills from Sharon Napier's apartment. For the first time, I was beginning to think those might be significant. I went through them with an abstract curiosity that felt ghoulish nevertheless. She was dead and it seemed obscene now to note that she'd bought lingerie that had gone unpaid for, cosmetics, shoes. Her utilities were a month behind, with dunning notices from several small businesses including her tax man, a chiropractor, and a health spa membership renewal. Visa and Mastercharge had gotten churlish and American Express wanted its card back in no uncertain terms, but it was her telephone bill that interested me. In the area code that included Santa Teresa, there were three calls in the month of March, not an excessive number but telling. Two of the calls were to Charlie Scorsoni's office—both on the same day, ten minutes apart. The third number she'd called I didn't immediately recognize but the Santa Teresa exchange was the same. I picked up my Cross-Reference Directory. The number was for John Powers's house at the beach.

I dialed Ruth, not allowing myself to hesitate. Surely Charlie hadn't told her I'd broken with him. I couldn't picture him confiding his personal affairs to anyone. If he was there, I'd have to think fast and I wasn't sure what I intended to say. The information I needed was from her.

"Scorsoni and Powers," she sang.

"Oh hi, Ruth. This is Kinsey Millhone," I said, heart in my throat. "Is Charlie there?"

"Oh hi, Kinsey. No he's not," she said with a hint of regret in my behalf. "He's in court up in Santa Maria for the next two days."

Thank God for that, I thought, and took a deep breath. "Well maybe you can help me instead," I said. "I was just going over some bills for a client and it looks like she was in touch with him. Do you happen to remember someone calling him a couple of times maybe six, eight weeks ago? Her name was Sharon Napier. Long-distance."

"Oh, the one who used to work for him. Yes, I remember that. What did you need to know?"

"Well I can't quite tell from this if she actually got through to him or not. It looks like she called on a Friday—the twenty-first of March. Does that ring a bell?"

"Oh yes. Absolutely," Ruth said efficiently. "She called asking for him and he was out at Mr. Powers's house. She was very insistent that I put her through but I didn't feel I should give out the number without checking with him, so I told her to call me back and then I checked with him out at the beach and he said it was fine. I hope that's all right. I hope she hasn't hired you to pester him or anything."

I laughed. "Oh heavens, Ruth, would I do that to him? I did see the number for John Powers and I just thought maybe she talked to him instead."

"Oh no. He was out of town that weekend. He's usually gone around the twenty-first for a couple of days. I have it right here on my calendar. Mr. Scorsoni was taking care of his dogs."

"Oh well, that would explain it," I said casually. "God, that's been a great help. Now the only other thing I need to check is that trip to Tucson."

"Tucson?" she said. Doubt was beginning to creep into her voice, that protective tone secretaries sometimes take when it suddenly occurs to them that someone wants something they're not supposed to get. "What is this about, Kinsey? Maybe I could be of more help if I understood what this has to do with a client of yours. Mr. Scorsoni's pretty strict about things like that."

"Oh no, that's something else. And I can check that out myself so don't worry about it. I can always give Charlie a buzz when he gets back and ask him."

"Well, I can give you his motel number in Santa Maria if you want to call him yourself," she said. She was trying to play it both ways—helpful to me if my questions were legitimate, helpful to Charlie if they weren't—but in any case, dumping the whole matter in his lap. For an old lady, she was adroit.

I jotted the number down dutifully, knowing I'd never call him but glad to get a fix on him anyway. I wanted to tell her not to mention my call but I didn't see how I could do it without tipping my hand. I just had to hope that Charlie wouldn't check in with her anytime soon. If she told him what I'd been asking about, he would know like a shot that I was on his tail and he wouldn't like that a bit.

I put in a call to Dolan at Homicide. He was out but I left a message, "important" underlined, that he should call me back when he got in. I tried Nikki at the beach and got her on the third ring.

"Hi, Nikki, it's me," I said. "Is everything okay?"

"Oh yeah. We're fine. I still haven't quite recovered from the shock of Gwen's death, but I don't know what to do about that. I never even knew the woman and it still seems a shame."

"Did you get any details from Dolan? I just tried to call him and he's out."

"Not a lot," she said. "He was awfully rude. Worse than I remember him and he wouldn't tell me much except the car that hit her was black."

"Black?" I said with disbelief. I was picturing Charlie's pale blue Mercedes and I'd fully expected some detail that would tie that in. "Are you sure?"

"That's what he said. I guess the detectives have been checking with the body shops and garages but so far nothing's turned up."

"That's odd," I said.

"Are you coming out for a drink? I'd love to hear what's going on."

"Maybe later. I'm trying to clean up a couple of loose ends. I'll tell you what else I need. Maybe you can answer this. Remember the letter I showed you that Laurence wrote—"

"Sure, the one to Libby Glass," she broke in quickly.

"Yeah, well I'm almost sure now that the letter was written to Elizabeth Napier instead."

"Who?"

"I'll fill you in on that later. I suspect that Elizabeth Napier was the one he got involved with when he was married to Gwen. Sharon Napier's mother."

"Oh, the *scandal*," she said, light breaking. "Oh sure, it could well be. He never would tell me much about that. Messy business. I know the story because Charlotte Mercer filled me in on that, but I was never really sure of the name. God, that would have been way back in Denver, just after his law-school days."

I hesitated. "Can you think who else would have known about that letter? Who could have had access to it? I mean, could Gwen?"

"I suppose so," she said. "Certainly Charlie would. He was working as a law clerk in the firm that represented the husband in that divorce and he lifted the letter from what I heard."

"He what?"

"Stole it. Oh I'm sure that's the one. Didn't I ever tell you the end of that? Charlie snitched the letter, just cleaned out all the evidence, and that's why they ended up settling out of court. She didn't do that well but at least it got Laurence off the hook."

"What happened to the letter? Could Charlie have kept the letter himself?"

"I don't know. I always assumed it had been destroyed but I guess he could have hung on to it. He never did get caught and I don't think the husband's attorney ever figured it out. You know how things disappear in offices. Probably some secretary got fired."

"Could Gwen have testified to any of this?"

"What *am* I, the district attorney's office?" she said with a laugh. "How do I know what Gwen knew?"

"Well, whatever it was, she's quiet now," I said.

"Oh," she said and I could tell her smile had faded fast. "Oh, I don't like that. That's a terrible thought."

"I'll tell you the rest when I see you. If I can get out there, I'll call first and make sure you're home."

"We'll be here. I take it you're making progress."

"Rapidly," I said.

Her good-byes were puzzled and mine were brief.

I hauled out my typewriter and committed everything I knew to paper in a lengthy and detailed report. Another piece had fallen into place. The night the storage bin was broken into, it was Charlie, not Lyle, who was planting the letter among Libby's belongings, hoping I'd find it, hoping he could shore up his own tale about Laurence Fife's "affair" with Libby Glass. Which probably also explained the key to her apartment that had been found on Laurence's key ring in the office. It wouldn't have been hard for Charlie to plant that one too. I typed on, feeling exhausted but determined to get it all down. In the back of my mind, I kept thinking of it as a safeguard, an insurance policy, but I wasn't sure what kind of coverage I needed. Maybe none. Maybe I didn't need protection, I thought. As it turned out, I was wrong.

27

I FINISHED MY REPORT AND LOCKED IT IN MY DESK DRAWER. I went out to the parking lot and retrieved my car, heading north toward Charlie's house on Missile Avenue. Two doors down from his place was a house called Tranquility for reasons unknown. I parked in front of it and walked back. Charlie's house was a two-story structure with a painted-yellow-shingle exterior and a dark shingled roof, a bay window in front, a long narrow driveway to the left. It was the sort of house that might appear in an establishing shot for a television family show, something that might come on at 8:00 P.M., everything looking regular and wholesome and suitable for kids. There was no sign of his car in the drive, no sign of occupants. I eased along the driveway toward the garage, looking back over my shoulder as I went. There weren't even any nosy neighbors peering out at me. When I reached the one-car garage, I went around to the side, cupping my hands so that I could peer into the window. It was empty: a woodworking bench along the back wall, old lawn furniture, dust. I looked around, wondering whose black car it was and why the cops hadn't gotten a line on it yet. If I could fill in that blank, then I'd have something to talk to Con Dolan about. I was going to have something concrete.

I walked back up the drive to my car and sat, a favorite occupation of mine. It was getting dark. I glanced at my watch. It was 6:45 and that startled me. I desperately longed for a glass of wine and I decided to drive on out to Nikki's. She had said she'd be home. I turned the car around, making an illegal U, and drove back down Missile to the freeway, heading north. I got off at La Cuesta, heading toward the beach by way of Horton Ravine, a large sprawling expanse of land that is known as "a luxury residential development." Horton Ravine once belonged to one family, but it is now divided into million-dollar parcels to accommodate the housing of the nouveau riche. In Santa Teresa, Montebello is considered "old" money, Horton Ravine the "new"—but nobody really takes the distinction seriously. Rich is rich and we all know what that means. The roads through Horton Ravine are narrow and winding, overhung with trees, and the only difference I could see was that here, some houses are visible from the road whereas in Montebello, they are not. I came out at Ocean Way and swung left, the road running parallel now to the bluffs, with a number of elegant properties tucked into the selvage of land that lay between the road and the cliffs.

I passed John Powers's house, almost missing the place since I'd come at it before from the other direction. I caught a quick glimpse of the roof, which was almost level with the road. I had a sudden thought and I slammed on the brakes, pulling over to the side. I sat for a moment, heart thudding with excitement. I turned the key off and stuck my little automatic in my jeans, taking the flashlight out of the glove compartment. I flicked it on. The light was good. There were very few streetlamps along this stretch and those I could see were ornamental, as dim and misty-looking as a lithograph, casting ineffectual circles of light that scarcely penetrated the dark. I got out of the car and locked it.

There were no sidewalks, just tangles of ivy along the road. The houses were widely spaced with wooded lots in between, ratcheting now with crickets and other night-singing insects. I walked back along the road to the Powers place. There were no houses at all across from it. No cars in either direction. I paused. There were no lights visible in the house. I headed down the driveway, shining the light in front of me. I wondered if Powers was still out of town, and if so where the dogs were. If Charlie was going to be up in Santa Maria for two days he wouldn't have left them unattended.

The night was still, the ocean pounding, a recurrent thunder like a storm about to break. There was only a faint crust of moon against the hazy night sky. It was chilly, too, the air smelling lush and damp. The flashlight cut a narrow trail down the drive, illuminating in a sudden band of white the gateway across the carport. Beyond it was John Powers's car, face-in, and even from where I stood I could see that it was black. I wasn't surprised. The white picket fencing that comprised the gate was padlocked but I eased around to the left of the carport toward the front of the house. I shone the light on the car. It was a Lincoln. I couldn't tell what year but the car wasn't old. I checked the fender on the left-hand side and it was fine. I could feel my heart beginning to thump dully with dread. The right-hand fender was crumpled, the headlight broken out, metal rim crimped and pulled away, bumper indented slightly. I tried not to think of Gwen's body at the moment of impact. I could guess what it must have been like.

I heard an abrupt squealing of brakes on the road above, the high whine of a car backing up at high speed. There was a sudden wash of bright light as a car pulled into the drive. I ducked automatically, flicking out the flashlight. If it was Charlie, I was dead. I caught a glimpse of blue. Oh shit. He'd called Ruth. He was back. He knew. The Mercedes's headlights were directed straight into the carport, with only Powers's vehicle shielding me from complete exposure. I heard the car door slam and I ran.

I flew across the yard, fairly skimming the rough cut grass. Behind me, almost soundlessly, came the low scuffling of the dogs in long loping strides. I started down the narrow wooden steps to the beach, my vision inky after the harsh glare of the headlights. I missed a step and half slid my way down to the next, groping blindly. Above me, only yards away, the black dog grumbled and started down, panting, toenails scrambling on the steps. I glanced up and back. The black one was just above my head. Without even thinking about it, I reached back and grabbed at one of his long bony forelegs, yanking abruptly. The dog let out a yelp of surprise and I shoved it forward, half flinging it down the steep rocky embankment. The other dog was whining, a ninety-five-pound sissy, picking its way down the stairs with trepidation. I nearly lost my balance but I righted myself, loosened soil tumbling down into the darkness in front of me. I could hear the black dog lunging at the cliffside but he couldn't seem to get a purchase, prowling back and forth rest-

lessly. I was nearly lying on my side as I slid down the last few
feet, tumbling onto the soft sand. The gun popped out of my
hand and I scrambled frantically until my fingers closed over
the butt again. The flashlight was long gone. I didn't even remember when I'd lost my hold on it. The black dog was loping
toward me again. I waited until he was almost on me and then
I lifted a foot, kicking viciously, bringing the gun down on his
head. He yelped. He'd clearly never been trained to attack. My
advantage was that I knew he was a danger to me and he was
just beginning to figure out how treacherous I was. He backed
off, barking. I made a quick choice. North along the beach, the
steep cliffs continued for miles, interrupted only by Harley's
Beach, which was too isolated for sanctuary. North, the dog was
blocking my path. The beach to my right would eventually
straggle past the town and it couldn't be more than a couple of
miles. I began to move backward, away from the dog. He stood
there, head down, barking vigorously. The waves were already
washing up over my shoes and I began to lift my feet, trudging
backward through the surf. I turned, holding the gun up, beginning to wade. The dog paced back and forth, barking only
occasionally now. The next big surge of waves crashed against
my knees, drenching me to the waist. I gasped from the shock
of cold, glancing back with a burble of fear as I caught sight of
Charlie at the top of the cliff. The outside lights were on now,
his big body sculptured in shadow, his face blank. He was staring straight down at me. I propelled myself forward, nearly
flinging myself through the waist-high water, edging toward the
rocks at the extreme southern limits of the beach. I reached the
rocks, slippery and sharp, a mass of granite that had broken
loose from the cliff and tumbled into the sea. I scrambled
across, hampered by my soggy jeans, which clung to my legs,
by my shoes weighted down with water, hampered by the gun,

which I didn't dare relinquish. Jagged barnacles and slime alternated under me. I slipped once and something bit into my left knee, right through my jeans. I pushed on, reaching hard-packed sand again, the beach widening slightly.

There was no sign of the Powers house around the bend. No sign of either dog. I had known they couldn't follow this far even if they'd tried, but I wasn't sure about Charlie. I didn't know if he'd come down the wooden stairs and trail me along the beach or simply wait. I glanced back with dread, but the hill projected, obscuring even the light. All he had to do was get back in his car. If he took a parallel path to mine, he could intercept me easily on the other end. Eventually we'd both end up at Ludlow Beach, but I couldn't turn back. Harley's Beach was worse, too far from streetlights and residential help. I began to run in earnest, uncertain how far I had to go yet. My wet clothes stuck to me, clammy and cold, but my prime concern was the gun. I'd already dropped it once and I knew sea water had curled up toward it as I crossed the rocks. I didn't think it had gotten wet but I wasn't sure. I could see somewhat better now, but the beach was littered with rocks and kelp. I prayed I wouldn't twist an ankle. If I couldn't run, then Charlie could track me at his own pace and I'd have no way out. I glanced back: no sign of him, sound masked by the breaking surf. I didn't think he was there. Once I got to Ludlow Beach, there were bound to be other people, passing motorists. As long as I was running, the fear seemed contained, adrenaline driving out every sensation except the urge to flee. The wind was down, but it was cold and I was wet to the bone.

The beach narrowed again and I found myself running in shallow water, slogging my way through the churning surf. I tried to get my bearings but I'd never been up this far. I caught sight of a wooden stairway zigzagging up the cliff to my left, the wind-bleached railing showing white against the dark tangle of vegetation clinging to the cliff. I followed the line up with my eyes. I guessed that it was Sea Shore Park, which ran along the bluff. Parking lot. Houses across the road. I grabbed the rail and started up, knees aching as I climbed, chest heaving. I reached the top and peered over the rim, heart stopping again.

Charlie's 450 SL was parked above, headlights raking the fence. I ducked back and started down the stairs again, a mewing sound in my throat that I couldn't control. My breathing was ragged, my chest afire. I hit the sand again and ran on, accelerating my pace. The sand was sluggish now, too soft, and I cut to my right, searching out the wet sand that was packed hard. At least I was getting warmer now, wet clothes chafing, water dripping from strands of hair matted with salt. My left knee was stinging and I could feel something warm ooze through my pantleg. The beach was interrupted not by rocks this time but by the sheer fear of the cliff, jutting out like a pie-shaped wedge into the black of the sea. I waded out into the waves, undercurrent tugging at me as I rounded the bend. Ludlow Beach was visible just ahead. I nearly wept with relief. Painfully, I began to run again, trying for a pace I could live with. I could make out lights now, dark patches of palm against gray sky. I slowed to a jog, trying to catch my breath. I stopped finally, bending from the waist, my mouth dry, sweat or salt water streaking down my face. My cheeks were hot and my eyes stung. I wiped my mouth on the back of my hand and moved on, walking this time, fear creeping up again until my heart was battering my ribs.

This stretch of beach was gentle and clean, looking pale gray, widening to the left where the high cliff finally dwindled away into sloping hillside, slipping down to the flat of the sand. Beyond, I could see the long stretch of parking lot and beyond that, the street, well lighted, empty, and inviting. The beach park closed at 8:00 and I thought the parking lot would probably be chained and locked. Still the sight of Charlie's pale blue 450 SL was a jolt—that single vehicle in the whole expanse of empty asphalt. His car lights were on, slanting forward into the palms. There was no way I could cut across the sand to the street without his seeing me. The darkness, which had seemed to lift before, now felt like a veil. I couldn't see clearly. I couldn't pick out anything in that smoky wash of darkness. The streetlights at that distance seemed pointless and whimsical and cruel, illuminating nothing, marking a path to safety that I couldn't reach. And where was he? Sitting in his car, his eyes scanning the park, waiting for me to crash through to him? Or out among the palms much closer to the beach?

I moved to the right again, wading out into the ocean. The icy water was making my blood congeal but I crept on, waves splashing against my knees. Out here, I would be harder to spot and if I couldn't see him, at least he couldn't see me. When I was out far enough, I sank down, half walking, half drifting through the undulating depths beyond the breakers. It cost me everything to keep the gun up. I was obsessed with that, arm aching, fingers numb. My hair floated around my face like wet gauze. I watched the beach, seeing little, searching for Charlie. Car lights still on. Nothing. No one. I had moved perhaps two hundred yards past the far-left extreme of the parking lot, almost even now with the concession stand: a small oasis of palms and picnic tables, trash cans, public telephones. I put my feet down, easing into a standing position, still angling to the right. He could be anywhere, standing in any shadow. I waded toward the shallows, waves curling at knee height, washing forward then across my shoes. Finally I was on wet sand again, moving quickly toward the lot, straining through the darkness for sight of him. He couldn't be looking everyplace at once. I crouched, shifting my gaze to the left. Now that I was forced into immobility, the fear took up where it had left me, ice spreading across my lungs, pulse beating in my throat. I slipped out of my wet jeans and shoes—lightly, quietly.

The concession stand was dead ahead: squat structure of cinder block, windows boarded over for the night. I moved to the right, through powdery sand, sinking down to my ankles, working harder on land than I had in water. I jumped. There he was—just a flash to my left. I dropped to a crouch again, wondering how visible I was. I eased down flat on my belly, pulled myself forward on my elbows. I reached the dark shade of the palms, which even at this hour cast clear shadows against the gray of night. I peered to the left, spotting him again. He wore a white shirt, darker pants. He disappeared into the shadows, passing into the grove of palm trees where the picnic tables were set out. Behind me, the ocean was hushed, a sibilant backdrop to our little cat-and-mouse. To my right, there was an oblong metal trash bin, chest-height with a hinged metal lid. I heard Charlie's car start up and I glanced back with surprise. Maybe he was leaving. Maybe he thought he had missed me and was moving now to intercept me farther down the beach. As he swung back to turn around, I darted toward the trash bin, lifted the lid with one thrust, and pulled myself over the metal lip into the crush of paper cups, discarded picnic sacks, debris. I wrestled out a place for myself with my backside, shifting my bare legs down into the garbage, wrinkling my nose with disgust. My right foot was touching something cold and gooey and the trash beneath me felt warm, like a compost heap, smoldering with bacteria. I pushed up slightly and peered over my shoulder through the crack, the metal lid tilted slightly ajar by the mountain of accumulated trash. Charlie's car was moving toward me, headlights slicing straight across my hiding place. I ducked down, heartbeat making my eyes bulge.

He got out of the car, leaving the lights on. I could still see a slice of light reflected from where I crouched. He slammed the car door. I could hear his footsteps scratch across the concrete.

"Kinsey, I know you're here someplace," he said.

I tried not to move. Tried not to breathe.

Silence.

"Kinsey, you don't have to be afraid of me. My God, don't you know that?" His tone was insistent, gentle, persuasive, hurt.

Was I just imagining everything? He sounded like he always did. Silence. I heard his footsteps moving away. I eased up slowly, peering out through the crack. He was standing ten feet away from me, staring out toward the ocean, his body still, half turned away. He started back and I ducked down. I could hear footsteps approaching. I shrank, pulling the gun up, hands shaking. Maybe I was crazy. Maybe I was making a fool of myself. I hated hide-and-seek. I'd never been good at that as a kid. I always jumped right out when anyone got close because the tension made me want to wet my pants. I felt tears rising. Oh Jesus, not *now*, I thought feverishly. The fear was like a sharp pain. My heart hurt me every time it beat, making the blood pound in my ears. Surely he could hear that. Surely he knew now where I was.

He lifted the lid. The beams from his headlights shone against his golden cheek. He glanced over at me. In his right hand was a butcher knife with a ten-inch blade.

I blew him away.

THE Santa Teresa police conducted a brief investigation but in the end no charges were filed. The folder on Laurence Fife contains the report I sent to the chief of the Bureau of Collection and Investigative Services regarding the discharge of my firearm "while acting within the course and scope" of my employment. There is also a copy of the refund check I sent to Nikki for the unused portion of the $5000 she advanced on account. All together, I was paid $2978.25 for services rendered in the course of that sixteen days and I suppose it was fair enough. The shooting disturbs me still. It has moved me into the same camp with soldiers and maniacs. I never set out to kill anyone. But maybe that's what Gwen would say, and Charlie too. I'll recover, of course. I'll be ready for business again in a week or two, but I'll never be the same. You try to keep life simple but it never works, and in the end all you have left is yourself.

Respectfully submitted,
Kinsey Millhone